ESCAPE INTO THE JUNGLE

Screaming into the wind, Hatch worked the rudder pedals to get the plane straightened out, and pushed the yoke forward to level off the nose. "Come on, baby," he begged the Maule, "come on, sweetheart. Fly, baby, fly!"

Through the shattered windscreen Hatch could see land approaching, a stretch of white beach and the thick, multi-hued green jungle beyond.

Suddenly his vision was blocked by the Hughes dropping in front of him as if it had been lowered by a rope. The shooter was taking aim.

Hatch kicked down the right pedal and twisted the wheel. The Maule took the rounds in its belly. Smoke poured from the engine into the cockpit.

The Maule was over the beach now. Hatch banked left and kept descending, only able to see ahead for occasional moments. Then the yoke began shaking in his hand and the tail seemed to be sliding backwards as the nose drifted up.

Then it hit. The plane came down on the surf line, the right wing over the beach and the left over the water. The plane skidded in the wet sand for twenty yards. Flames flicked from the engine cowling as soon as the plane stopped.

Hatch had enough time to pull out his weapons and the rucksack before the fire, surging along the bulkhead padding, reached the cargo compartment.

Hatch darted into the jungle as a black helicopter made its first pass over the wreckage. . . .

HATCH'S MISSION

Don Merritt

You cannot sit on bayonets,
Nor can you eat among the dead.
When all are killed, you are alone,
A vacuum comes where hate has fed.
Murder's fruit is silent stone,
The gun increases poverty.

—Delmore Schwartz,
*For the One Who Would Take
Man's Life in His Hands*

BANTAM BOOKS

TORONTO • NEW YORK • LONDON • SYDNEY • AUCKLAND

HATCH'S MISSION

A Bantam Book / September 1987

ISBN 0-553-26868-6

Published simultaneously in the United States and Canada

PRINTED IN THE UNITED STATES OF AMERICA

O   0 9 8 7 6 5 4 3 2 1

For
Peter Matson

Wellington, New Zealand

Ξ

The explosion was spectacular, lighting up the evening sky like a bomb. You could see it all the way down on Customhouse Quay; at first witnesses to the fiery blast thought the Kelburn cable car had gone up—more French government terrorists making some trouble over nuclear testing.

The house, now a pick-up-sticks heap of burning rubble, belonged to an American immigrant couple; they kept to themselves and had been in the neighborhood for only two years. The husband, who had been alone in the house, was on the faculty of Victoria University. None of the neighbors was able to recall exactly what he lectured on there. Mrs. Wilkins, who lived next door, said the wife was pretty, but wasn't it odd how she was missing the little finger of her left hand? Mrs. Wilkins also remarked that the young woman spent quite a bit of her time outdoors and often sat on the balcony, from where she had a view all the way down to the bay. She was friendly enough, although certainly not pushy. It was a terrible way to lose one's husband, even if, thank goodness, he must have gone quickly.

Mr. Hammond, from across the road, said he smelled gas just a bit before the explosion, but Mrs. Hammond said she could not recall anything untoward in the air.

The house had stood on a large hillside lot, but the fire crews were able to contain the inferno without its engulfing any of the other gingerbread Victorian homes.

Because the heat was so intense and the fire so slow to slacken, they did not recover the husband's body for another ten hours. The bullet hole in the back of the skull was evident even to the fireman who first uncovered the corpse.

Part One

Ξ

Tuva, Olowalu Atoll, Austral Islands

It was particularly hot. There was no shade on the pier except in the late afternoon, when you could get down low behind the stretched-out shadow of the water barrel, or lie among the burlap copra bags waiting in the white sun, which was where Hatch had more or less chosen to pass out a couple of hours earlier.

The wind had slackened under the weight of the approaching evening and the accumulation of the day's heat and humidity settled over Tuva like a wet wool blanket. From the copra factory on the lower reaches of Kilohana Mountain, workers shuffled past mounds of drying coconut meat and down the trail toward the village; multicolored fishing skiffs on their way home labored under aging Johnson outboard motors; and inside Papa Jack's bar, Hattie, Tuva's fat whore and Papa Jack's only waitress, waddled around the tables lighting decorative hurricane lamps, anticipating the thirsty copra workers and salt-burned fishermen.

Stopping suddenly, burning match held flickering above a red lamp, Hattie turned her head to a faint, alien sound. The approaching drone of the twin radial engines on the Canadian-built CL-215 amphibian sounded to her like the guttural hum of Suji Fukimoto's 1952 Yokohama-model dental drill. Leaving her lamps and going out to the plank sidewalk in front of Papa Jack's, she threw one beefy arm over her forehead and squinted hard against the fat red sun.

In the Government House, Mr. Jolly Malcolm, the Australian government's administrator on Tuva, rolled his homemade wheelchair away from the desk and leaned over to get a look out the window. It had been Mr. Jolly's experience that nothing good ever came to Tuva from the air. Scooting closer to the windowsill so he could see around the side of the building to the banyan

tree where Kimo and Kalaka would be napping, Mr.
Jolly called out to awaken his chair-bearers.

The seaplane banked hard right out of the sun and
skimmed over the reef as if its wingtip were tracing the
line of a runway, finally climbing again to circle the
perimeter of Tuva Bay. By then there were forty or fifty
people gathering on the pier.

The amphibian banked again and under full flaps
flared just as it cleared the jagged coral reef and smacked
into Tuva Bay; it bounced three times before settling into
the foamy green water like a sun-dazzled albatross.

As the plane taxied toward the dock, brown, naked
pier boys perched hopefully, ready to dive for coins.
Women backed away and held their woven pandanus
hats against the wet gale blown back by the props. Two
men went forward to take lines, a door opened on the
side, and a man in a white shirt with shoulder epaulets
stepped out.

By the time Mr. Jolly and his chair-bearers arrived,
the seaplane had disgorged its single passenger and was
already revving its engine for takeoff. Ducking against
the spray, holding their hats and the hands of children,
the crowd on the pier watched the plane leap off the bay
and back into the sun, where in a moment it sounded
again like Suji Fukimoto's dreaded drill.

Mr. Jolly gestured forward with his arm, and the
escorts pushed his chair onto the pier. When the crowd
parted for him, Mr. Jolly could see the *haole wahine*
passenger from the plane removing a passport from one
of many pockets on her sweat-stained khaki shirt.

"My name is Jolly Malcolm. I am what passes for
government here."

"Jan Moss," the woman said, offering her passport, her
real passport, for she was through with hiding.

"An American." Mr. Jolly noted the customs stamp
from the provincial headquarters at Olowalu, dated that
day, although he could tell without the passport. She had
that look of possessiveness he had seen in plenty of other
Americans.

"Hope I don't need a visa," she said, pushing down her sunglasses slightly and rubbing the bridge of her nose. Her eyes were closed.

"Not for a stay of less than fourteen days."

"That was my understanding, Mr. Malcolm."

"'Mr. Jolly' will do."

Jan Moss nodded, flicking aside a long strand of yellow hair stuck to the sweat on her forehead; a movement, thought Mr. Jolly, more of distraction than impatience.

Mr. Jolly returned the passport and Jan dropped it into her pocket. Even through the dark sunglasses, it was obvious that her eyes were on the tapa cloth over Mr. Jolly's lap.

"Not crippled. No legs a-tall," Mr. Jolly said.

"I'm sorry. I was staring."

"Never mind. May I ask your business on Tuva, Miss . . . ?" Mr. Jolly figured that she was in her late thirties, but he was not good at guessing the ages of women; not good, in fact, with much of anything where women were concerned.

Curious Tuvans jostled one another to get closer to the blond *haole*, and children gathered expectantly around her legs. Jan Moss patted a boy on the shoulder and smiled indulgently.

"Shoo," Mr. Jolly commanded, waving his hand at the children. "Go on, now. Shoo. Get off the lady's feet, for Chrissakes."

"I don't mind them," Jan said courteously. "And it's Mrs., although I hope you'll call me Jan."

"They're your shoes," Mr. Jolly responded. "Seems you plan to stay awhile. Your ride has left."

"If I may, sir, for a day or two. I am looking for an American who is said to live here on this island." Jan jerked her foot away when two wrestling boys fell on her toes.

"Momona, get your bloody heathens off our guest!" Mr. Jolly yelled to a woman in the crowd.

Jan smiled, receiving in response one from Mr. Jolly,

who found himself softened by the beauty given to her face by the smile.

"American, you say?"

"Yes, a . . . ah, Caucasian . . ."

"White man is acceptable," Mr. Jolly said, smirking a little at her American's notion of tact.

"A white man who calls himself Hatch," she continued.

The group's intake of breath behind her made Jan turn around suddenly. Then someone laughed, then a woman giggled, then another, and others.

"I see." Mr. Jolly raised his voice to express his displeasure over the laughter.

"He does live here?" Jan asked, fatigue and confusion softening her already low voice.

"He is there," Mr. Jolly said, pointing into the crowd, which separated before him like a human Red Sea.

Jan Moss turned toward the opening and looked down the aisle of bodies. There, at the end of the dock, curled up in a pile of burlap bags, lay the man she had come to see. When Jan made a move in that direction, Mr. Jolly stopped her.

"I would let him be."

Jan turned back to Mr. Jolly.

"My God, is he all right?"

"Not a-tall, actually," Mr. Jolly said.

2

The night was warm, soft, quiet; even the surf rumbled lazily, muffled against the barrier of the reef. Torchlights illuminating the pier and seawall flickered against the purple backdrop of the dark, sharp mountains, and the yellow glow of kerosene lamps gave life to the small houses dotting the thickly vegetated slopes.

At the end of the pier an old man fished alone. His name was Makaavana and by day he fished far out in a skiff with a red lateen sail. Silhouetted against the evening sky, he and his long, arching pole gave the night a kind of permanence, captured like a charcoal sketch hanging on a wall.

Occasionally a halyard slapped a mast on the *Blowing Cold*, the ketch at anchor in the bay—Hatch's boat. And sometimes, when a moment of time was caught between swells breaking at the reef, it was so quiet you could hear the wooden boat creaking as she rolled and tugged against her anchor.

Janet Henry Moss, changed from the khaki shirt and skirt into a silk aloha blouse and white shorts—fine, long, tanned legs stretched out in front of her—sat on a dock bollard by the pile of copra sacks and stared at Frank Hatcher, who was still passed out cold among the burlap bags. An eruption of laughter from Papa Jack's turned Jan's head for a moment. How strange, she was thinking, that there aren't any mechanical noises. Almost spooky. Then she turned her attention back to the man sleeping like death just off the end of her feet.

Even curled up against himself, she could see the long muscles in his strong legs outlined below the skin like ropes wrapped in flesh-colored cellophane. His face was turned away, hidden beneath a crooked arm and mat of tangled hair. But she knew him by the power in his body and did not need to see his face for confirmation.

Jan had been sitting on the bollard with a can of Foster's for half an hour. During that time, Hatch had not moved; his breathing stayed steady and coarse; otherwise he could have been dead. Jan had intended to let nature take its course. A man could hardly sleep all day and all night as well. But she was getting bored, so she reached out with her foot and nudged Hatch's leg, then harder. "Hatch," she said, then repeated it in a louder voice.

The man among the bags tightened his body defensively but did not open his eyes or make a sound except for a catch in his breathing.

"Come on, wake up," Jan persisted, poking at him again.

Hatch started, rolled sideways, and drew up his arms to cover his eyes.

"Hello," Jan said softly, assuringly. She got off the bollard and knelt next to him.

She was astonished. She would not have recognized Hatch's face if they had passed on a street somewhere. She had last seen him at Andrews Air Force Base in the security hangar a little over two years ago. Now Hatch had a long, ragged beard and his black hair—tangled and streaked with white—hung almost to his shoulders.

Hatch's dark eyes were open when he moved his arms away. Jan turned her face slightly, so with the light from the torches, Hatch could see her clearly.

"Jan?" The voice was heavy with disbelief.

She thought he looked like Rasputin but decided not to say it.

Hatch sat up quickly, but the sudden movement jostled his equilibrium. Hanging on to his head with both hands, he swallowed hard and leaned back until the rough copra bags supported his weight.

"Hangover, huh?"

Hatch tried to stand but slipped to one knee. Jan reached out and grabbed him under the arms to pull him up. "Steady as she goes," she said lightly.

"I'm okay," Hatch said, shrugging her off even as he stared at her incredulously. After a momentary wobble, Hatch got his balance and straightened up. The world settled down before his eyes and he eased into the moment.

"Beer?" Jan asked, producing another can of Foster's and offering it.

Hatch pulled the tab and drank deeply, swishing the beer around in his mouth for a moment before swallowing.

"Thanks," he said, then took another drink.

The horizon undulated in front of him again and Hatch sat down on a copra bag. Jan sat back down on the bollard. Guitar music with an Elizabethan sound came from Papa Jack's. Jan turned to it.

"That's Dennis Lindsay," Hatch said to explain the music. "He's a Brit rummy; a painter when he can get some paint and canvas. Been here longer than I have—fifteen years, I'd guess. All he knows how to play are those damned English folk songs."

"He plays them well," Jan said.

"Who wouldn't if he played the same six songs over and over for fifteen years."

"There's something to be said for doing one thing well." Jan looked back toward Papa Jack's, attentive to the guitar for a while, as if she needed to rethink something.

"Jan?" Hatch repeated her name, as if by saying it again he could find an explanation for her presence.

"You certainly picked yourself an out-of-the-way place, Hatch." She gestured expansively. "Even knowing the name of this place didn't make it easy to find, or get to. They told me I'd either have to wait in Papeete for the copra freighter, which might or might not be coming to Tuva this month, or hire a plane."

"What plane?"

"You slept through it."

Hatch occupied himself with the beer. He knew by then what she would tell him in her own time; he had known it at least tacitly the moment he saw that Jason was not with her.

Finally, turning to look at Hatch, Jan said, "The government man here, Mr. Jolly, told me about Kukana."

"Two years ago, day before yesterday," Hatch said, then drained the rest of the beer from the can, some of it falling into his beard. "Did you bring any more of those?" he asked, looking at the can she held.

"Afraid not," Jan said. "But here, finish this one. These cans are too big for me, and actually, I've never become accustomed to warm beer." She handed over the can and Hatch accepted it without thanks.

"Around here, ice is as expensive as fuel."

Hatch drained the rest of Jan's beer, then looked out across the dark water; he began talking as if he were picking up a conversation he had just left off. "She never spoke again, not from the moment we left you and Jason in Maryland, not on that cavernous, empty Air Force plane they put us on, and not here, not at home, not a word. But she cried. Christ, did she cry. No, actually, it was more a whimper. She ate, but showed no interest in doing it. You had to put the food into her mouth most of the time. She slept usually. She had become like a child, only worse, because at least a child tries, and has the urge to survive.

"The first time I left her alone—I went fishing with Tioni, her brother—she left our house, walked half a mile up the slope of that mountain back there, and threw herself off the *pali* into the sea.

"We did not find her body for two days; by then she was bloated and the fish had gotten to her.

"Probably she never would have recovered from what happened to her in the States."

"I'm very, very sorry about Kukana," she said, wanting then to tell Hatch what she had also lost, but knowing he was not ready to hear it. It was too dark for Hatch to see how moist her eyes were.

"Want something to eat?" Hatch asked.

"Where can we go?"

"Over there's the only place," he answered, pointing toward Papa Jack's.

"Where's Jason?" Hatch asked finally as they headed off the pier, as if he had only just then noticed her husband's absence.

"He's not with me," Jan answered, putting off the subject.

But Hatch already knew. Because she would not have intruded upon his sanctuary for anything less.

3

It went badly in the bar.

Alapaki, the bartender, had taken out the prized record player and cranked it up. The locals, dancing to a stack of scratchy 45's, made the walls tremble.

"Can't we get out of here?" Jan screamed over the music.

But Hatch, who was drunk again, either did not hear or intended to ignore her. He leaned his chair back to the wall, propped his feet on a bar stool, and watched the dancers, clutching a bottle of Japanese Scotch to his chest like a shield.

So Jan gave up and turned her chair toward the space cleared for dancing, and after a while found herself attracted to the beauty and grace of the dancers. The blend of Little Richard chanting "Good Golly, Miss Molly, you sure like to ball," and the Tuvans' native dances brought a smile to Jan's face, the first unforced one in weeks. It felt good to forget for a moment. She had never seen anything quite like these people.

A few minutes later, Hatch was spinning across the dance floor, knocking into dancers like an errant pinball bouncing off bumpers. At first Jan thought he was trying to dance, but then she could see that he was trying to reach the record player on the bar. He careened off one woman, knocking her into her partner, and shoved two men backward until they lost balance and fell to the hard-packed dirt floor. The others quickly parted for him.

Alapaki, seeing Hatch headed toward the prized RCA Victrola, lunged across the bar just as Hatch made a grab for it, both men reaching it as Chuck Berry sang: "Lucille, you don't do your daddy's will," and the needle scratched out the rest with a sound like rending a live cat. Alapaki jerked the record player off the bar and backed up with it held protectively against his chest.

"Nogut, Hatch, nogut," Alapaki cried, pressing his back to the wall, guarding the record player. "Go 'round bilong me oltaim, bilong yu nevah."

Hatch turned around, leaned back with his elbows on the bar, faced the Tuvans standing quietly before him, and took a drink from someone's glass. "These joys are false. Can't you see that the struggling to repeat and perpetuate pleasures necessarily and inevitably turns into pain? Nothing is ever the same as it was before; while trying to recreate something that meant or gave pleasure . . . you cannot, and what you have from failure is pain. Pleasure breeds disappointment." Stumbling over a tongue numbed by alcohol, the last few words were unintelligible.

Tioni Makani, brother of Hatch's dead wife, came from the Tuvans massed on the dance floor and put his hand on Hatch's shoulder. Hatch shrugged him off.

"I see it in your eyes," Hatch went on, weaving back and forth like seaweed in the surf line. "'Ah hah,' you say, 'the hero of Tuva is a coward and a drunk.' I always was. God damn you all for showing me joy. God damn you all!" Hatch was shouting now. "If you had not shown me happiness, I would never have learned to recognize pain."

Hatch slumped to the floor again, and this time did not shake Tioni away when he pulled him up.

"Hele mai," Tioni told Hatch. "Taim yu bilong hale."

Tioni put his arms around Hatch and moved him toward the door and outside.

Alapaki set the record player back on the bar, cranked it up, and put on a fresh stack of records. One woman was crying, tears heavy on her cheeks. Until the first record fell and began, there was silence in the bar. You could hear the surf tumbling over the reef. Then, a few bars into "Jailhouse Rock," life crept cautiously back into Papa Jack's.

"Yu wan' mo' same kine?" Hattie asked Jan Moss, looking at the empty glass in her hand.

Jan looked at her glass, then up at Hattie's bulk, and

shook her head. When Hattie left, Jan put some money on the table and made her way through the crowd toward the door. She thought of Jason, how much he would have liked Tuva and its people.

Outside, Jan moved quickly away from the bar to escape the racket, then slowed down to a stroll. Hatch and the man who had taken him out of Papa Jack's were nowhere to be seen. Jan walked up Alii Street, the only street in the village, following the curve of the bay toward the Keena Hale—the Government House—and beyond to where, there being no hotel on Tuva, she had taken a small room on the second floor of Mr. Lee's Emporium.

She thought about Frank Hatcher, about how much she needed him, and about what she had witnessed in the bar. She let herself remember California and better days, hoping the memories would temper the throbbing behind her eyes.

Lost in thought, Jan nearly tripped over Mr. Jolly. He was seated in his wheelchair below the spreading banyan tree, reading a book by lamplight.

"Please excuse me," Jan said quickly, readjusting the chair's alignment in the dim yellow light.

"Think nothing of it," Mr. Jolly said.

"What are you reading?" she asked, killing time to keep from going up to the hot, dismal room.

Mr. Jolly held up the cover for her to see: *Martin Eden*.

"That's one I haven't read," Jan told him "Do you mind?" she asked, sitting on one of the large exposed banyan roots.

"Please do," Mr. Jolly replied. "I would welcome a bit of chatter with someone new. We don't get many visitors, you see."

She nodded. "I've actually never read any Jack London."

"We have a limited supply of books here. I've read all of them many times."

"When I get home, could I send you some books? How would I do that? Do you have mail service?"

"We are visited six times a year by the copra freighter from Olowalu, the provincial headquarters. Mail is delivered at the same time. It would be very kind of you to send along a few books. I shall provide you with an address before you leave."

"That would be fine. Any preferences? I'd hate to duplicate ones you have already."

"I'm partial to British writers. Anything Iris Murdoch might have published in the last ten years. Would you know if Graham Greene is still alive and publishing?"

"I'll find out."

"No more Herman Melville, please. We have three of *Moby Dick* and four of *Typee*. People suppose that one living out here in the southern islands must like reading about them as well."

"Tuva is extraordinarily beautiful," Jan said, toying with a stick. "But I would have rock fever pretty badly after a while, I think. I haven't traveled widely out here, but something about islands unhinges me."

"What sort of business are you in, Mrs. Moss?"

"Please, call me Jan. I'm a widow, Mr. Jolly. I guess I'm what you would call a housewife, or I was. In my younger days I was a nurse."

"Your younger days are hardly over, Jan."

"Why, thank you, sir."

"My sympathy for the loss of your husband. Has it been long?"

"Half a year," Jan said softly.

Mr. Jolly opened his mouth as if to speak, and the light caught his bad teeth. He was an odd-looking, small man. Jan wondered how Mr. Jolly had lost his legs, if maybe it had happened when the men who had tried to kill Hatch came to Tuva for him. Hatch had told her about it in California when everything had just started. Even if he were able to stand, Jan guessed, Mr. Jolly could not have been more than five-two or -three.

"Why have you come to see Hatch?" Mr. Jolly asked after they had been silent for a minute.

"Actually, Mr. Jolly, it's simply personal business. I don't mean to be secretive, it's just that it's, well, just personal."

"Let me tell you why I ask. Maybe you already know about the things that happened here a few years ago. If you are Hatch's friend you probably know enough. I am referring to the time I lost these . . ." He put both hands on the tapa cloth covering where his legs would have been. "Hatch was the hero of all Tuva. I cannot begin to tell you how important he was to these people, how respected and loved he was. He was given everything an extremely giving people could offer."

"You're right, he did tell me what happened here. I've known Hatch for a long time. We first met when we were young—barely out of our teens. He was a friend of my first husband, who was killed in Vietnam. I didn't see Hatch for twenty years after that. Not until two years ago. But I guess you know—"

"Yes. Rather, I figured—"

"He's changed."

Mr. Jolly nodded. "If you know Hatch, then you know better than to judge him too hastily. The slovenly, belligerent drunk spouting senseless aphorisms, begging for fights, and sleeping where he falls does not come from in here." Mr. Jolly pointed at his head. "But here." He pointed at his heart. "It is what he became after Kukana fell from the *pali*. Jumped. Why pretend it was otherwise? No one knows what happened to her in the United States, what things she saw through her heart's eye."

Mr. Jolly stopped and looked at Jan as if he expected her to provide an answer, but she shook her head and poked holes in the dirt with the tip of a stick.

"We are all right here, Mrs. Moss . . ."

She noticed the change from "Jan" to "Mrs. Moss."

". . . when left to ourselves. But it seems that every time an outsider comes to our island, there is trouble. Are you bringing trouble for us?"

"I hope not. I intend not to."

"I, too, hope not. One of Hatch's many layers is self-destructive, and we are working to repair that part of him. If you bring trouble for Hatch, I can assure you that your leaving of this island will be bloody less friendly than your arrival."

"That's a chance I'll have to take," Jan said, standing. "There is more than one way to repair a soul. Consider that, sir." She dropped the stick, reached out to shake Mr. Jolly's hand, and said good night.

Jan stopped before heading up the stairs to her room and looked back at Mr. Jolly, who had opened the book in his lap again but was gazing up at the intricate sky.

4

When Hatch saved Kukana's life and then married her, Kukana's father, Kamuela, the chief of all Tuva until his death, built for them a grand house on the mountain slope above the village of Tuva, where the breezes of the southern trades were cool and fragrant. Hatch had not been back to that house since the day Kukana's body was found floating in the lagoon. The child of that marriage lived with Tioni and his wife, Jenny, a Peace Corps leftover.

When he was not too drunk for the long walk or when someone took him there, Hatch was home at the shack he had built years ago on the coastal lava flat wedged between the sea and the jungle a mile or so from the Tuva pier. The tin-roofed, rust-streaked, unpainted shack squatted in waist-high weeds like an abandoned Buddha.

Sweat stained Jan's khaki shirt by the time she had worked her way along the narrow jungle trail to the beach at Kaiwe Point. Sunlight steamed through the double canopy of vegetation and gnats caught in the warm air currents darted like bits of ash blown by a fan; Jan took breaths behind a cupped hand to lessen the number she swallowed. Then the jungle opened onto a sandy clearing. She could see the ocean beyond a grove of palm trees and smell the scent of salt air borne on a fresh breeze. Hatch's shack sat at the back of the beach.

Hatch, dressed in old shorts and a ragged T-shirt, was on the beach working on an outboard motor mounted in a water-filled test barrel. A film of grease and motor oil defined the cords of muscles in his arms, and his tanned skin glistened like a polished gun barrel. The image of strength and power clashed with Jan's memory of Hatch passed out among the burlap bags.

Jan announced her presence early by calling out and waving. Hatch looked up, shielding his eyes from the morning sun, then went back to the motor as if no one had been there.

"I thought I was dreaming," Hatch said when Jan came up.

"That's quite a hike through the jungle," she said.

Hatch nodded, his concentration still on the stuck spark plug.

"Can I offer a hand?" she asked.

Hatch looked up, then tossed Jan an oily rag. "You can hold the head while I torque this mother."

The frozen plug did not move. Hatch squirted more lubricant on it, nodded for Jan to tighten her grip, then reapplied pressure to the wrench.

With a grotesque screech, the plug gave and Hatch lost the skin off three knuckles when the wrench came around.

Jan followed him down the beach and knelt beside him at the edge of the lagoon while he rinsed his hand in the warm salt water.

"Jan," Hatch said without looking up, "you reminded me of something I thought I could forget."

"I understand. Please forgive me."

"Forget it. It never leaves, not really."

Hatch stood, shook the water from his hand, then dried it on his shirt. Jan followed him back to the test tank, where Hatch installed a new spark plug, attached the gas hose, and test-started the motor. Then he carried the motor to the lagoon and mounted it on a bracket at the stern of his outrigger skiff. Jan sat on a palm stump watching him bring fishing gear from the shack down to the boat. When the boat was ready, Hatch started to push off, but he stopped and looked up the beach at Jan.

"I have to go fishing," he said.

"Must be nice," she answered.

"It's how I earn a living."

She nodded.

Hatch gestured by tilting his head to the side and back.

Jan stood, walked down to the boat, and helped Hatch shove off. It was impossible to talk over the motor. Soon they were through the reef passage and heading away from Tuva. A fine mist from spray over the bow cooled Jan's face. Terns, gulls, and a solitary hunting frigate bird joined the boat as they all moved out to sea. In the distance, Jan could see a number of other boats, some under sail, some with no sails that were moving under power.

Jan watched Hatch rig hand lines while reaching back occasionally to adjust their course. The bilge held coils of line, hooks, and baits. Every once in a while Hatch glanced up and scanned the sea. Jan kept out of the way except when Hatch gave her some little chore to do.

They had been heading out for twenty minutes when Hatch reached back and cut the motor.

"We'll drift with the current," he explained to Jan's confused expression. "Here it runs along the fifty-fathom break." He began streaming out a coil of baited line. "Out there the bottom drops off rapidly, the current moves in like this and runs into the fifty-fathom ledge, pushing plankton, shrimp, small squid, and other foods toward the surface, where the bigger fish, mainly tuna, feed. And sometimes we get blue marlin in here chasing the tuna."

"You've caught marlin on a hand line?"

"I've *lost* plenty of marlin on a hand line."

"Last year, Jason caught a twelve-hundred-pound

black marlin fishing off Cairns. We trolled the five-hundred-fathom ledge outside the Great Barrier Reef. Why don't you troll with the motor and cover more area in the same time?"

"Because gas for this motor is shipped in barrels from Tahiti and I have to pay about six dollars Australian for a gallon of it. This isn't Cairns."

"Too bad you can't tune it to burn Scotch." Jan immediately regretted the catty remark, but Hatch ignored the comment and was watching the line sag between the Clorox-bottle floats.

There were other boats in the area, although none particularly close. Jan looked back at the island, the multihued greens becoming shades of purple as their distance from the island slowly increased, and believed she understood one of the reasons Hatch had abandoned the world for this place: it was beautiful.

She watched Hatch working, tending the trailing lines, scanning the sky for signs of birds feeding. She also noticed when Hatch took drinks from the bottle of whiskey wrapped in a rag kept out of the sun.

It was a time of quietness, only the sea lapping against the hull and the birds calling. "Jason is dead," Jan said.

Hatch nodded. "Hand me that bundle of 10-0 hooks. Yes, there by your right foot."

Except for the incongruous nod, Jan could not tell if it had registered with Hatch, but she went on, "And Michael Laser killed him."

Hatch occupied himself tying a hook to a thick monofilament leader and only responded with a quick look at Jan before going back to his chore. He had been both surprised and not; having surmised Jason's death by his absence, but not connecting Laser, and not thinking of his friend as murdered.

Jan opened the flap over her breast pocket and removed a yellowed newspaper clipping. She carefully unfolded it, then handed it over to Hatch.

The headline read: "MAN KILLED BEFORE BLAZE."

Above it was a picture of the ruins of a house. The dateline was Wellington.

According to Metropolitan Police Inspector Nigel Hunnicutt, the man found dead in last night's Kelburn Park blaze had been murdered before the fire, which, it is speculated, was deliberately set.

Found on the floor in a rear bedroom was John W. Miller, 47, a visiting professor of political theory at Victoria University. Mrs. Miller, a housewife, was not in the house at the time of the blast.

According to a neighbor, Mr. Fred Small of Old Terrace Lane, the fire. . .

Hatch looked up, folded the article, and handed it back to Jan. He did not need to read the rest of it.

"John and Joan Miller were the names the Company gave us," Jan told Hatch, putting the article back into her pocket. "He had been shot once through the back of the head, here"—she pointed to a spot on the back of her own head—"then the house was set afire. There was hardly enough left to make an identification. I was supposed to be there that afternoon, but . . ." Quiet tears fell steadily from her eyes, embarrassing her with their spontaneity.

Hatch looked away, out to sea, his lips set in a hard, straight line. Then, without turning around, he said, "Laser. You're sure?"

"Yes. Jason knew something about Laser, something he had stumbled across, but he wouldn't tell me what it was. He said I'd be safer if I didn't know. But he was planning to come here, to see you, Hatch, when he was murdered. I don't know why. He was very nervous about it. I think he wanted to warn you."

Hatch's head tipped downward until his chin rested against his chest, his eyes closed, and he mumbled something. Then he looked up at the sky and nodded, as if answering an unasked question.

"I'm sorry, Jan. How long ago?"

"Six months. I miss him, Hatch. The case, as they call it, remains unsolved. I know it was Laser. I can't tell you how. Some things you know. Who else had any reason to kill Jason? It certainly wasn't robbery. I told the station chief, but he doesn't believe me. He says Michael Laser is dead. But I heard things, that Laser was alive and hiding somewhere in Southeast Asia—Thailand or Laos, maybe—well, here I am."

Fifty yards ahead of them gulls dropped into the water as if they had been shot; the surface boiled.

"Bait, bait on the surface," Hatch said then. "That's what the birds are diving on, mackerel shad pushed to the surface, where the birds can see them. The shad trying to escape a danger from below is what makes them churn at the surface. They're trying to fly." Dozens of sea gulls dove into the froth like kamikazes in a death spiral.

Hatch pushed hard with a paddle to urge the boat faster in the current, striking the water with the blade as if to kill it. "We'll trail our lines through the bait; the tuna are in a frenzy now and will hit anything that moves."

"What do I do?" Jan asked.

"Put on those gloves and when I tell you, pull in the forward line as fast as you can. Dump any fish into the bottom and kill them with that club."

"Kill them?"

"So they don't flop back out."

"Oh God, really?"

The skiff drifted into the bait school. Birds fell so close to them that Jan ducked to avoid being hit. She could see the silver shad flashing just below the surface, and below that, darker, larger shapes moving fast.

"Now, now, now!" Hatch cried.

Jan grabbed the surprisingly heavy line and began pulling it hand over hand toward the boat. "It's getting heavier the closer I bring it," she shouted.

"More fish," Hatch said, standing in the stern and pulling in the aft line. "Can you do it?"

"Christ," Jan groaned, putting her back into it. "I can try."

The skiff rolled in the swells and Jan and Hatch had to

brace themselves with legs spread wide to keep from being pitched out. Hatch's laden line was in the boat now. He stood amid five flopping bonita tuna, smashing their heads with the billy, then watched as Jan pulled the last four fish into the boat. They were both splattered with fish blood. Following Hatch's lead, Jan picked up the club and chased the flopping fish around the boat like a madwoman, the boat still pitching and yawing as if attacked by the sea.

Finally Hatch took the club out of Jan's hand. "Jan they're dead. Stop, they're dead now!" Hatch still held her hand, the one from which her little finger was missing. Now he had to shake off the memory of the day she had been mutilated.

Jan stared at him, shaking, then looked down at the mutilated fish between her feet.

"I don't . . ."

"Sit down. We'll start back."

She sat down hard and leaned back. The bilge was filled with blood and fish.

"I had this sickening image," she said after a while, "of Eskimo hunters on an ice floe bashing out a seal pup's brains. Isn't there some other way to do this?"

Hatch did not answer. He knelt in the bilge, removing hooks and coiling line.

"Here," Hatch said, pulling out the whiskey bottle and offering it to Jan.

"I don't think so," she said, unsure of her stomach in the rolling, pitching skiff.

Hatch took a long drink before putting the bottle back.

"There's more than a hundred pounds of tuna here," he said.

"Is that good?"

"About average for *aku*—bonita. This one's about fifteen pounds, the rest between ten and twelve. They run a lot bigger sometimes."

"What's all this worth to you?"

"About three quarts of Scotch."

Hatch started the engine and headed the skiff toward

Tuva Bay. Jan wondered how long they had been out. Her skin felt hot and tight. She pulled back her watchband and saw the striking white, contrasting skin under it.

Over the engine noise Hatch called out. "They've got some coconut-oil stuff you can put on that. It works pretty well."

Jan nodded, watching Hatch steering their course toward the reef slot and into the bay, where they would unload the catch at the pier.

Maybe, Jan thought, survival is a condemnation all its own; finding yourself the only survivor, the only one left, after so much death. Jan understood him better now. The solitude had enforced a kind of moral emptiness on him. It had hardened her; she could feel the hate inside her chest like a stone. Hatch, living out here by the wayside for so many years, had looked bewildered over the news of Jason's murder. But bewildered he was not. Jan could still see in him, no matter how deftly Hatch tried to cover it, the man who had once been Captain Frank Hatcher, the Green Beret about whom a commander once wrote in a report, "Captain Hatcher is the best damned man to have on your side in a fight that the U.S. Army ever had the guts to produce." It was still there, his eyes, his way of staring, looking, taking it all in—they made him seem downright virulent. Jan could see the man who two years ago had leapt onto a magnesium grenade meant for the President of the United States and knocked it away—a grenade tossed by Michael Laser, the man Jan believed had killed her husband.

Jan had lied before about seeing seal pups. In the blood of the twisting fish she had created an image of Michael Laser, a man she had never met. And Hatch was the only person she knew who had ever seen him.

The bay was glassy in the late-afternoon heat, the air above the concrete wharf shimmered. Standing on the dock above the boat, Jan had to grab the fish hoist to steady herself, her body not yet adjusted to stability. Hatch got the fish off-loaded. Other boats came and the fishermen called to one another in a private language. Jan stepped away and let them work.

There was tranquillity, even beauty, in the way the islanders went about their tasks, and Jan remembered the ironic necessities of life in the world away from this as a stab of memory, painful and familiar. Suddenly she hated Tuva because it distracted her from her fury, tempered her compulsion for revenge.

When Hatch climbed up to the pier, Jan fell into step beside him as they headed for Papa Jack's.

"Go away, leave me alone. I'm not going to kill him for you or anybody else. There's been too much killing already."

Jan grabbed his arm. "You don't get it, do you? *I* want to kill him; all I want you to do is teach me how and help me find him."

"Get away from me," Hatch said, shrugging Jan off and heading toward the bar.

"Wait!" she stopped him. "God damn you to hell, Frank Hatcher!" Jan cried, her face red and streaked with angry tears. "You *owe* me this! Dammit! You *owe me*! And I owe it to Jason!"

Hatch pushed by her and stormed into the bar.

5

When Papa Jack's closed at five minutes to midnight— so it would not be open on the Sabbath—Hatch, who had had plenty to drink but still remained uncomfortably sober, walked across Alii Street and onto the long pier. The torches along the street had been snuffed hours ago and the last lights in the houses were blinking out one by one as if wired in series. The full moon hanging midway to its zenith cast long shadows. A dark, fat cloud hung below the moon like an ambitious bowl waiting to catch it. As Hatch walked to the end of the pier, his shadow stretched behind him farther and farther until it washed out in the light from torches on the seawall.

He stopped when another step would have put him into the bay, and he stood very still there, his eyes looking straight out to the reef where the rumbling surf sent sheets of white spray shimmering in the moonlight to fall back like glitter through a sifter. The surf was loud and compelling. Hatch strained against an all-too-familiar urge to swim through it, and beyond.

The surf pounding against the reef disguised the rhythmic squeaking of the wheels of Mr. Jolly's chair. To avoid startling Hatch, Mr. Jolly announced his presence with an obvious cough.

"Oh, good evening, Mr. Jolly," Hatch said, taking his hands from his pocket and clasping his fingers together at his stomach.

"Hatch," Mr. Jolly acknowledged the greeting, nodding his head. "What do you see?"

"Out there?" Hatch glanced seaward. "The reef, the ocean, the moon, stars, the usual."

Mr. Jolly rolled himself closer to the edge and Hatch sat down on a dock bollard so Mr. Jolly would not have to look up to see him. They did not speak for some time.

Then Mr. Jolly said, "So, you will be leaving us again."

Hatch turned quickly. "Did she tell you that?"

"No one has said anything. No one has to."

"I'm not going anywhere."

"So, your *wahine* friend has come only to say hello?"

Hatch offered no response.

"You aren't drunk," Mr. Jolly continued.

"What?"

"You have been drunk a goodly portion of the last two years, my friend, and continually since the approach and passing of the anniversary of Kukana's death. But tonight, you are not drunk."

"An oversight I assure you will be corrected shortly."

"You are preparing yourself for something, I think, and for that you want to be sober."

"Preparing myself for what?"

"Why ask me? What do you think?"

"You seem to know everything else, why not ask yourself?"

"I will admit that I am knowledgeable about many things, most of them utterly useless in this practical world. For I cannot fix plumbing or electrical lights, nor can I fly a plane or sail a ship; I cannot grow my own food nor can I cook what is grown by others; I do not understand algebra or physics; I cannot heal the sick; Christ Almighty, *hell*, man, I can't even bloody walk, a result, more or less, of my inability to understand that you should not confront a man with an automatic weapon." Mr. Jolly allowed himself a small laugh. "But I have an appreciation for poetry and music, literature; I am concerned with the soul and the mysteries of the human heart; I can think and ponder the philosophical verities, and I can love, in my style."

"You know enough, and certainly more than I do. I can fly a plane, sail a ship, fix plumbing, wire for electricity, cook—well, sort of—speak many languages, handle all weapons . . . I"—Hatch slapped his chest hard—"have no soul, no heart, and no love."

"Which, my old friend, is why I think you have decided to go on this journey with the woman."

"How is that?"

"To fill the deep emptiness in your soul, Hatch, so that maybe once again you will know how to live."

"Do you know why she has come for me?"

"I don't think it matters."

"To find a man, Mr. Jolly; a man she wants killed. Not to find life."

"Finding this man is necessarily killing him?"

"In this case, one implies the other absolutely."

"The only absolute is that there are none."

"That's philosophy, Mr. Jolly. This is killing."

"Well, of course, some men need killing. We are restored by their deaths."

"Name one."

"Hitler."

"Name another."

"Mussolini."

"Name one not associated with World War II."

"The man who kidnapped Kukana and took her from her home, from her child, from her husband, and who left her empty and ashamed. How many is that? This man she seeks, could he be one of them?"

Hatch stared at the reef. Michael Laser was the only one of those still alive. And now he had murdered Jason Moss, without whose intervention Hatch would be rotting in a U.S. prison.

"Go with her, Hatch. Face this demon. Slay it or not, but face it. Otherwise you will remain among the dead, in search of a grave, useless to everyone, to yourself, to your daughter, to the honorable memories of those who have died with you. Go, Hatch, and recover your life if you can."

Hatch realized Mr. Jolly had moved away when the squeaking wheels broke through the wall of his concentration. When he looked back, Mr. Jolly had turned and was rolling his chair off the pier in the direction of the Government House.

Hatch stood and turned to follow Mr. Jolly. Somehow he had known where it would lead when he saw the way Jan killed the tuna.

From the window in her room above the store, Jan Moss watched Hatch turn off the pier and enter the jungle trail leading to his shack at Kaiwe Point. What, she wondered as she pulled away from the window and sat on the narrow bed, what would she do if Hatch refused to come? Could she do it alone? She knew the answer was no. But maybe she could hire someone. She had considered that. Whom could she trust? Who would even believe her? Certainly not Jason's *friends* from the goddamn CIA.

Jan lay back on the wrinkled, sweat-dampened sheets and propped her head against the wall. The room held only the bed, a wicker chest of drawers, and a washbasin; almost as an afterthought, a framed picture obviously cut from a travel brochure, showing the Sydney Opera House, hung askew on the wall behind the bed.

Jan's eyes slowly closed and sleep caught her unawares.

6

She awakened when the sun refracted off the jalousie slats in the window, laying a swatch of primary colors across her eyes.

The village awakened with her: the rooster whose cackling invaded Jan's dreams through the night now attacked the morning sun with renewed vigor; a pack of small flies buzzed in rising circles inside a shaft of light as the warmth pulled them upward; a dog chased a chicken down Alii Street; the surf pounded against the reef.

Jan lay in bed for a few moments until curiosity about a swishing sound pulled her to the window. She had slept nude in the heat and took the sheet with her as a wrapping. The Chinese man from whom Jan had rented the room was sweeping the board sidewalk in front of his store with a palm-frond broom.

Something moved to her right, a flash, an intimation of movement, and Jan jumped back. The gecko lizard, feet spread, spun left, then right, then climbed into the corner of the ceiling. During the night Jan had heard them feeding and clicking to one another.

She ditched the sheet and wrapped herself in a towel, then went downstairs to the toilet. The shower stall was streaked with rust and Jan chose to wash herself quickly from the basin.

Through the wall she could hear the Chinese arguing in pidgin with someone who answered in a high-pitched female voice. Dishes and cups rattled. Maybe they were preparing the breakfast that was reputedly included in the two-dollar price of the room.

In the stairwell back up to her room, Jan passed a chubby, plain-faced teenage girl she guessed had been the point of the Chinese's squealing rage. Jan smiled and said good morning while stepping aside for her. The native girl smiled, then raised her hand and covered her yellow teeth.

Breakfast waited in her room. The sheets had been stripped from the bed. On the bare mattress sat a bowl of sliced mango, pineapple spears, a thick slice of French bread, and bits of sashimi. Jan ate while dressing, then headed down to the village to look for a place that might serve coffee.

From the seawall Jan could see that two boats had already put out and were headed for the opening through the reef; a dozen others were at the pier and the fishermen were preparing their gear before setting out. Jan did not see Hatch among them.

There was very little to the village: a single seashell-paved white street running parallel to the sea for about three hundred yards—a church at one end and the Government House at the other; a couple of stores, an open air market, two bars, a few houses, and a one-room school finished off the street. There was an abandoned warehouse on the pier that looked from the paint and faded lettering to have been built by the Australian Navy during World War II. Jan had started onto the pier when a faint whiff of coffee turned her head. She followed her nose into Papa Jack's.

Hattie was now lazily wiping down the small round tables with a rag, occasionally using it to pop flies out of the air with admirable accuracy. Jan recognized the man behind the bar from last night; now he was washing glasses. A boy no older than twelve raked cigarette butts off the dirt and sawdust floor, puffs of dust following the blades of his bamboo tool like dirty ghosts.

Then Jan saw what had drawn her—an old-style stainless-steel coffee urn perking noisily on the far end of the bar.

"Good morning," she said to any or all of them.

Hattie popped a fly and did not look at her. The boy smiled. The man behind the bar nodded and said, "Bar bilong open short taim, ahet klok. No taim drink likkur Day bilong Sabbut."

As far as Jan could figure, the bar would open at eight o'clock, no liquor because it's Sunday. "Could I get a little coffee now? I'll take it outside." She glanced at her wristwatch—it was a little after seven-thirty.

"We'll just help ourselves and go outside, Alapaki." Jan heard a voice behind her and turned to see Hatch standing in the doorway.

"O-kay-do-kay, Hatch," Alapaki said, waving.

"You use anything?" Hatch asked Jan as he went to the coffee urn, lifting a couple of cups on the way.

"No, nothing," Jan answered.

Hattie turned and knocked a fly out of the air.

"Good shot," Hatch told her.

"Fo-die," Hattie said, twisting the rag in front of her chest with both hands.

"She's killed four," Hatch translated for Jan.

Hatch filled two mugs, handed one to Jan, and they went outside.

"When you weren't at Mr. Lee's, I figured you'd follow the smell of coffee down the street," Hatch said as he sat down on the long bench running along Papa Jack's front.

"I'm continually amazed by your ability to recover," Jan said after testing the hot coffee.

"Recover?"

"From drinking."

"The key is to avoid becoming sober."

"You seem sober now."

"It's a disguise. Beneath this glib, coffee-drinking facade lurks a pickled brain."

Jan laughed. She appreciated the effort it took for him to be offhand.

They looked across the street and over the seawall toward the bay, the reef, and the ocean. More boats had gone out, most under sail. The last boats were just leaving the pier.

"I envy you this, having it for so many years," Jan said. But she was thinking about what she had lost, about how suddenly Life seemed to have turned against her. Life?

She thought. Had she meant God? Hatch spoke and got her attention.

"I didn't know what I had here all that time, not until it was mostly gone. So there's nothing to envy. For all practical purposes, what you don't know or understand does not exist. The cruelty was in discovering it, coming to need it, only to then have it taken away."

"Pardon the cliché, but isn't it better to have loved and lost than never to have had the experience at all?"

"No."

"For you, maybe. I could not have lived without it."

"You would have lived."

Hatch sipped his coffee quietly and watched the fishing boats heading out.

"I like the one with the red sail," Jan said, wanting to change the subject.

"Makaavana. He's a good fisherman. He's very old and he has children to help. But on Tuva no one can be hungry or thirsty or want for love. That isn't why he fishes still. He goes out because he doesn't know how to do anything else." After a long pause Hatch added, "Like men who keep going to fight. Once you have defined yourself, to deny it is to cease to exist."

Jan knew then, at that precise moment, that Hatch was going to help her, but she would let him find his own way of telling her.

Two elderly women dressed in Sunday finery passed them on the plank sidewalk. Hatch greeted them, introducing Jan Moss when they stopped to pass a moment's time. Around them, the village came fully awake: children ran playfully down the shell and coral street ahead of their parents, young boys careful of their best clothes showed off for girls in dresses, and men walked in stately discomfort behind their wives—as if being led was the only way to get them to the church; only the heathens, Chinese Buddhists and men of the small Hindu population, were at work; and the fishermen, who were a breed unto themselves. The church bell tolled for the faithful, both dubious and sincere.

"I just found the source for the feeling of *déjà vu* I've been having," Jan said after the women had left to answer the bell. "I've seen this in half a dozen movies."

"God," Hatch said with a wistful tone, "I haven't seen a movie in . . . I can't remember the last time . . . since 1963?"

"You probably haven't missed much."

"I always kind of liked movies," Hatch said.

Alii Street was deserted then, except for the man and woman sitting side by side on the bench in front of Papa Jack's. A dog, fat and docile, explored the trash heap at the edge of the alley by the church, and ever-present gulls circled the bay, their cries now commingled with the rise of *a cappella* voices in harmony from the church, making "A Mighty Fortress Is Our God" sound as if it had been written by some sad South Seas romantic.

Hatch saw Jan check her wristwatch, then he said, "There is a radio in Mr. Jolly's office through which you can contact Tahiti."

Jan looked up a bit confused.

"To call for the plane," Hatch went on.

Jan nodded her understanding, then asked, "For when?"

"Tomorrow. Noon. They'll have high tide in the bay."

Jan nodded again, knowing better than to stretch it out, certainly not to thank him for agreeing to come. They both knew what it meant. They both understood about debts and payments.

"This will be more difficult than you can possibly imagine," Hatch said then. "We will do this my way entirely."

"Yes," she said.

Jan stood, set her coffee mug on the bench, and headed off toward the Government House. The stone in her chest glowed like heated metal.

7

There was no one home when Hatch reached the upland house of Tioni and Jenny Makani; he sat in one of the wicker chairs on the veranda to wait. From there he could see all of the leeward side of Tuva, and the breeze at that altitude was cool and free of insects.

Emma was only ten weeks old when Kukana was kidnapped and taken to the United States, and only ten weeks older when Kukana threw herself off the *pali* into the sea. Hatch did not know how to care for her. The child was mysterious; he was perplexed by her inability to communicate in a language he understood. Since she could not speak intelligently to him, how, he wondered, would he know if she needed something? If she hurt, how would he know where? He was overwhelmed by the responsibility, and terrified by his love for her.

Hatch had fallen asleep in the chair; Emma's voice woke him.

"Papa, Papa, Papa," Emma cried, pulling free of Jenny's hand and waddling across the yard to the veranda.

Hatch got up and went down the steps, kneeling at the bottom to wait for Emma to jump into his arms. Beyond Emma, Hatch could see Jenny puffing up the hill in her tent of a muumuu. Vastly overweight, she barely managed the heat.

"Hello, my darling," Hatch said into Emma's ear when she threw herself into him.

"We bought my dress," Emma said excitedly. She pulled herself away from Hatch and took off toward Jenny, yelling, "Show Papa my dress."

Grabbing Jenny's hand, the child tugged her back toward Hatch, who was now standing and walking toward them.

"Hello, Hatch," Jenny greeted him. "We've been to the Emporium, as you can see, I guess."

"Show Papa, show Papa," Emma insisted, pulling Jenny's arm.

"She's growing so fast I can hardly keep her in Sunday dresses," Jenny said.

"This one's beautiful," Hatch said about the yellow dress Emma was wearing. "Your dress is beautiful, honey," he said to Emma.

"No, Papa, see my new one." Emma pulled the paper sack away from Jenny and brought it to her father.

Hatch pulled from the sack a white sundress with yellow flowers sewn into wide shoulder straps. Emma took the dress and held it up in front of her, spinning like a miniature model.

"It's a very beautiful dress," Hatch told her.

"Why don't you go put the dress in your room," Jenny said, finally reaching them. "Then you can come back outside and see your father."

"You put it," Emma challenged.

"Emma," Jenny said in a no-nonsense voice.

"You put it," Emma repeated.

"Do you want your papa to think you're a spoiled little girl?"

"Do what Jenny says, Emma. I want to talk to her for a minute, then we'll go to Pupukea Beach for a swim. Okay?"

"Okay, Papa." Emma gave him a quick kiss and ran inside with her new dress.

"Lay it neatly on your bed," Emma called out.

Hatch sat down on the steps and Jenny sat next to him, the empty sack held in front of her knees. She exhaled heavily.

"She's a lot, isn't she?" Hatch said.

"She's a continual joy . . . and a lot, too." Jenny smiled.

"I've asked too much of you and Tioni to keep her."

"You've given Tioni and me a great gift, Hatch. It is not only the honor of caring for the future *Alii Nui* of Tuva, but watching her becoming Kukana incarnated, her mother in miniature. She's a wonderful little girl."

They were quiet. Hatch put his hand on Jenny's shoulder and left it there. There were child noises coming from inside the house.

Then, after a time, Jenny said, "We know, Hatch."

Hatch nodded and took his hand off Jenny's shoulder.

"How long?" Jenny asked.

"I really don't know. Not very, I hope. Maybe a few months, maybe a few weeks."

"She will miss you, but at her age the impact will not be so strong."

"Maybe not on her."

"Yes, of course. But on you . . ."

"I love her very much, I just don't know what to do with her."

"I understand. Emma knows how much you love her, Hatch."

Emma exploded through the door and flew across the veranda, landing on Hatch's back, yelling, "Giddiyup, Papa, ride, ride."

Hatch jumped up and galloped a small circle in the yard in front of Jenny with Emma laughing hysterically. When Jenny stood to go into the house, Hatch said, "I'm going to take this cowgirl down to Pupukea. When we come back, would you do something about this?" He tugged at his beard and hair.

Jenny waved, calling out after them, "Reverend Walters is coming for supper tonight at six. Come early if you want me to cut all that off and make you look reasonable."

Hatch waved over his shoulder and galloped Emma down the hill.

That night Hatch's body sought new, more terrifying tricks to fool his brain into giving it alcohol. His heart beat furiously fast, then slowed suddenly, contracting prematurely, putting two beats on top of one another so the heart seemed to miss a beat. His fingers trembled so erratically that he could not hold a glass without spilling some of the water inside. Sometimes his vision clouded. He could keep nothing in his stomach.

He slept intermittently, awakened by frequent nightmares. He tried to exhaust himself to sleep by running wind sprints on the beach and swimming out to the reef and back, but each time he managed to fall asleep, it was only for half an hour or so before the dreams shook him awake. Finally he gave it up and went out to sit on the *lanai* and watch the sea.

Later, in the morning darkness, he pulled from beneath his bed an old footlocker. He worked on the locks by kerosene lamp—the key had been lost years ago—but finally gave up and cut through the top of the locker with a Ka-bar knife.

Rotting inside the locker lay the residue of a life so long repressed that it seemed to belong to a stranger; a life so old and distant that it felt like a masquerade once worn to a forgotten party—a party Hatch had attended disguised as Captain Franklin Jefferson Hatcher, combat intelligence officer with the Fifth Special Forces group, a party he left early because the music made him sick.

Hatch reached into the locker and pulled out a faded green beret with the red Fifth group flash and his silver captain's bars on it; the bars had oxidized, turned dark against the flash, which had itself faded to deep yellow. He held the beret in front of him for a moment as if to put it on, but he pitched it onto the table and probed inside the locker again.

A folded khaki uniform shirt lay on top of everything else in the locker, and Hatch took it out, holding it up by the shoulders. Above the left pocket were three racks of ribbons, his silver master-parachutist wings, and the combat infantryman's badge. His index finger roamed over the multicolored ribbons, passing over the Bronze and Silver stars, the commendation, campaign and service medals, pausing over the Purple Heart, which was covered with clusters—as if to touch them was to touch the scars on his body. He ran his hand down the shoulder and folded the sleeve to expose the shoulder patch: the sword and lightning bolts inside the arrowhead pointing upward to the Airborne and Ranger tabs. He folded the shirt again and put it on the table next to the beret.

He threw aside a set of tiger-stripe camouflage fatigues and a bush hat, uncovering a shoe box which rattled metallically when he picked it up. Inside the box were the medals corresponding with the ribbons on the shirt, his original set of silver jump wings, an extra set of captain's bars, a silver signet ring, as well as a packet of letters and a manila envelope filled with photographs.

His hands were shaking too badly to study the pictures, and anyway, he told himself, they would only show a young, fresh kid, ready and gung-ho to a fault, and a family long gone in reality and memory. He put the shoe box on the table.

Fishing around in the locker's bottom, he came up with his Randall fighting knife. He put the knife aside.

Everything went back into the locker except the shoe box and its contents, and the knife.

He carried the locker down to the beach, set it inside his skiff with a half-dozen heavy stones. Then he paddled out beyond the reef and dumped it over the side. Spontaneously he blew the sinking locker a kiss.

It was dawn by the time he finished the note to Tioni and Jenny. Writing "In the Event of My Death" across the envelope, he put it with the shoe box on the floor next to his bed. Should he write something to Emma? No, she would forget him soon enough, and all the better for it. Even the note to Tioni and Jenny was terse: *Let Emma think of you as her parents. I know you love her, and she you. I know you will see to it that she has a life filled with possibilities, which is all I can ask. If she ever wonders, tell her that I did love her.*

Then he opened the top drawer of his wicker dresser and removed an ornately framed photograph of Kukana and himself, taken on their wedding day by Mr. Jolly. He removed the photograph and replaced the frame.

He put the photograph into a small bag, along with his

new passport—issued, along with a full pardon, two
years ago, by direct presidential request—a little Australian and American money, the Randall knife, and finally
he slipped the ring over the third finger of his right
hand.

It was dawn then and he snuffed the lamp.

Hatch took the bag and went outside, leaving the door
open. Let the Tuvans help themselves to any of that
junk, he thought.

As he started off through the jungle toward the village,
he did not look back. Michael Laser was only the excuse.
Hatch had been handed a ticket in the Laotian jungle
more than two decades ago, and now he had to take the
ride.

From Tuva they flew by seaplane to Papeete, Tahiti,
and from there got a series of UTA flights that hop-
scotched them across the South Pacific to Cook, Fiji, and
finally Wellington.

They had not talked much on the plane. Hatch slept
solidly and Jan intermittently. They seemed almost as
strangers. It was as if they were afraid to talk, afraid of
what might be said.

Jan noticed that Hatch took only a Coke from the
stewardess when the drink cart went by, and she,
although wanting a drink badly, asked for coffee. Hatch
drank the Coke quickly, chewed the ice cubes, then laid
his head back on the seat and fell directly to sleep again.

She looked at him for a moment, still surprised just a
little by the way he looked with his hair neatly cut, the
beard shaved off with only a thick mustache remaining,
and dressed in long pants and a cotton shirt; so
surprisingly handsome again. But then, he had always
surprised her, that was his way. His ability to recover
from self-neglect, to adapt instantly to abrupt changes,
still astonished her.

Watching him sleep, Jan remembered the first time
she had seen him asleep—more than twenty years
earlier on a beach south of Rosarito on the Baja peninsula

of Mexico. She was lying on a blanket between her two men: on one side of her, his hand lying casually but possessively over her breast, was Greg Henry, a lieutenant with the SEALs, who would in a few months become her first husband; and on the other, his hands tucked under his head for a makeshift pillow, was Frank Hatcher, a Green Beret first lieutenant, asleep, and unaware that Jan's hand lay warmly against his chest.

Jan smiled, remembering how much of that weekend Hatch had been asleep. Hatch and Greg were then at the Special Warfare School in Coronado, California. It was a rare two days off. A year later they were both somewhere in Southeast Asia. Greg never returned, which left Jan a widow at twenty-one.

Jan's smile faded and she leaned her head against the window. There was nothing to see below but a layer of clouds lying so thickly over the ocean that it seemed a floor. A widow again, she closed her eyes and played out scenes of revenge against the screen of her eyelids.

Part Two

Ξ

Koh Phuket, Thailand

8

She had first taken Hatch to see Tom Considine, the political officer at the American embassy in Sydney, the Company man who told her to stay away from Michael Laser. But Considine, they were told, had returned to Washington.

They flew to Wellington then. The Company man at the embassy, who had been the Mosses' contact in New Zealand, and whom Jan had overheard mention Laser at an embassy party, told them that Michael Laser was dead and that Jan must have been confused. He absolved the U.S. government of any further responsibility in ensuring Jan's safety unless she would put herself under his control and take a new identity in England.

"Now we do it my way," Hatch told her then. "This is just a lot of bullshit."

That night at a TraveLodge in Rongotai, they ate a quick, quiet dinner in the motel restaurant, retiring to their adjoining rooms before nine o'clock.

An hour later Hatch knocked on the door to Jan's room. Pulling closed her bathrobe, she let him in. Hatch strode across the room, then turned back to face her. Jan closed the door and sat on the bed.

"What?" Jan asked when Hatch stood there silently.

"I've thought about it," Hatch began, speaking as if reading from notes, "and even though I know you've been thinking all along that you'd go with me, you can't, and that's all there is to it. It's not something I came over here to argue with you about, either. I'll take care of it, don't worry about that. But you'd hold me up. You can see that. So I can't take you and that's all there is to it." He walked to the door and opened it, then turned and added, "I'm sorry, Jan." He closed the door quietly behind him.

Jan sat on the corner of the bed and stared at the back of the closed door. The emotion that began its rise from the pit of her stomach as fear reached her throat as fury. She stood abruptly, jerked the Chinese robe tightly to her chest, and banged on the door between their rooms.

Hatch opened the door and stood aside as she pushed by him into the room. She turned and stood face-to-face with him, her index finger poking the air in front of his chest.

"Where the hell do you get off telling me *I* can't go with *you*? The man killed my husband! He's responsible for this"—she held up her hand and displayed the missing little finger—"remember? And besides, *I* have the money, *I* have the contacts, and *I*, goddammit, have the goddamned desire! Don't you dare try to put me aside, Hatch. Don't you dare!"

Nodding her head authoritatively, Jan backed up and blew out of the room like a white squall.

Hatch sighed heavily, then smiled in spite of himself.

They had flown to Manila and changed planes to Bangkok. They spent the night at a small hotel on the tiny street behind the *klong*, the canal, near Jim Thompson's house. Hatch had run into Thompson in 1964 at a bar on Phya Thai Road, and Thompson, the sometime spy who created the Thai silk industry, secured for Hatch his first job after he walked out of the war—as a bodyguard for the family of a Chinese banker in Singapore.

If there was anything of interest going on in Southeast Asia, Hatch figured that Jim Thompson would know about it. What Hatch did not know was that Thompson had disappeared on a trip into Malaysia in 1967 and had not been heard from since. The fancy house, which Thompson had filled with antiques and priceless, exotic works of Thai art, had been turned into a museum, which was what Hatch and Jan found there.

"What now?" Jan asked as they stood on the walk in

front of Thompson's house, a flood of people parting to pass them like rocks in a stream.

"I don't know yet," Hatch said, looking around as if an answer might be found in the face of someone passing by. He turned to say something to Jan, but it was drowned out by the sputtering roar of a half-dozen *tuk-tuks*, the omnipresent three-wheeled minibuses, going down Rama I Road.

"What?" Jan shook her head.

But Hatch had already turned toward a group of women dressed in Thai sarongs who were selling books and postcards of the Thompson house. Greeting them in *wai*, the prayerlike clasping of the hands and inclining the head slightly, Hatch asked if any of them spoke English: "*Ti ni mi kai pud pa sa ang-kid yipun dai mai?*" he asked, hoping that his grammar and pronunciation were, after so long a time, still sensible.

"Yes, speaking good," one said, smiling politely and returning the *wai*.

"My Thai is *mai di*," Hatch said. "I wonder, would you happen to know where the man is who used to live in this house?"

"Mr. Jim Thompson?" the girl said. Her friends giggled, politely covering their mouths.

"Yes, Jim Thompson. I knew him a long time ago."

"Mr. Thompson, he disappear on Malaysia, also long time ago. This his house. Museum now."

"He's dead?"

"Probably, maybe. Dead, yes. Gone anyway."

"*Kob khun,*" Hatch thanked her. Bowing in *wai*, he went back to Jan.

Well? she inquired with a look.

"Check out and get a *tuk-tuk* back to Don Muang."

"We're leaving Thailand, just like that?"

"We're leaving Bangkok." Hatch's memories of Thailand's capital were not good.

The late-afternoon Thai Airways turboprop flight to Phuket arrived as the sun was setting into the Andaman

Sea. The lush, subtropical island, connected to the mainland of southern Thailand by a causeway, was populated by an amiable mix of Thai, Malaysians, Chinese, Indians, expatriate Americans, mercantile Europeans, pirates, sea gypsies, and, lately, tourists, who came for the pristine beaches, coral-laced clear seas, and distinctly more pornographic delights.

After being chased back to the curb by a speeding, rocking billboard truck advertising an American gangster movie in Thai and English, Hatch and Jan flagged down a *samlor*, a motorized pedicab, for the fifteen-kilometer trip west of Phuket City to the beach town of Patong.

"This looks like Little Acapulco," Jan said when they walked along Patong's central street.

"I don't know, I've never been to Acapulco," Hatch said, grabbing her bag and walking off down the street.

"Well, neither have I," Jan said, following behind him. "I just meant that . . . Never mind." She hurried to catch up, wondering what she had done to make him so abrupt.

There were rows on rows of bars, most hardly larger than a small motel room, with tin roofs and open sides through which Jan could see rows upon rows of beautiful doe-eyed Thai women in sarongs cut to their hips, or tight white shorts and fluorescent tube tops, perched on wicker stools, displaying their legs like market meat, their oiled skin reflecting like still water the light from strands of multicolored light bulbs. It gave the place the atmosphere of an eroticized small-town street carnival, enhanced by the cacophonous blend of a half-dozen jukeboxes blaring against the volume of VCR movies playing on screens above the bars. Only the bartenders, methodically wiping out glasses, seemed to watch the movies.

"Do you know where you're going?" Jan asked a little breathlessly, having run to catch him.

"Hey you guy, big man, hey you," a girl called out from a bar below a red-white-and-blue neon sign proclaiming "Old Glory" in both Thai and English.

"Come on in, handsome," another cried out. "Hey, you can bring you wife too."

"We get a boy for you wife," another yelled.

A *samlor* putt-putted by, weaving around a pair of staggering rented bicycles on which were perched two obviously drunk American sailors.

"Oo, sailor boys," a bar girl called out, but she did not move from her stool or break her pose.

"You big like you look?" another cried, holding her hands a foot apart.

"Come here, come here, come here," offered another, emphasizing the double entendre, singing the first word.

The young sailors rode their bikes up onto the board sidewalk and crashed into the bar, spilling girls, drinks, and stools. The bartender jumped over the bar, pool cue in hand.

Hatch grabbed Jan's arm and jerked her into the street. They dodged a *samlor*, then Hatch flagged down an empty pedicab.

"Do you know the Black Pearl?" Hatch asked as he helped Jan into the cab.

"I know," the old Chinese man answered with a bow.

"How much?"

"Not much."

"How much?" Hatch insisted. "Tell me first."

"Black Pearl long way from here."

"Come on, get out," Hatch told Jan, taking her arm again.

"Twenty *baht*," the old man said quickly.

"It's not that far. Ten."

"Fifteen. I have many children."

"Ten *baht*," Hatch said, climbing into the cab and handing over the note. "Buy a rubber."

The old man muttered in Chinese and pedaled away.

At the Black Pearl, which was indistinguishable from all the other bars around it, as well as those on Patong's main drag, the bartender had to be pulled away from *Rocky IV* on videotape.

"Boone Buchannan," Hatch repeated, yelling over the jukebox version of "A Whiter Shade of Pale," playing loud on top of fight music from the movie.

"Mr. Boone not here," the bartender said, looking back and forth between Hatch and the movie.

"Will he be here?" Hatch asked.

"Maybe. Maybe no. Mr. Boone not owner of Black Pearl now. I am owner." The bartender pointed to his own chest.

"Do you know where I can find him?" Hatch asked. But he had lost the bartender's attention to the choreographed blows being delivered on the video screen.

"Hey, you!" Hatch yelled, trying to regain the man's attention.

Someone tugged on his arm and Hatch looked around into the dark oval eyes of a bar girl.

"Why you look for Mr. Boone?" the girl asked.

"Do you know him?"

"Maybe. I been work here long time."

She looked it. She had to be pushing thirty; twenty was getting old for a Patong bar girl.

"I am a friend of his," Hatch said, straining his voice to be heard over the music and loud laughter from surrounding bars.

"You like buy me one gin?" the girl asked, letting her hand rest on Hatch's shoulder. "Okay for you wife too. I can be with boys and with girls, same time." She looked around Hatch and gave Jan a smile.

Jan, embarrassed, quickly looked up at the television, as if she had been watching it all along.

Hatch put a twenty-*baht* note on the bar. "Buy yourself a drink. None for me. I'd like to find Boone."

"Mr. Boone live by Karon Beach, between there and Kata, before you get to Club Med place."

"*Kob khun,*" Hatch thanked her with the *wai,* which she returned.

"Do you know what a Club Med place is?" Hatch asked Jan as they went back to the street.

"Of course, it's a kind of—"

"Good," Hatch interrupted. "Show me." He hailed a

taxi for the bumpy, dirt-road drive south to the tip of Koh
Phuket.

9

Boone Buchannan's house sat on the beach just
beyond the high tide line; a tangle of palms and
bougainvillea came down the slope and enclosed the
back. In front, a rickety plank pier extended from the
veranda a hundred feet into the bay; a holding tank made
of sticks tied with hemp floated in the calm black water at
the end of the pier. Chunks of rotting Styrofoam kept the
tank from sinking with the weight of hundreds of large
oysters held inside; oysters that had been impregnated,
as it were, with mother-of-pearl beads planted into the
mantle tissue as irritants, and which were now halfway
through a four-year gestation. Kerosene lanterns vaguely
illuminated the end of the pier and each end of the
holding tank. A small dark man dressed in black silk
clothes squatted in the shadows on a floating platform
beneath the end of the pier; on his lap lay an automatic
rifle with a collapsible metal stock.

Hatch first saw the man as the swelling and falling red
glow from the tip of his cigarette. The guard was only a
dark profile in the shadows, but it was enough for Hatch
to determine that the man was guarding something and
that the object extending across his lap was probably a
machine gun. Hatch put out his hand and stopped Jan.

"What—"

"Sssh," Hatch whispered, putting a finger to her lips.

Hatch looked in the direction he wanted Jan to look,
but she could not see what he had seen in the darkness
below the pier. She shook her head.

"Holding tank for pearl beds, cultured pearls," Hatch
whispered into Jan's ear. "It's guarded."

There was light in the house. The jungle was quiet.
They could easily hear water from the bay lapping over
the top of the holding-tank frame. When Hatch held his

breath and listened carefully, he could just hear music—mainly a thumping bass beat—coming from somewhere behind them, probably the bars at Karon Beach, from where they had just hiked along a narrow path.

"Can't we just say hello or something?" Jan wondered. "I mean, you think he would shoot us if we just walked up to the house?"

"Without a doubt."

There was a burst of laughter from the tile-roofed house—a man's and a woman's. Then the front screen door, which led onto the pier, opened and a human figure filled it. The man took a cigarette from his mouth and flicked it in a high arc into the water, where it disappeared like a miniature meteor. Hatch saw the guard stand attentively. The woman's voice called out something in Thai from inside the house, where a light had just come on, and the man in the door waved her off as he headed out onto the pier. The man said something in Thai to the guard, and they had a brief unintelligible conversation. The woman appeared in the doorway, backlighted from inside the house, nude, hands on her hips. "Poo-oon," she called out in a plaintive singsong voice, giving the word two syllables and heavily accenting the first.

"This might not be a good time," Jan whispered, smiling.

Hatch shrugged. He put Jan behind a nearby tree in case the guard was quick-triggered, then called out to the man on the pier: "Boone Buchannan. It's Hatch, Frank Hatcher."

The guard crouched and leveled his K-50M Chinese submachine gun in the direction of the voice, but the man put out his hand before the guard could fire. "*Mai chai*," Boone said.

"You got your man calmed down?" Hatch yelled.

"I thought you were dead," Boone yelled back.

"I've got someone with me," Hatch said, "a woman. We're coming out to the beach now."

Boone Buchannan said something to the guard, who

then went back to his position below the end of the pier. Boone walked back toward the house to meet Hatch.

"A woman?" Boone said when they came into the dim light. Boone Buchannan, his thinning black hair wet and slicked back over his wide scalp, wore a pair of baggy khaki shorts and a ragged gray sleeveless sweatshirt with the logo of Harvard University stretched over his chest. He was taller than Hatch, about six-three, but seemed forty pounds lighter.

"Jan Moss," Hatch introduced them, "Boone Buchannan, scoundrel extraordinaire and"—Hatch feigned a slap at Boone's nonexistent belly—"ex-fat-man. Some diet, Boone. Or is it the girl?"

"Hey, what can I say?" Boone winked.

Boone took Jan's hand and made a show of kissing it. "Madame," he said lavishly. Then he reached out and grabbed Hatch, pulling him into a bear hug as they slapped one another on the back. Behind them, the naked woman stared.

"Well, piss on my match, you old lunatic," Boone was saying. "How come you're still alive, huh?"

"Not that a few haven't tried, I tell you that," Hatch said, pulling back.

They held each other by the shoulders, Boone still pounding on Hatch with one hand.

"Poo-oon," the native woman sang for attention.

"Don't you just love hearing a woman call you 'poon'?" Boone smiled and looked over at Jan with a wink.

"Coming, Lotus Blossom," Boone said over his shoulder to the woman in the doorway. "Christ A-mighty, Linn, cover thyself, you heathen lovely." Boone turned back to Hatch and said, "Now ask me, go ahead, ask me, ask me why I live in this godforsaken, sinful cesspool at the end of the known world. Go ahead, ask me."

"I'm asking," Hatch said.

"How can you ask me a thing like that, man? Come on with you both, now, let's get out of the landing path of mosquitoville airport."

Linn, whose name was actually Khunying, the nine-

teen-year-old daughter of the man crouched beneath the
pier with a Chinese submachine gun in his hands, held a
flowered sarong in front of her as she opened the door for
her fifty-year-old lover and the two Americans.

Boone introduced them.

"Linn is *not* a Phuket girl," he said, arching his
eyebrows. Linn wound the sarong around her body.
"She's a mainlander, a Bangkok broad. Phuket girls don't
like to have fun, do they, Lotus Blossom?"

"Phuket girls' pussies dry up like old durian, smell just
the same," Linn said, spitting on the wooden floor.

Jan blushed in spite of herself.

Boone sent Linn into the kitchen for a bucket of ice,
then excused himself and went into the back for a fresh
bottle of gin. "We'll toast whatever devil led you here
with some fizzes."

When they were gone, Jan turned to Hatch and asked,
"What is a durian?"

"A native fruit that's hard and spiny on the outside,
soft and gooey on the inside; tastes all right, I guess, but
the smell . . . imagine sucking a rotten egg, wearing a
shirt on which a baby just puked, while standing in a
sewer."

"Uck. You're kidding."

"Afraid not."

"That's a rather crude analogy the girl used."

Hatch nodded. He was looking around the room,
which seemed to contain symbols of its own, acquisitions
representing Boone Buchannan's near-thirty years in
Indochina. Many of the weapons were antiques, most of
the native masks and shrunken heads were authentic and
of museum quality, and the collection of East Indian
wood carvings was probably worth thousands of dollars.

Jan was inspecting a head when Boone returned with
the gin-fizz makings.

"From a tribe near Morobe, New Guinea. A chief,
killed in battle. That head is just about seventy years
old."

"You mean they were shrinking heads just seventy years ago?" Jan asked.

"My darling beauty, they were shrinking heads in the mountains of New Guinea last week." Boone let out a bone-rattling laugh, then called out something in Thai to Linn.

Boone made their drinks and Linn brought them fresh pineapple spears, soda crackers, and fillets of marinated raw fish. While they ate and drank, Boone told them about selling his bar and massage parlor in Patong Beach and retiring to his house and the pearl farm. Linn flirted silently with Hatch, which, to Jan's dismay, she found infuriating. How could Hatch put up with such a whorish come-on? And from a veritable child!

"Well, it's settled then," Boone said after finding out that Hatch and Jan had arrived only that day and had not yet taken a room.

"We didn't come out here looking for a free room," Hatch said.

"Don't be silly." Boone waved his arm expansively. "*Mi casa es su casa*. This place has four bleeding bedrooms. You, of course, are welcome to share one if that's how it is."

"That's how it isn't," Hatch said quickly, without looking at Jan.

"So be it."

Jan thought it rude of Hatch to have answered so quickly, as if she did not exist. If it had not been for Boone's courteous attention, she might as well have been invisible.

"Up off your pretty butt, my little bubble," Boone said to Linn. "Rooms for two guests. *Wiki wiki*. Chop-chop." He clapped his hands like a potentate.

Linn left them after giving Hatch a look that blended regret with offering.

"Can I help?" Jan asked, standing.

"Don't you dare," Boone said.

"In that case," Jan said, looking around, "I would like to clean up a little before bed."

"Oh God"—Boone feigned a chuckle—"don't you love it when a round-eyed, classy broad talks dirty?"

"You are the most incorrigible man I've ever met," Jan said, having to laugh.

"Incorrigible. Did you hear that word? Oh, how you get to me, darling." He patted his heart. "The facility you seek is down the hall, last door at the end."

"Thank you, Mr. Buchannan."

"Boone, Boone."

"Boone." Jan laughed, shook her head, and went down the hall.

Boone turned immediately to Hatch and said, "You're missing the boat with that one, old friend."

"I like your consistency, Boone. The world needs some constants."

Boone stood with some effort and poured two fingers of gin into two glasses, handing one to Hatch.

"Enough bullshit for one night?" Boone asked.

"I'm looking for Michael Laser," Hatch said. "What can you tell me?"

"One thing, one thing you better hear. Mike Laser is the fucking devil incarnate, and I don't care what kind of horse you're riding, you don't want to be chasing him."

"You know where he is?"

"I know where he was. Nobody ever knows where he is. Very few people even know what he looks like, not any who are still alive. He has many names, many faces."

"Where he was will do. I know what he looks like."

"No matter what I say, whether I help you or not, you're going to go chasing after Laser?"

Hatch nodded and took a deep drink.

"Tomorrow. I'll ask around, see what there is."

"I'm asking nothing more," Hatch said, toasting Boone with a raised glass before gulping the rest of the gin.

The humidity rose during the night as clouds of the marine layer hugged the coastline, trapping the day's heat and the sea's salty moisture like steam in a sauna. As Jan lay nude on top of the damp, warm sheet, she began to understand Linn's aversion to the sarong. Above her a fan spun on its fastest speed, but its breeze was muffled and diffused by the mosquito netting around the bed. She felt drowsy, groggy in the heat, and could not sleep.

She folded the pillow behind her neck and looked down over her body, which glistened with sweat in the soft yellow light from kerosene lamps burning on the veranda and pier. There was something intensely erotic about it, the heat, her shining body, the wild, distant noises of birds and animals in the jungle, mixed with the sense of threat, of danger. Plus the anonymity. She could die here and no one would know, no one would care. Or she could kill a man with impunity. Sometimes, when it was very still, she could hear water lapping over the pearl-bed holding tanks, and it reminded her of the steady rhythms inside her own body.

Slowly, cautiously, as if the body were not her own, but some new and foreign thing, Jan slid her hands over the wet skin of her breasts and down across her stomach, leaving tracks in the sweat like the paths of tandem twisting snakes. She thought of Boone and Linn, visualizing him lying between the pretty young girl's legs, watching him grow thick, hard, and long, slowly entering her. In her mind Jan could become one and then the other, the man and the woman, feeling what each would feel, giving what each could give, as now she gave to herself for one of the few times since her husband had died.

Afterward, lying in bed was like lying in a pool of warm water; she got up to let the night air cool her skin and dry the bed. The house was quiet. Her weight made the floorboards creak slightly as she walked to the window. The lizards scattered into dark corners. But the window, which faced the jungle side of the house, offered no breeze. Jan pulled on a pair of shorts and a T-shirt, then tiptoed quietly through the house and out to the veranda.

Jan hoped that Linn's father would not shoot her when

she went outside. She could see his dark form at the end
of the pier. She thought of waving or making some sign,
but was afraid of calling attention to herself. She slipped
out the door and walked quietly to the end of the long
veranda, where there were some wicker chairs and a
table. She could already feel the slight breeze blowing in
from the bay, carrying with it air cooled slightly, but
effectively, by the sea.

The end of the veranda was away from the lamps and
hidden in darkness. Jan put out her hand and felt along
the wall as she moved cautiously forward. As she
reached down to probe for a chair, her hand touched
warm flesh.

10

"Just me," Hatch said, leaning forward until his face
met a tiny strip of lamplight running around the outer
edge of the veranda railing.

"That just about stopped my heart," Jan said breathlessly.

"Light attracts the bugs."

Jan found a chair and sat opposite Hatch. Now she
could see his outline, the flashes of light reflected in his
eyes, and occasionally the glints from his watch and a
ring on his right hand when he moved in a certain way.

"I was trying to be quiet so Linn's father wouldn't take
a shot at me," Jan said, turning to look toward the pier.

When she turned, Hatch could see the shape of her
breasts pressed against the damp T-shirt. He looked
away.

"That's not her father," Hatch said.

"Oh? But I thought Boone said . . ."

"I mean, the guard shift changed about an hour ago.
There's somebody else out there now."

"Oh. You've been here for a while, I guess."

Hatch nodded.

"You know more about this part of the world than I do,

but it's hard for me to fathom how Linn's father can sit out there guarding Boone's oyster farm while his daughter, hardly grown, runs around up here naked, sleeping with a man who must be nearly three times her age. If I were Boone, I don't think I'd want the girl's father sitting outside my house with a machine gun!"

"The girl looks rather grown to me."

"Well, physically, of course. She has an admirable body. You know what I mean."

"The Thai are a proud people, strong, moral, religious, brave."

"Then how—?"

"Linn and her father are from Bangkok. Bangkok is a city. Like New York, Los Angeles, Manila, Paris, cities everywhere. Money corrupts. I'd say the answer to your question is that Boone Buchannan has what is, to people like Linn's family, a helluva lot of money. People who've never had any want some."

"He doesn't seem rich."

"It's perspective. Boone has plenty. He's been around a long time, time to acquire a lot of things, including a reputation for having the inside track on most of the undercover deals made in this part of Asia.

"I've known Boone since our days at the JFK Spec War School, at Bragg. He was good, but the Army held him back, cramped his style; he was too smart, too independent to stay in the military for very long. He started free-lance ghosting for a couple of American intelligence agencies, including the CIA. Ironic, isn't it? Jason might have known, or at least known of, Boone.

"He had a business moving uncut gems out of the boonies for transport to Singapore and Hong Kong for cutting and distribution. But he was also the leading conduit of what you might call raw, uncut information, which he traded and sold like the stones people kill for out here. He did all right. Although there was a time some people would have liked to see him killed.

"Last time I saw Boone was here, in Phuket, in 1967. A long time ago. We did each other some favors. He's still alive, so I think I'm one ahead."

"Boone told you?" Jan asked, leaning toward him.

"Not really. But at least he knows who the man is. He's going to ask around."

Jan felt her heart pounding, unable to distinguish between feelings of fear and of anticipation.

"It will happen, won't it?" she said, still leaning close to Hatch. "Tell me it will happen."

Hatch stood and walked to the veranda railing. He was now visible in the lantern light. Jan got up and went to stand beside him.

"I'm sorry," she said. "I don't mean to push you."

"You're not, it's all right."

Jan put her hand on Hatch's arm and urged him to turn toward her. "Hatch . . ." she said, unwilling to complete the thought.

When Hatch turned, their faces were close. Jan moved. It was nearly imperceptible, but her head tilted back slightly and her eyes lowered. Hatch looked at her mouth, at the sweat beaded above her lip and on her chin, and had an impulse to touch his tongue to her there, to taste her.

But the sudden flare of a match jerked his head toward the pier. The guard had stood and was lighting a cigarette, the machine gun propped over his shoulder like a worker's shovel. Still illuminated by the match, the guard turned and looked toward the veranda, then shook the match out. Hatch turned away from Jan and said, "We should try to get some sleep."

"Good night," Jan called softly after him, but Hatch continued into the house without another word, and Jan put her hands on her shoulders, holding herself in the sudden chill.

11

Hatch surprised himself by sleeping two hours past
sunrise, missing the coolest part of the day. The air in his
bedroom was already thick and laden with moisture. He
dressed quickly, slipping on a pair of shorts and a
sleeveless khaki shirt, then walked barefoot to the
bathroom, passing Jan's door, which was still closed.

He found Linn in the kitchen, seated at the glass-
topped table with a tall, sweaty glass of fruit juice and a
large book in front of her.

"Sawaddi klap." Hatch said good morning to her.

"Sawaddi ka," Linn answered, looking up from the
book.

"Ti nai Boone?"

"English talk, please, for I will to practice," Linn said.
"Poon go Phuket City . . ." She seemed to be searching
for the rest of the sentence. "How, in English, you say
neung?"

"The number? You mean 'one'?"

"Chai, yes. Poon go one hour back."

Hatch nodded, going to the refrigerator for something
to drink. "What are you reading?" he asked.

"English book." Linn displayed the cover for him. The
cover said *Business English for Secretaries.* "Very hard
book." Linn shook her head in frustration.

Hatch took out a glass jug that seemed to hold juice
from a papaya or guava, or maybe passion fruit. He
poured a glass and tested it. Guava. Leaning back
against the counter, he watched Linn's lips move as she
silently mouthed each word.

"Why do you want to learn English?" Hatch asked,
making conversation as long as they were in the room
together.

"I am have desire for . . . to be secretary, work for
big American office in Bangkok, have apartment there,

maybe too finding American husband for to take me to America. Poon pay for me to go at the secretary school."

"That's nice of him."

"Poon a good man, nice man. I always give honor to him for help me for secretary school. When Poon gone, then I get the money he promise."

"When he's gone where?" Hatch asked, unable to believe Boone Buchannan would ever be pulled away from Thailand.

"Do you say 'dead'? Like, 'when he dead'?"

"'When he dies,'" Hatch corrected. "Are you saying that Boone is dying?"

"I can have hard time to say it for the sad it give me." As if to prove the sadness, tears formed in her eyes.

"Is he sick? What's wrong with him?"

"I have not English words for it."

"Speak Thai. Speak slowly and I can follow you."

In Thai, Linn said, "The doctor in Phuket City and the doctor in Bangkok both tell Poon that he is dying from the disease where the body attacks and kills the body," which Hatch understood to be cancer. "The sickness is in his blood."

Hatch shook his head and turned around to look out the jalousie window above the tin sinks. Boone was dying of cancer. So that was where the weight had gone. Boone had been as thick and stocky as a water buffalo the last time Hatch saw him; in fact, Boone's code name in the recon days had been Buffalo.

"How long he live?" Hatch asked in Thai.

"Not more than a year," Linn answered in her language. "Maybe not that long now."

"I'm glad you tell me," Hatch said, "but do not tell Boone I know. Okay?"

"Yes, I won't tell him. You are right, you are his friend, I can see. It would dishonor him to have people act differently in his presence."

"I go to swim," Hatch continued in Thai. "Tell the lady time she wakes from sleep that I go to the bay, she to wait for me here."

"Okay," Linn said in English, putting her face back into the book.

Hatch rinsed the glass and left it in the sink, then went out the kitchen door and around front to the pier. The sun was well above the jungle canopy and the morning bay mist had risen to form the first layer of what later in the day would become towering, rolling stratocumulus clouds to drop a few inches of rain over the inland mountains.

Divers worked the oyster beds. A sampanlike skiff was tied up at the end of the pier, and tied to one side of the holding tank was a narrow, motorless wicker boat, not unlike a *hang yao*—the thirty-foot motorized canal boats called "long tails" in Bangkok. The night guard had been replaced by a new man, who was holding the same Chinese K-50M, as if there were only the one weapon and they passed it from guard to guard as the shifts changed.

Hatch made his presence known with a loud approach to the pier. You should not surprise a man holding a submachine gun.

When Hatch walked out onto the pier and pantomimed that he was going for a swim, the guard waved him off and called out, "*Mai chai*, no swim here."

"Okay," Hatch said. "*Ti nai*? Where?"

"Other side," the guard told him, pointing across the spit of land on which the house sat.

Around the point was a narrow, sparkling white beach behind which tall coconut palms arched toward the water and a reasonably young banyan tree offered shade. Hatch left his shirt over one of the banyan's lower limbs and walked into the bay, warm as a bath and flat as a pond in a calm. He dug in with his arms and stroked ahead with no sense of destination or time.

The swimming, and the solitude, would give him time to think, to focus his attention on the apparent inexorability of his return to Indochina. For Hatch did not think his chances of surviving another incursion into those jungles any better than Boone's of escaping cancer's death warrant.

Which is what Jan could not understand, and why he was not going to take her any farther than they had already come. He no longer needed her. Not the money—where he was going it would be irrelevant; not the contacts, which were useless and had probably already alerted the wrong people; certainly not her dangerous eagerness, which would probably get her killed. No more people were going to die because of him.

He had wanted to kiss her last night on the veranda. He had wanted to pull her close, hold her, make love to her, as if it were only in that way he could grasp the last shreds of his life and hold on for a while longer, although knowing he could not erase the last quarter-century's failures by fulfilling a desire he had carried around since being left stranded on a Mexican beach on a summer night in 1963, when he decided not to fight his best friend for the girl they both loved, when by holding back he gave Jan to Greg. It was just another reason for leaving her behind.

No, Jan's journey would end in Thailand. He would ask Boone to see to it that she got out safely. Hatch owed that much to Jason; that and the death of Jason's killer. Hatch intended to clean his slate, leave no debts owed, no more punctures in the shredded fabric of his karma.

Boone called late in the morning and told Linn to ask Hatch to meet him at Wat Pratong, a temple about a dozen miles north of Phuket City.

After a short walk to Karon Beach, Hatch got a *samlor* for the ride to the Buddhist shrine.

After removing his shoes, Hatch entered and found Boone waiting where he said he would be, by the Enlightened One's gilded statue. Seeing Boone there, with his eyes focused on the complacent Buddha image, Hatch felt weighted by sadness. He stopped to compose himself. Hatch touched Boone's shoulder. "Interesting Buddha image," he said, looking at the top half of the statue. "What happened to the rest of it?"

"Somewhere in Burma there are people worshiping a pair of crossed legs and a golden butt," Boone laughed.

The laugh, Hatch noticed, was muffled, almost respectful. Hatch had not known Boone to be particularly respectful of anything or anyone who had not demonstrated his worth.

"No, really," Boone went on, "according to local legend, a boy working in the fields tied one of the water buffalo to this weird rod sticking out of the ground. He went off for a nap and was found dead; the buffalo had also died. Trying to remove the buffalo from the spike, the villagers began digging around it, and what they uncovered was a gold-plated Buddha—this one. They worked and worked, trying to dig the thing up, but to no avail. So, I mean, what would you do? They built this temple around the statue they couldn't unearth."

"But why is there only half of it here?" Hatch asked.

"So the story goes, some Burmese tried to steal it. They didn't have enough men to carry it in one piece, so they cut it in half. They were discovered coming back for the top and were killed. Which means there was no one left to tell them where the bottom half went."

"Ah, I see," Hatch said. "So instead of a reclining Buddha, somewhere in Burma there's the *wat* of the golden legs."

"Interesting way to put it."

They moved aside for a group of worshipers, then Hatch followed Boone outside.

"Let's find some shade," Boone said, leading Hatch to a grove of trees at the side of the temple. Nearby, a group of local women swept and raked a stone garden, using bamboo implements. A teenage boy on a moped bike showed off for his girlfriend by spraying her in a shower of pea gravel spun from beneath his tires. Boone sat down and leaned back against a tree trunk. Hatch squatted Asian-style next to him.

"I've lived in the East too long," Boone said, his expression placid.

"How's that?" Hatch asked, letting Boone find his place.

"This stuff's starting to make a little sense to me."

"Stuff?"

"All this spiritual mumbo jumbo."

"Like Buddhism?"

"The lot if it. There's not much of a barrier between these Asian spiritual philosophies. We've got them all here—Buddhists, Hindus, Muslims, various Christians, animists, the whole bunch. The space between Buddhism and animism gets pretty narrow here. Did you notice the spirit house at the edge of my veranda?"

"Yeah, I saw that."

"Things were happening in the house, weird stuff, things missing without explanation, things broken, people getting sick—"

Hatch nodded and waited for Boone to continue.

"So I put the spirit house up, and another, larger one on my property in the jungle. You never can tell."

"Yeah, I guess you're right about that."

"Don't make fun of me, old friend."

"I wasn't, Boone. Did it have that sound? That's not the way I meant it. You should know—"

"Sorry. I get jumpy. Part of aging, I guess."

"There's never been anything you'd need to apologize to me for, Boone."

Boone nodded.

For more than two minutes they quietly watched the scene around Wat Pratong. Clouds were building towers in the distance to the east. It would probably rain in a couple of hours as the clouds backed up to the coast. It would not be a long or a hard rain; it was still a month before the monsoons would start.

"Do you ever wonder what death is like?" Boone asked after a while.

"Who can help it?"

"What do you think?"

"I don't know. I guess I think nothing, that there's nothing after life, in death. Although I can't really imagine nothing, a mental impossibility. You?"

"I don't want to go." Boone smiled. "I want to stay here, forever, with this body . . . well, maybe a better body, with my friends and my house and my things, everything staying like it is forever."

"You don't mean that."

"I do. But I'll take coming back, reincarnation."

"With memories?"

"Exactly, with my memories intact."

"Me, I'd skip the memories."

Boone looked at Hatch and nodded.

"Are you afraid of dying?" Boone asked.

"No."

"Do you mean that?"

"Yes."

"I don't know whether to envy or pity you. It scares the piss out of me, Hatch."

Hatch pulled his lips tight in thoughtfulness.

"Does that make me less a man in your eyes?"

"Of course not. But this is pretty morbid shit, Boone, old man."

Suddenly Boone let go with a belly laugh that plastered his back to the tree and squeezed his face tight. The laughter was infectious and in a moment Hatch was lying on his side laughing as hard as Boone, who was now slapping the ground in ecstatic pain.

Two boys and a dog stopped to watch the two strange old *farangs* laughing together like children.

"This is all I could get," Boone said later.

They had walked around the temple talking about Buddhism for almost an hour. The walk had eventually taken them down the road a short distance to an outdoor bar where now they were at a back table drinking ice-cold beer from bottles.

"Michael Laser is probably over in Laos. What it looks like is, Laser's the top security adviser for one of the drug warlords in the northern mountains, man named Som."

"The one they call Prince Phoun Som?" Hatch asked, the name sparking a fire in his guts.

"Yeah," Boone said. "Well, yes and no, really. The prince is an old man. I don't think he's very active these days. It's his son, Kaysone Som, who's actually running things up there. Laser works for him.

"Listen, Hatch. I know that once you set your mind to doing something it's going to get done, but shit, friend, just walking into those mountains, not even looking for a bunch of goons like Som's troop, is no less than walking into the gates of hell expecting to kick the devil's ass. I'm going to ask you to forget this thing, whatever it is, let it go. I know you probably won't listen to me, but I've got to know I tried, I've got to live with myself. I owe you that.

"Are you listening to me, Hatch?"

He was not. He was already back in Laos.

12

Hatch had twisted half out of the sheet, which was now wrapped around one of his legs, and lay on his stomach near the edge of the bed, one arm hanging out of the mosquito netting. The overhead-fan motor could have used a few drops of oil. It squeaked like a metallic metronome, its blades slowly stirring the heat like sticks in mud.

But Hatch felt cool, having in his dream just come from bathing in the river with Mai. A breeze teased their wet skin like feathers. Mai was playful and wanted to make him chase her back into the village, where she would let him catch her, then tease him into making love. But Hatch, who with his team had been going in and out of Toulan for many months, knew Mai's ways. He worried about her pregnancy. Their child had been growing in Mai's womb for eight months. Mai thought Hatch was silly, the cautious way he treated her. Mai had seen women squat in the fields, push out a baby, slice through the cord, wrap the baby in a cloth, and walk home to clean it. Mai, who was seventeen and pregnant for the first time, thought it must not be too bad a thing to have a baby. But Hatch acted as if even laying his head on her belly to hear the fast heartbeat might kill it; he would always jump back when he got a kick or a turn.

Mai loved Hatch so much that some nights when he was away she thought she might die from the emptiness where he had lain beside her many other nights. That he had promised to marry her and take her to America was little comfort when he was always in danger, always in places where he could be killed. He was safe only when she could touch him.

But this day, this night, there was in both of them a sense of dread, for Hatch and his team were to leave Toulan in the morning.

"It won't be so long," Hatch said to Mai, speaking Lao because Mai had not been able to learn very much English yet. "Only three days, probably. We aren't going far this time."

"I, who am desperate when I lose sight of you for a minute, think three days is the sum of all time," Mai told him, looking away because the reminder made her want to cry. She tried never to cry in front of him because she could see his discomfort over her tears, his endearing inability to cope with it.

That night, in the deepest darkness, Hatch had awakened with his arm lying over Mai's distended belly, and unable to go back to sleep, had moved carefully away from her and gone out of the small bamboo-and-thatch house to smoke.

But Mai had awakened when his arm left her, and she turned over to watch him squatting to smoke just outside the doorway. All she could see was the shadowed outline of his back and the gray smoke rising above his head in the dim moonlight. Then it was safe to cry.

In his dream Hatch could see what he had not been there to see, but what he had not been able to keep from imagining during many tormented nights over the past twenty years. The nightmares were so familiar that they had become the reality. He saw Prince Phoun Som's drug bandits come into Toulan and terrorize the people who had sheltered the seven American commandos of Prairie Fire Recon Team Two, letting them use the village as their base. He saw them shoot the village mayor dead in the doorway of his house. He saw them beat the few old men left in the village—all the young men having already left to fight with or against the Pathet Lao. He saw them burn houses, abuse children and women. He saw all the things that Mai's uncle had, while hiding Hatch in a mountain cave, described in such solemn and terrible detail.

But what he saw with the clarity and detail of slow motion was Mai being dragged from her house, by men who ripped the simple dress from her body and kicked her where she had fallen in the mud by the washing stream, and then being staked spread-eagled and exposed to the villagers, who were forced to watch as one of the drug bandits knelt over Mai with his long knife poised above the rise of her belly.

Unable to break out of the dream, even when somehow Hatch recognized that it was a dream, he focused on the knife.

Torchlight ricocheted off the bright metal like sparks as the blade cut and Mai screamed. Then he saw the rat, its teeth oversized and snapping at the air, lowered into the opening in Mai's belly. Suddenly Hatch is inside Mai, with the fetus of their son, pressing himself back, back, back into the womb as the rat rushes toward them. . . .

Jan pulled Hatch up from the depths of his subconscious by pushing his arm and loudly calling his name.

"You were screaming," she said when Hatch opened his eyes.

She had pulled back the netting and Hatch remembered where he was. Beyond Jan, who was beside his bed, he saw Boone and Linn in the doorway; Linn, as usual, naked, and Boone wearing a garish pair of flowered boxer shorts, his belly distended below stark ribs like a water bag in a cage.

Hatch was as wet as if he had just stepped from a river. Beads of sweat dripped from the tips of clumps of his hair like a faucet not fully closed. His eyes, which had opened with a wild, crazy look, were now focused and dilated.

Jan sat on the edge of the bed where she had thrown back the netting and picked up Hatch's hand, which felt cold, clammy, and trembling. "Are you all right now?" she asked.

"Yes," Hatch said, his voice rough from disuse.

Boone put his arm around Linn's shoulders and guided her back to their bedroom. Boone knew about dreams.

Hatch pulled his hand free and rolled out the other side of the bed, forgetting that he was naked until he was already up. He reached down, picked up his shorts from the floor, and slipped them on. He went to the window and stood looking out at the bay.

"Some dream," Jan said, getting up and walking around the bed to stand beside him.

Hatch picked up a cigarette and his lighter from the night table, cupping his hand around the flame even though there was no breeze. The exhaled smoke curled around his head for a moment, then drifted out the window like a departing ghost. The exhalation relaxed the tightness in Hatch's chest.

"What was it? Do you remember?"

"No," Hatch lied to her. "I was never very good at remembering a dream."

"I used to get up and write mine down. It was like training my memory, so now I remember a lot of detail from dreams."

Hatch nodded and took another drag.

"But I guess some dreams you don't want to remember," Jan went on.

"That's probably true," Hatch said.

He had in fact remembered everything in the dream. He always did remember that one.

"Well, I guess I'd better go back to my room," Jan said
with a tone asking him to tell her to stay.

"Sorry I woke you," Hatch said, crushing the cigarette
out.

"That's all right, really."

Hatch noticed then that Jan was wearing only bikini
panties and a small white T-shirt. The moonlight through
the jalousie slats left shadow stripes across her chest.

"Well," Jan said as she began walking toward the door,
"see you in the morning."

"Yes, see you then," Hatch said, smiling politely.

When Jan was gone, Hatch sat down on the side of the
bed and put his face in his hands.

It was useless trying to go back to sleep. It always was.
Dawn would come in a couple of hours and the devils in
the darkness would be replaced by the gremlins of light.

Hatch went outside to the veranda; it was too hot to
stay in the room. There was some breeze and it came
from the bay, taking with it a little of the cooler air over
the water. He waved to the pearl guard and got a return
wave. Then he lit a cigarette.

He had talked with Boone about supplies and equip-
ment. Hatch decided he would need an automatic pistol
and a shotgun, four clips for the pistol, and a box of
shells. Boone said he could get Hatch a newer version of
the old Special Operations group's pump twelve-gauge, a
basic Remington 870 chopped and converted with a
pistol-grip handle, sling, twelve-and-a-half-inch barrel,
with a modified Mossberg Accu-Choke. "You'll find the
870 to be a lot like the sawed-off Ithaca Model 37 you
took into Laos in the old days," Boone had said, "except
that, unlike the Ithaca, this Remington requires you to
release the trigger each time for it to reset. Okay?" It
was okay with Hatch. Hatch had asked for shells with the
twelve-pellet Magnum 00 buckshot load, but Boone said
it would cause an unacceptable increase in the recoil for
a pistol-grip, and Boone recommended the Federal
Premium 00 nine-pellet loads, which, Boone had said,

"will give you a more uniform pattern at up to thirty-five yards."

Hatch had asked for a standard military-issue Colt forty-five-caliber automatic, but again Boone redirected him. Boone had said, "I can get you a brand-new, far superior semiautomatic the Commies have been turning out in Czechoslovakia; the CZ Model 83. It's a pocket pistol very similar to the Walther PPK series, with a few improvements. The magazine carries thirteen 9mm Kurz cartridges and it's a double-action blowback without a locked breech. It weighs a tad over twenty-six ounces, with an overall length of six-point-eight inches. It's cleanly disassembled, simple to operate, totally dependable, and best of all, I can get it for you tomorrow."

Hatch had his Special Forces-issue Randall knife with him. The rest was easy enough: a series of terrain maps, water-purification tablets, canteen, dried-fruit packs, a dozen pairs of socks and a pair of good boots, two sets of tiger-stripe fatigues, a good hat, a Ka-bar knife, bug juice, rain poncho, a rucksack, and a medical kit including compresses, sulfa, Dexedrine, Percodan, tape, snake-bite kit, and diphenoxylate for any severe stomach cramps with diarrhea.

Boone wanted four or five days to put the package together. That was all right with Hatch, who would use the time to work on his conditioning and try to get some more information on contemporary Laos and Laser's whereabouts. Unlike the climate of Tuva, which was also hot, that part of Laos, particularly as the monsoon season neared, was hotter and extremely humid. Hatch intended to swim three times a day now, increasing the distance to a mile each time, and run in the nearby jungles for half an hour twice a day—in the cooler morning air and again late in the evening.

As of today, he was no longer going to eat at Boone's table, but go into the town for local fruits and try to find snakes and lizards in the nearby jungle.

Hatch crushed out the cigarette and threw the butt

into the water beyond the veranda, wishing it had been
his last one, but knowing better. The trees behind the
house were now silhouetted against a brightening sky.
Dawn was nearing. Birds, the first of the jungle creatures to acknowledge the arrival of a new day, were
already tuning up. A parrot cried.

Hatch peeled off his T-shirt, stepped out of his thongs,
and walked along the beach to the back of the house
where the guard allowed him to swim.

The water, cooler than the air, enveloped him like a
friend's enclosing arms, and Hatch pushed out toward
the sentinel rock a half-mile out.

Jan left the window in the living room and went back
to change into her swimsuit. From now on she did not
intend to let him out of her sight.

13

Jan had not been able to keep up with Hatch, who had
finished the half-mile out to the island and was coming
back when he passed Jan swimming out. She stopped
and trod water until he reached her.

"Are you okay?" Hatch had asked.

"Yes," she had answered. "Just waiting for you."

Hatch continued stroking toward the beach.

"You really don't intend to take me, do you?" Jan had
asked when they got back to the beach.

Hatch picked up the towel he had left over the
banyan-tree limb and began drying his face and hair
briskly.

"Why?" Jan went on, bending over to pick up her
towel.

Hatch turned to the sound of her voice but did not
respond.

Jan reached out and grabbed his arm, jerking the
towel away from his face. "Answer me, God damn you!"

Hatch faced her then. "Because you couldn't possibly

keep up with me; because I'll be going part of the way through the jungle on foot and it will take many long, hot, agonizing days to reach the mountain camps; because having you around will make an already difficult trek impossible; because going into Laos is illegal and if you were found you would be executed, or maybe worse; because I want Michael Laser, and if I take you in, the chances of getting to him are cut substantially; because—"

"*Shut-up!*" Jan had screamed, reaching back to slap him.

Hatch caught her hand an inch from his face and held it there.

"I hate you!" Jan cried, tears filling her eyes. "You never did plan to take me, did you? You just played me along like a child, teasing me to keep me contented. I bring this to you, asking for help, and you take it from me. You bastard! Let go of me!"

Hatch let go of her hand and Jan held it with the other as if her fingers were hurt. She stared hotly at him, but Hatch's eyes would not give in.

Jan turned abruptly and ran back to the house.

Boone, drawn by the sound of crying, found Jan in her bedroom. He hesitated by the door, which was not fully closed, then shrugged and knocked.

"Are you all right, my darlin'?" he called out as he pushed the door open a few more inches.

"I'm okay," Jan answered.

"You're sure now?"

"Yes. I'm all right." Jan wiped her face with the corner of the bedsheet.

When Boone did not respond, Jan called for him. "Boone, don't go yet, please."

The door opened and Boone came into the bedroom.

"Had a little spat, did you?" he said.

"How could you ever be friends for so long with such a bastard?"

"We don't see each other very much." Boone smiled widely, happy with that explanation.

"He has lied to me, cheated me, made me feel like shit . . ." Jan stood and went to the window.

"Let's take a walk, shall we, darlin'? Let me show you some of this Eden." Boone held out his hand for her and Jan took it.

They walked away from the main road back toward Karon Beach, keeping to the jungle side on a trail that twisted along the path of least resistance through a maze of vines, trees, flowers, high grass, and ferns. The sun reached the jungle floor only in isolated spots, like light shining through cheesecloth, and, although moist, it was cooler out of the sun. They walked slowly, almost sauntering, and Jan put her arm through his. They could have been a retired British couple on a spring-day walk through the War Memorial Park across from the Raffles in Singapore.

"Have you ever taken notice of the ring Hatch wears on his right hand?" Boone asked Jan as they walked deeper into the forest.

"Yes, the silver one," she said, "but not closely."

"Actually, it's rather simple: a signet-type oval with a thistle inside it; smaller, but identical, thistles on either side."

"Thistles? You mean, like the weed?"

"Yes, that kind of thistle."

When Boone did not speak right away, Jan said, "Suits him. He's kind of prickly, wouldn't you say?"

"So it does. There were once eight of those rings made, identical to the one Hatch wears. The thistle is the Scottish national emblem. England is the rose, Ireland the shamrock, and Scotland the thistle. The Scottish national slogan is *'Nemo me impune lacessit,'* which can be loosely translated from the Celtic as: 'Who dares fuck with me.'"

Jan smiled and asked, "Is Hatch a Scot? I didn't know."

"Yes. On his mother's side. His grandparents emigrated just before the turn of the century." Boone stopped walking. He seem winded. "Let's go over this way." He pointed to a trail off to their right. "There's a place . . ."

They walked another thirty yards along the new trail until coming upon a shrine that looked like a dollhouse on a rock base with a bamboo altar before it. There were wildflowers planted nearby, and Jan thought that the place was quite beautiful. In the trees beyond, white-faced monkeys chattered and darted through the middle limbs.

"How nice," Jan said with slight amazement. "What is this?"

"It's called a spirit house," Boone told her.

"For prayer? Like a Catholic grotto?"

"Not at all, actually. It's a house where spirits live. This land, this forest, is inhabited by the spirits of people who lived here in the past. We make this house for them, to keep them happy. I'm not saying I believe in stuff like that, but, well, you know? The dead often haunt us. So, it can't hurt."

There was a bench, a split log resting in a V-frame, and Boone gestured for Jan to sit, then he joined her.

"The ring," Jan reminded him.

Boone nodded. "Hatch's recondo team was put together back at Bragg in 1962."

"I first met him the next year," Jan said.

"Yes, at the Special Warfare, UDT/SEAL school in California; that was part of the same training. They were an experiment; specially trained and conditioned to live in jungles without support, without guidance, and, for that matter, without accountability; a rather creative and bold step for such a lumbering behemoth as the U.S. Army.

"First a man had to volunteer. Thousands did. Then they were tested, physically and mentally, to cull the group down to a hundred or so. After extensive background checks—not for security as much as to determine the kind of instincts a man might be able to call upon—each man was sent out on a mission, absolutely secret, of course, and the result of that gave him a slot on the team, or not.

"Actually there were five such teams, comprising

eight men each, all living in small Laotian highland villages from where they ran recon patrols, and on occasion performed political nullifications—they assassinated folks. At the time it seemed, well, necessary. Regardless, those men were trained to kill in ways that would make the Mafia proud.

"They were called ghosts or spooks by the regular Green Beret troops who were in Laos during those earliest days as part of the White Star Mobile Training Forces. They didn't wear symbols of rank or unit, they had no direct lines of accountability, and generally all anyone outside their AO's—areas of operation—ever saw of these men were vague shadows moving silently through the forests, or, some might have thought, like banshees. You could drop them into the middle of any jungle, anywhere in the world, anytime day or night, and they'd know their way around in an hour. They were the forty best all-around soldiers the military system knew how to produce.

"During their training at Fort Bragg, Hatch discovered that five members of his eight-man team, including himself, were Scots by ancestry. It wasn't long before the other teams were referring to Hatch's men as Scotties.

"There was an intense and not altogether friendly rivalry among the men of these special recondo teams during the training at Bragg. A number of practical jokes were pulled, and sometimes the humor was pointedly lacking. Anyway, the day the training was finished, the command at Bragg held a kind of private ceremony on the grounds behind the barracks. The men were in full dress—berets, spit-shined boots, the works—and there was a band, as well as a sort of reviewing stand thrown up, on which top brass from the JFK school as well as the post commander and his contingent perched for inspection. This 'contingent' consisted in the main of mental cripples from the intelligence agencies. No offense to your late husband."

"None taken."

"All the teams lined up in their numerical sequence before the stand, but when time came to begin, team two, Hatch's team, was conspicuously absent.

"Suddenly, from behind one of the barracks came this squawking bagpipe, damn thing so loud you could hear it over the band. Team two came marching onto the grounds dressed head to toe in the full-dress kilts of the Scottish Royal Highland Regiment, better known as the Black Watch. They passed in review, then turned smartly and took their places in the conspicuous hole between teams one and three. And just as the bagpipe finished, Hatch stepped sharply out from the line, did an about-face, and saluted the men of his team British-style; you know, palm out. And as his hand dropped back to his side, the whole parade ground seem to explode. There were M-80's, cherry bombs, whistlers, and all kinds of firecrackers; they were under the reviewing platform, in the hedges, in holes scooped from the grass . . . everywhere. Team two had rigged this thing the night before and wired it all to go in sequence when one of their cohorts, a Green Beret sergeant hiding in one of the nearby barracks, got the signal and hit the detonator."

Boone stopped for a moment to laugh.

"What happened?" Jan asked.

"It was all assholes and elbows," Boone continued. "Men flying every which way. Old General Bishop did one helluva swan dive off the reviewing stand."

"How do you know all of this?" Jan asked, laughing a little herself.

"Well, because I was one of the assholes and elbows trying to turn himself into a mole and burrow into the parade field. I was the intel/commo officer on team five."

Jan looked up at Boone but did not say anything. Her eyes expressed the surprise. She thought it better unsaid.

"Anyway, the rings," Boone said. "Hatch had them made up by a jeweler in Raleigh; eight identical rings, which Hatch paid for with his own money. He gave them to his men the day they shipped out for this godforsaken piece of the killing fields."

"I assume you're trying to tell me something? This wasn't just to entertain me, was it?"

"Just a story. Take it for what it is, unless you see something in it. I just want you to know what kind of man Hatch was."

"Was?"

"Was, is. You can see it in him, like you can still see the child in the man, in spite of the fact he has shed and replaced his skin a few thousand times. Hatch is slow to move, slow to anger, reticent to fight; but once angered, once moving, is like a truck with momentum. You have to kill Hatch to stop him from completing a mission. It's like the Scots' meaning in the thistle—you rile a man like Frank Hatcher at your peril."

A minute passed, then Jan said quietly, "Boone, I envy what you men have had together. Even when it was all wrong, which that stupid, phony war was, you got from it something the rest of us will never know."

Boone nodded.

"But," Jan went on, "neither of you is going to keep me from going after the man who killed my husband." She pushed herself up from the log bench and walked directly back to the trail.

Boone got himself up more slowly, and instead of following her, he stood in front of the spirit house for a moment. He had not finished his story. He had not told her about how Hatch took off his ring that day in the Laotian jungle when every other member of his team was ambushed and killed. Or about the day he found Mai and their child murdered in Toulan. When Boone had seen Hatch wearing that ring again, he knew that Hatch was going back into Laos to finish the slow-motion suicide he had begun that day more than two decades ago.

14

At the Lido Bar in Patong, Hatch had taken a small table in the back to wait for the man Boone said would meet him there at six o'clock. The CZ 83 automatic inside the waistband of his khaki shorts and covered by the tail of his flowered shirt felt obtrusive but comforting. Hatch ordered a beer and drank without taking his eyes off the bar's open front.

It was dusk. The strands of multicolored lights grew brighter against the darkening backdrop. Flickering light from the television over the bar in the saloon across the road cast an eerie greenish glow over the faces turned up to it. Since it was still early and there were few customers, the Lido's bar girls chattered to one another like frenzied parrots. A trio of drunk Thai sailors wobbled down the street singing "Mamas Don't Let Your Babies Grow Up To Be Cowboys." It was obvious, Hatch thought, that their mothers had failed.

Hatch could hear three different rock-and-roll songs coming from three separate jukeboxes down the way, although the Lido's jukebox was quiet, its lights flashing sequentially in expectation. It was still quiet enough in the Lido to hear the *zzit* of moths being electrocuted in a crematorium disguised as a long, friendly-looking green lamp. Two moths, older and wiser than the others, Hatch thought, circled his head in lazy, patient spirals.

Jock's arrival was signaled to Hatch when suddenly three of the bar girls spun around on their perches and began their usual singsong pornographic routines, telling the usually embarrassed customer he was the sexiest, handsomest, most-well-hung hunk they had ever seen. The man, who from Boone's description had to be Jock, pushed through the girls as if they were bushes blocking a trail.

"Get off my case, you sleazebags," Hatch heard Jock say.

Then their eyes met in recognition.

Jock swaggered to the small rear table like a sailor leaving a ship and took a seat opposite Hatch without extending his hand to shake.

"There's not a clean cunt in the bunch," Jock leaned over and said conspiratorially to Hatch. "You couldn't *pay* me to fuck a Thai broad. Name's John Robinson, but my friends all call me Jock. You Hatch?" Jock extended his hand over the table. Hatch nodded but made no move to shake Jock's hand.

"I see," Jock said, pulling his hand back. "Right-o."

"How do you know Michael Laser?" Hatch asked, wanting to get to it and get out.

"How do you get a drink in this place?" Jock asked, looking back and forth over each shoulder. "Hey, honey!" he called out to any of the bar girls. "Gin and tonic, chop-chop." He clapped his hands twice, then turned back to Hatch. "Ready for another brewski?"

"No, I'm fine," Hatch said, holding his beer bottle by the neck as if it might soon become a club.

Jock fidgeted and Hatch waited for Jock's drink to arrive, only to have Jock send it back for ice. Hatch figured Jock was homosexual—something distinctive in his mannerisms, a careful style in his way of speaking— and that, not whether the girls were clean, was why he ignored them.

"These people will fuck you any way they can," Jock griped, "from ice cubes to diamonds. This *Joe* in Phuket City last month tried to sell me some Cubic Zirconia, claiming they were diamonds." He expelled something like a laugh.

The drink returned with ice and Jock held it out in toast before tipping it back and swigging half of it in a gulp.

"Now," Jock said and wiped his lips, "where were we?"

"Laser," Hatch said, taking a drink from the bottle of beer.

"Boone tells me you're not with none of the agencies, but Boone can tell a lie when it's to his benefit."

"I'm alone, entirely."

"What's in it for me?"

"Depends on what it's worth."

"And I suppose you're to be the judge of that, eh?"

"Look, do you or do you not know where Laser is?"

Jock reached down for his pocket and Hatch's hand went behind his back for the pistol.

"Whoa!" Jock said, lifting both hands into the clear. "I'm just getting a little package out of my pants pocket. What's your hand holding on to back there?"

"Go ahead, get your package," Hatch said, leaving his hand around the pistol grip.

"Boy, kind of edgy, ain'tcha?" Jock put a small brown envelope on the table, then opened both hands palms_ up.

Hatch brought his hand back around to the table and left it in sight.

"Here's my deal," Jock said, shaking a fine white powder onto the envelope flap. He bent over and covered one nostril with a fingertip while inhaling the powder up the other through a straw. He then switched nostrils and repeated it. Shaking his head and blinking, Jock pushed the envelope a little toward Hatch, offering it to him.

Hatch shook his head and waited for Jock to put the cocaine away. The last thing he needed was to get busted for dope by the Thai, who were notorious for hanging suspected smugglers. Jock was, Hatch thought, so bold that he was either utterly stupid or he had some kind of in with the police.

"Oh, shit," Jock blurted out, shaking his head and sniffing hard. "Have mercy!" He exhaled loudly through his mouth and blinked a couple of times. "Do, Lord, remember me," he sang.

"Your deal," Hatch prodded.

"Sure you won't . . . ?" Jock indicated the envelope. "No, I guess not," he said when Hatch gave him a hard look. He put the envelope back into his pocket and it was not until both of Jock's hands were in view that Hatch took his hand off the pistol grip and brought it back to the table.

"Here's the deal," Jock said again. "Boone tells me you've got no major funding, and that's all right, since I really don't need the money. What I need is a favor." When Hatch offered no response, Jock continued. "Mike Laser has something of mine and I want it back. I'll tell you how to find him and if you get out of there alive, all you've got to do is return my property."

"What is it?"

Jock looked around the bar, apparently to ensure that no one was close enough to overhear. Then he leaned toward Hatch slightly.

"There's this young man, a boy really." Jock lowered his voice and kept his eyes on the table. "He's a Meo, an amazingly pretty boy, as you know how beautiful those people can be when they are young. His family farmed poppies for the Soms. His name is Kithong Sangsom. He's eighteen now. Kaysone Som, that fucking little tyrant, populates his army by abducting young men from the villages under his control. That's it. I want Kithong Sangsom brought to me here in Phuket city. That's my deal. Boone says I can trust you to keep your word. Do I have it?"

"But, as you said, Boone sometimes lies."

"I have no choice. Besides, you've got about as much chance as a flea crawling up an elephant's ass with rape on his mind of coming out of Prince Som's little kingdom with your head connected to your body. But just in case you might . . ."

The look on Jock's face saddened Hatch. He had at first thought of teasing Jock, making him squirm before agreeing to his terms, but now he could not.

"I'll bring the boy out *if* he wants to come," Hatch said.

"Oh, he'll come all right," Jock said, looking up and smiling. He finished his drink and held the glass over his head, rattling the ice cubes until one of the girls came and got it for a refill.

"You're sure we're talking about the same Michael Laser?" Hatch asked when the girl left. "He has a scar—"

"On his chin, here." Jock ran his index finger in a line along his chin from high on the jawbone down to the middle below the lip. "BAR got away from him."

Hatch figured the scar came as a result of letting a Browning automatic rifle get loose on rapid fire. It was a characteristic scar.

"There could be only one," Jock said. "Mike Laser is the only completely amoral, psychopathic madman I've ever known. I knew him from way back, from Nam. I was in the Air Force, stationed in Bangkok. I made some deals with him, you know? Moved some stuff for him. The Air Force bugged out of the country, but I stayed around, you know? I was doing a deal for Laser about a year ago. I got into their little kingdom, stayed there three months."

"Doesn't Laser ever leave the camps?" Hatch asked, thinking it would be better to catch him on more favorable terms, on neutral ground.

"Not lately. He's carrying some bad baggage from some escapade a couple of years back, too many big guys from the civilized world want a piece of him, if you know what I mean."

Hatch knew too well. "But," Hatch said, "in mid-January, he was in New Zealand."

"No way, brother. Impossible. I was there from just after Christmas through the end of March. I can tell you for certain that Laser was not in New Zealand or New Nowhere-else during that block of time. I saw him every day. I understand that lately he's been coming into Bangkok for who-knows-what. He's been down here a couple of times I know about. We did some deals, arranged some meets."

"Meets with who?"

"Some arms dealers. No-name boys."

"You're sure Laser did not leave Laos last January?"

"Hey!" Jock held out his arms, palms up.

Jock could be lying, Hatch figured, except that he had no reason to. But that meant someone else had hit Jason.

"Okay, so Laser stays close to base. What's he doing for
the drug bandits?"

"Bandits? Prince Phoun Som and his son are more like
warlords, old-style. Bandits don't live in palaces and
control territories more vast than the Lao People's
Democratic Whatever-they-call-it government can claim
control of. Laser? I don't know. He's up to something
big, though, I can tell you that. Within Som's kingdom,
I'd say Mike Laser is the right-hand man. He's in charge
of Som's army. You might say he's like the chief of staff.
There's about a dozen deserters and leftovers, crazy-ass
Americans who wouldn't give up, you know? They work
with Laser."

There was some commotion at the open front of the
bar, but Hatch ignored it. "Americans? What do you
mean? MIA's?" A movement and a cry behind Jock
pulled Hatch's attention to the bar.

A man shouting in Thai pushed his way across the bar
floor toward their table, and Hatch instinctively turned
sideways in his chair while reaching back for the pistol.
Jock turned around to the noise.

The pistol, a Colt .45 automatic looking like an
oversize stage prop in the man's small hand, came up
from the man's side in one fluid motion and leveled at the
front of Jock's head. Hatch had flipped backward out of
his chair and pulled out his pistol just as he heard the
automatic boom three quick times. And the Thai man
was still screaming.

Hatch did not have to see Jock to know that the blood
and flesh splattered against the back wall had been a
large part of Jock's head a moment earlier. He rolled
against the wall, using the overturned table as a shield,
and looked out to find the shooter.

Already Thai police were filling the place. From
Hatch's vantage point all he could see of them were
crisply creased khaki pants bloused into polished jump
boots. Hatch put his pistol behind a large potted fern
and slowly eased himself into the open, keeping his
hands out and in the clear.

As he got up and stepped over Jock's body, which had been thrown into the table and against the back wall before falling back, he could tell that two of the shots had hit the target, one striking the center of the forehead directly and the other snapping the spinal cord as it ripped through Jock's neck. Pretty good shooting for a wild little man with a very big pistol, Hatch thought.

Suddenly two cops grabbed Hatch's arms, waved pistols around in front of his face, and pulled Hatch out to the street. They were all yelling at him in Thai. The street in front of the Lido Bar was filled and the police van had to nudge its way through the crowd, siren wailing, to get to the front. When they shoved Hatch into the van, he found Jock's killer already there, handcuffed to a ring on the floor, two guards on either side. The man kept saying in Thai: "He fucked my wife, he fucked my wife." Two new guards followed Hatch into the van and he was also handcuffed to a floor ring, which, because of Hatch's height, required him to ride bent over.

"What the hell did I do?" Hatch asked first in English, then repeated in Thai.

"Keep quiet," was all one of the guards would say.

In a few minutes they reached the police station in Phuket City and Hatch was put into a cell, alone, without being processed.

The odor of stink did not come only from the open urinals, Hatch decided.

15

Hatch had been in the dark cell less than two hours when he heard a noise at the end of the hallway and a light came on. Two Thai guards escorted a man to Hatch's cell and opened the door. In good Thai, although spoken with a heavy Western accent, the man told the guards to leave them alone and that there would be no need to lock the door behind him.

"Mr. Hatcher," the man said as he pulled a package of cigarettes from his shirt pocket, "I'm Perry Nelson, State Department." He knocked up a couple of cigarettes and offered them to Hatch, who took one and waited for a light.

"I didn't know there was a consulate in Phuket," Hatch said, leaning forward to light the cigarette from the Ronson Nelson produced.

"There's not. I'm at the embassy in Bangkok."

Nelson looked back at the bunk, then sat down on it. Hatch leaned against the wall in the corner. Smoke rose above his head, curled, and flew out the tiny window near the ceiling.

"Wondering how I got here so fast?" Nelson asked, smiling. "Actually, I was at the Club Med place on Karon Beach when I heard an American had been involved in a shooting and was being held in the jail here in Phuket City. Figured I'd better check it out."

"I didn't shoot the man. Do you know what I'm charged with?"

"I can tell you that much. The Thai are holding you for possession of two grams of cocaine, as well—"

"That wasn't my junk," Hatch interrupted.

"Yes, well, anyway, they are also holding you as a material witness to the murder of John Robinson. I might as well mention further that possession of that much of a controlled substance in this country can get you life imprisonment."

"Yeah."

"Be thankful you weren't in Malaysia. They'd hang you for it there."

Hatch shook his head, took a last drag, and crushed the cigarette out on the concrete floor.

"Another?" Nelson asked, holding out the pack.

Hatch waved it off and said, "No, thanks."

Hatch noticed that Nelson did not take a cigarette himself, and he imagined that the man did not smoke.

That would be consistent with Hatch's feeling that there was nothing honest about him.

"What can you do for me?" Hatch asked, sitting on the bunk opposite Nelson, who had leaned forward, resting his forearms on his thighs and clasping his hands together.

"Actually, I don't think they will pursue the cocaine charge. It could have belonged to Robinson as easily as you, and, in point of fact, he seems the more logical candidate for a doper, given his background. But the Thai don't like people getting killed in their resorts; bad for the tourist business."

"They have the man who did it. They took him away in the wagon with me. And he's a Thai."

"Yes, they had him."

"Had?"

"Actually, he seems to have escaped."

"Escaped? How? They must have been holding him in a tent on the lawn. Look where they've got me."

"Yes." Nelson looked around the tiny, secure cell.

It was obvious that Nelson was an intel man, but not which agency, and not why he would be involved in such a crude setup, and certainly not why they wanted Hatch. The clothes—a preppie's lightweight summer poplin suit, old loafers recently shined, yellow button-down-collar shirt with the collar open—suggested a pol-sci graduate from Princeton or Yale doing his stint with the Foreign Service; but the sunglasses sticking out of the coat breast pocket were what Hatch in the old days called "diddy-bop" glasses, and they had always been popular in the civilian intelligence community; Nelson's eyes flashed with a young intel man's consuming curiosity; and Hatch did not believe that a vacationing functionary from the embassy in Bangkok would have taken an interest in a situation like this without some kind of direct request.

"It might help me to help you, Mr. Hatcher, if you wouldn't mind telling me what happened in the Lido this evening."

"The man the police picked up came into the bar, walked directly to the table where Jock—or Robinson— sat, raised what looked to be an old military-issue Colt forty-five automatic, and put two rounds into Robinson from about five yards. That last part I didn't happen to see. I was on my way to the deck at the time."

"Did the shooter say anything? Or did he just fire?"

"He said plenty, although I only managed to get a little of it. My Thai isn't too hot and he was running his words together like freight-train cars derailing."

"Interesting image."

"That's what it sounded like. All I got was that he seemed to be accusing Robinson of sleeping with his wife."

"So the shooting was probably the result of an unfortunate domestic situation?"

"You could put it that way if it makes your books balance."

Nelson looked up as his only response to the sarcasm.

"You were a friend of his?"

"Nope. I'd never seen him before the Lido, maybe half an hour before he got hit. There's nothing to connect between us, and the only drugs I abuse are alcohol and nicotine."

"I believe you, Mr. Hatcher, and I think the Thai will, as well. Actually, they are pretty good people." As if he were only wondering about the time, Nelson asked, "What were you and Robinson talking about?"

"What does that have to do with anything?"

"Actually, I should be direct, Mr. Hatcher."

Hatch stood, crossed his arms over his chest, and leaned against the wall below the window. This is where the shit starts getting deep, he thought.

Nelson looked at Hatch for a moment, then continued. "John Robinson, commonly known as Jock, had been under suspicion for some time by both Thai and U.S. intelligence groups. They were aware of his petty business operations—a little smuggling in semiprecious stones, some narcotics trafficking, small time only, and even a little faggot pimping for rich tourists.

"But we also know that he has made a number of surreptitious incursions over the border into Laos, and not for his usual illegitimate purposes."

"I couldn't tell you," Hatch said when Nelson paused.

"Anything he might have said, any hints at all, might help us determine what Robinson was doing over the border. Did he, for example, say anything about the drug warlords operating over there?"

"Not a word."

"I see. Let's stop beating around the bush, shall we? I would like for you to tell me the purpose of your meeting with Robinson."

"There's nothing to tell," Hatch said. "I was having a drink, apparently he spotted me for a fellow American, came over and offered to buy me a beer, which I accepted, and we were just passing time when he got hi~ brains plastered to the wall. No shit."

"Very well, Mr. Hatcher. But if you happen to think of anything else, remember something that could be helpful, would you call the number on this card?" Nelson took a card from his inside coat pocket and handed it to Hatch.

There was nothing on the card except "Perry L. Nelson" and a phone number. "This the embassy?" Hatch asked.

"My office, Bangkok. I'm returning, regretfully, to-morrow. Phuket is quite a place."

Nelson went to the door and yelled down the hall for the guards. Then he turned back to Hatch and offered him another cigarette.

"Shall I have the guards bring you a pack?" Nelson asked.

"No, thanks. I'm trying to quit." But Hatch took the offered cigarette and a light from Nelson.

"What about getting me out of here?" Hatch asked after lighting the cigarette.

"I'll see what I can do. Maybe we can do each other favors?" Nelson proposed, winking.

The guards came and escorted Nelson back down the hall, locking the door to Hatch's cell behind them.

"I wouldn't mind something to eat," Hatch called after them.

An hour later, hearing another commotion at the end of the hall, Hatch hoped it was his dinner. It turned out to be Boone Buchannan.

"I can't take you anywhere," Boone said, smiling broadly as the guards unlocked Hatch's cell door. "Come on, let's vamoose before they change their minds."

"Thanks for fixing this thing," Hatch told Boone when they got outside. "How much do I owe you?"

"The least I could do, my friend. After all, who sent you to Jock in the first place? The poor sucker."

Outside, the street was still wet from the evening rain, and steam rising from the gasoline-soaked tar turned a variety of colors in the glow of the carnival lights strung between the lampposts. Boone's aging Mercedes sedan was parked across the street and as they walked to it Hatch said, "Let's stop by the Lido on the way. I left something behind a planter there."

"Wonder what that could be?" Boone said.

"Ever hear of a guy called Perry Nelson? Says he's with State at the embassy," Hatch asked when they were in the car.

"Nope," Boone answered. "You had a visit?"

Hatch nodded. "A very curious one. Asked a lot of questions about Jock."

"What'd you tell him?"

"Nothing."

"What'd you get?"

"Enough."

Boone pulled up in front of the Lido and Hatch asked him to wait. Then Hatch went inside and retrieved his automatic from behind the planter. Jock's blood and brains had already been scrubbed from the bamboo wall, but the clean spot stood out against the rest of the grimy walls. The bartender was yelling at Hatch, mostly urging him to get out, and Hatch offered a wave as he went back to the car.

Boone gave Hatch a questioning look as he started the motor, and Hatch responded with a nod. Boone pulled out onto the narrow street and headed out of the bar district, although not alone.

"I'm sorry about what happened," Boone said. "Feels like I set you up or something."

"Forget it. How could you know?"

"We all used to joke about getting it from a jealous husband," Boone said.

"Yeah. But this thing smells pretty bad, Boone."

"How's that?"

"Jock's a queer—was a queer, that is. So what's he doing fucking that guy's wife?"

"Bisexual?"

"Maybe. But I don't think the guy liked women at all, sexual or otherwise. Also, the shooter was good. Even at that range it's pretty hard to put two forty-five slugs into the most critical spots of a man's head, especially have one of them sever the spinal cord at the neck. You know what a jolt those things have. You have to have emptied a lot of clips through one of those old Colts to be able to hit anything with it."

"You got a point there," Boone said, turning onto the road toward Karon Beach.

"Did you know the guy escaped from the police tonight?"

"No, I didn't hear that."

"That's what Nelson said. Pretty slick, don't you think? I mean, I was just a material witness and look where they had me. Doesn't that seem odd to you?"

"Everything about the police here has always seemed odd to me."

"I tell you what else: I doubt if Perry Nelson, or whatever his name might be, just happened to interrupt his vacation because he heard some American had been involved in a bar shooting in Patong. I make him for some agency, probably CIA."

Boon nodded. "Maybe. But what are you saying?"

"Nothing yet. Just talking it out. Boone, who told you about Jock Robinson? I mean, who told you that he had been in Laos recently and could have information on Laser?"

"You just hear things. Really, I don't remember where I got the word on Jock. You know how things go around. Maybe from one of those Vietnamese spooks always hanging out at the Black Pearl. Jock used to hang out there. I'll try to remember."

"Yeah, okay. But I tell you what, this has the stink of some intel operation all over it."

"You could also be getting a little paranoid, my friend."

"Then I shouldn't tell you that I think we're being followed," Hatch said.

Boone parked the Mercedes inside the garage behind his house and locked it up. The tail had fallen back and disappeared as they turned onto the bay road.

Thinking about something else Jock had said, Hatch went ahead to the house. If Jock had not lied about Laser being in Laos at the time Jason Moss was murdered, then who had killed Jan's husband? And Jock? The jealous-husband story did not wash. None of it did. If the CIA knew where Laser was, why not just go in and tap on his head? Certainly they weren't going to let a man who'd attempted to kill the president sit untouched just because he was in Laos.

16

They had eaten dinner. Linn and Jan were putting things away in the kitchen, and Boone, who had lain down on the sofa in the main room, was asleep. Hatch asked Jan if she would take a walk with him, and Linn happily urged them to leave the kitchen chores to her familiar routine.

They walked out onto the pier, which stretched nearly a hundred feet from where it connected to the veranda, and stopped at the walk ramp around the pearl bed's holding tank. The guard, who was now used to the presence of those two *farangs* around the house of his employer, squatted on his perch below the pier with the automatic rifle in his lap, his eyes scanning the dark, quiet bay for signs of approaching poachers.

Hatch reached over to his shirt pocket for a cigarette and felt an initial panic when the pocket was empty, then remembered purposely leaving the package in the nightstand drawer in his room, trying to wean himself. He was not concerned that the cigarettes would kill him; if not that, then something else—you're dead all the same. He wanted to recover some of his wind for the long trek through the high jungle mountains, when his body would need all the oxygen he could put into it. He had managed in three days to cut back to about ten cigarettes a day, down by half from his usual. Still, he wished he could find something to do with his hands.

"I have some apologizing to do," Jan said into Hatch's self-centered silence.

"Never," Hatch said, thankful she had broken the ice.

"Thanks, but yes, I do. Not for dragging you into this; I don't think your life as I saw it on Tuva was worth very much, and maybe this way you can . . . I don't know, recover. But that's none of my business. No, what I'm sorry about is asking you to do something for me, then not letting you do it, handicapping you. If I didn't trust you, I wouldn't have come to you in the first place. It's just so hard . . . I just want to . . . can you understand why this is so important to me, why I need to be part of it?"

"Laser didn't do it," Hatch said.

"What?"

"Laser was in Laos when Jason was murdered."

"But—"

"The man I was with today said that he was in Laos with Laser from Christmas last year through March;

Jason was killed in the middle of January. The man says he was with Laser every day during that period and that he didn't leave the country."

"And you believe him?"

"I have no reason not to. There was nothing to be gained lying about it."

Jan turned her back to Hatch, gripped the pier railing, and leaned out over the water slightly, her eyes staring straight ahead into the distant jungle across the way. There were lights, dim and amber, glowing through the thick vegetation, the lights of faraway Karon Beach resorts. Hatch concentrated on rubbing his fingers one by one as if it were some mandatory daily ritual. He was on the verge of asking the guard for a cigarette.

"Why? I don't see what . . ."

"I'm not saying I have the answers, but maybe we've been asking the wrong questions."

"Then who killed Jason?"

"I don't know, Jan."

"What are you going to do about Laser?"

"I'm still going in after him. There's momentum here that compels some action. I do owe that to Jason. And something Mr. Jolly said before we left. Besides, we've been led this far for some reason, and now I'm a little curious to know what it is. Whether Michael Laser killed Jason or not, he did try to set me up for the attempt on President Phillips, and he is responsible for *that*." Hatch's eyes glanced down at Jan's missing finger. "There's a debt here, regardless."

"And me?"

"I'd like to ask you to go home, to Wellington, or anyplace besides here, but I don't think you will."

Jan's look confirmed it.

"So I want you to stay here with Boone and Linn. I've asked Boone and he's pleased to have you. I made him promise not to hit on you." Hatch smiled.

"Okay," Jan said so softly that Hatch could not be sure he'd heard correctly.

"Okay?" he questioned.

"Yes, okay. If you won't take me, there's not a whole lot I can do about it. I can't go alone, you know that. You succeeded in taking that away from me. So okay, God damn you. But if I were a man you wouldn't ask me to wait, and that really pisses me off, Hatch."

"Not necessarily. I can move better on my own. You notice that I didn't ask Boone to go."

"Boone's dying."

"How did you know? Did Linn tell you?"

"I used to be a nurse. You can tell from his clothes that he's lost a lot of weight quickly, and he hasn't much energy, his skin has an anemic tint. If I were to guess, I'd say it's cancer, blood or liver maybe."

"I haven't probed. Please don't tell him you know," Hatch said. "From what Linn told me, I think it's leukemia. Sharp guess, lady."

"I'm not *completely* worthless." Jan spit the words at him, then turned away and started walking off the pier, the anger coming more from her own embarrassment at having lied than from anything Hatch had done; Linn had told her about Boone's cancer.

Hatch watched her go into the house, then bent over the railing to the guard and said, "*Bu ri nung song.*" When the guard stood and gave Hatch a strange look before handing over the entire pack, Hatch realized that he had indeed asked for a pack of cigarettes rather than one. "*Neung, ka ru na.*" Hatch laughed and held up one finger.

After letting his eyes readjust to the darkness after the flare of the match, Hatch headed back to the house.

Boone and Hatch sat across a wicker table from one another in the backyard next to a stand of bamboo trees. Between them, its curled edges held down by a Ka-bar knife on one corner and a coffee cup opposite, lay two maps, a smaller terrain map on top of a much larger Indochina area map.

Boone, using a pencil for a pointer, jabbed a spot on the area map and said, "So, I'll take you by car to the airstrip, here, between Phangnga and Kapong. Buzz

Killion will wait for us up to noon, then he and his STOL
plane have to split, with or without you. We shouldn't
have any trouble reaching the strip with at least an hour
to spare.

"Okay. You and Buzz will head directly east across the
Gulf of Thailand to your first refueling point at the old
Air America field just south of Pattaya. Buzz knows the
place like the back of his hand from the old days. You
should be in and out of there in under fifteen minutes.
You and Buzz part company at the jungle strip between
Kantaralak and Det Udom, here. It should be a couple of
hours before dawn by then."

Pulling over the terrain map, Boone pointed to a spot
near its center and said, "Head north by northeast.
You've got just a little under a hundred klicks before you
pick up the Mekong at the border. If you don't bear more
north than south of east, you'll be too far south, too close
to the Kampuchean border." Boone followed the northern border of Kampuchea with his pencil. "Too much
straight east and you'll run into the Dam Noi lake, here;
it'll cost you most of a day getting around it. It's
impossible to tell how far upriver you'll have to go on
foot before finding an opportune boat.

"Once you hit the river, there are no border crossings,
no checkpoints of any kind south of Ban Khemmarat, but
you aren't going that far upriver. You see this big curve
the Mekong takes into Thailand here, just east of Ubon
Ratchathani? That's where you should pick up the river.

"You can see that the terrain here has to be next to
impassable, so you'll head south on the river until you
reach this branch, the Done, and cut back north, here,
where it parallels the road. My understanding is there's
nothing out there but jungle until you reach the village
of Khong Sedone; that should be, I figure, four days from
tomorrow night.

"At Khong Sedone, take the easterly branch of the
river, here, and go to Bung Sai."

Boone drew a large dark circle on the map by going
over and over it, enclosing all of southern Laos south of a

line from Savannakhet, Laos, across to Khe Sanh, Vietnam. "This is Prince Phoun Som's country, his nation within a nation," Boone told Hatch again—what they had already discussed a half-dozen times. "Along with his psychopathic son, Kaysone, and an army as well-equipped as the Pathet Lao counterrevolutionaries, certainly more dangerous. Understand this, Hatch, even the Vietnamese Army doesn't go into Phoun Som's territory and make trouble."

"I'll be careful," Hatch said in a teasing tone.

"Don't bullshit around on this one, Hatch. I'm serious."

"I know you are, Boone. I appreciate it, really. But remember, it's country I know pretty well."

Boone shook his head. "Pretty goddamned old knowledge."

With the point of the pencil he pressed a hole into the map at a 1,572-meter mountain just south of Saravane, and said, "Here. Phoun Som's fortress is supposed to be here."

The heat seemed to creep over the windowsill and move lightly, like a cat prowling, over Jan's bed. It had rained late. Through the eye of Jan's imagination she could see heat waves bending the air. She wanted to sleep but could not close her eyes; there were demons in the dark, and her heart, stimulated by the confusing fight-or-flight message coming from deep within her brain, thudded and fluttered against her chest, beating so furiously that she could not muffle its sound by pulling the pillow against her ears, sound carried throughout her body on a highway of arteries so that even her fingers and her toes throbbed like an engine out of sync.

Suddenly there was terror. It had no source and no focus, but it was as real and as terrible as anything Jan had ever felt before, terror annihilating reason. If she did not move, do something, her heart would burst inside her chest, her brain would swell until it exploded, her lungs would collapse and suck the life from her throat like a vacuum, she would die.

Jan swung her legs off the bed and jerked back the mosquito netting. She stood naked by the window, but there was no breeze to cool her wet, dark skin; the play of lanterns over the bay and the jungle beyond created unbearable creatures, monsters of the night and the shadows borne on yellow, weak light.

She had to move or die. Pulling a khaki shirt from the back of a chair, she draped it over her shoulders without inserting her arms through the sleeves. Clutching it closed over her breasts, she went out into the dark hall and moved down one door to Hatch's room. As she reached out to push open the unlatched door, a lizard clicked on the nearby wall and scurried away, unseen in the darkness. Jan gasped without crying out.

Hatch had heard the sharp intake of breath, as well as the padding of bare feet in the hall. As the door to his bedroom opened slowly, he reached over to the nightstand and picked up the pistol lying there. He put his left hand over the barrel and gripped the slide to chamber a round, but waited, listening.

Dim light from the open window bounced off Jan's eyes first, then her skin, and Hatch quietly replaced the pistol.

Jan pushed the door closed behind her and stepped into the room. For a moment she looked at Hatch, who was sitting on the side of his bed holding back the netting with one hand. Neither of them spoke. She turned away, stopped, then turned back. Jan was sure Hatch could hear the syncopated drumbeat of her heart, that he could surely sense her terror, that he could feel the heat pulsing from her like a strobe. She took two more tentative steps toward him and waited.

"Jan?" he said.

"Would you hold me, please," she answered.

Hatch flipped the mosquito netting over the top brace and moved to one side of the bed.

As if she had been pushed from behind, Jan stumbled forward and landed on the bed next to Hatch, in his arms. Hatch held her, lightly stroking her hair. But after a moment Jan turned her face from the breadth of his shoulder and let her lips glide up his neck to his face, urging him with soft kisses to turn toward her. After a hesitation, Hatch turned his face toward Jan and she put her lips over his, opening her mouth.

She shrugged her shoulders and the shirt fell from her back and she pressed her breasts against Hatch, reaching behind his head to pull his mouth harder into hers, kissing him hungrily like food to the starved, drink to the thirsty, love to the empty, urging into him the terror until it was thinned into invisibility and replaced by desire. Their bodies, wet from the heat, slid together on the bed and Hatch moved on top of Jan, pressing her deep into the bed with his weight. Surrendering her need to him, Jan reached behind her head and gripped the brass bed frame with both hands, the metal warm to the touch, slippery. After that, all the moments fused into a single piece of time and Jan did not know when they actually began making love, nor when they stopped. She remembered neither of them speaking at all.

17

Jan woke slowly, luxuriously; still on the border between asleep and awake, she stretched her muscles like a cat rising from a long nap, pushing her toes straight out and arching her back, pulling her arms above her head. Smiling, she opened her eyes and rolled over, expecting to put her arms around the man she had made love to last night. But the other side of the bed was empty.

Jan sat up quickly and swung her legs off the bed. The sun was well up. There were noises from the kitchen. Of course, she told herself, reaching over to pick up her shirt off the floor, he's having breakfast, he wouldn't leave without seeing me, saying something, doing something!

It took three tries to get her arms through the sleeves, and she was in too much of a hurry to fiddle with buttons. She clutched the shirt to her chest and went back down the hall to her room.

Dressing quickly, Jan ran a brush through her tangled hair, washed her face, touched up a little around her eyes and lips, then hurried toward the kitchen, slowing to a nonchalant walk just before going through the wide door.

"Good morning," Jan said to Linn, who was in the kitchen alone.

Wearing a pair of black nylon panties and a deep-cut red bra, Linn turned from the sink and greeted Jan. Her hands were buried in dishwater.

"Where are the others?" Jan asked, crossing the kitchen to peer expectantly out the back door.

"Gone," Linn said.

"Gone?" Jan went over to the counter by Linn. "Let me help you with those," she said, picking up a drying cloth. "Gone where?"

"Gone, gone," Linn said, handing Jan a wet coffee mug.

"Gone . . . you mean, Hatch and Boone have left to meet the plane already? But I thought . . ."

"Gone one hour," Linn explained, holding up one soapy finger.

Jan turned around and leaned back against the edge of the counter, drying the mug as if in a trance. That son of a bitch, she said to herself.

"Hatch say give you that letter," Linn said, nodding her head toward a folded piece of paper on the kitchen table. "There"—she drew Jan's attention to it.

Jan put down the towel and mug and went to the table. She picked up the note and sat down before opening it. Linn went back to the dishes.

The letter was folded over once. There was, when Jan finally made herself open it, very little inside. Only:

Jan,
  I couldn't wake you, you looked so peaceful, and so
beautiful. Thank you for last night. I wish I had

some years to live over again. Don't be too angry, you must have known all along I couldn't take you. Thanks again for giving me this smile.

Hatch

Jan read the note again, hoping her eyes had maybe skipped a line. But there was no more. She had read every word.

"You goddamned asshole," she muttered, wadding up the note and throwing it on the table.

Jan stormed out the back door and plopped down in one of the wicker chairs beneath the shade umbrella, looking back at the house. Just the two women, Jan thought, abandoned to the house while the men go off to do manly things. She saw Linn pass before the door and pick up the wadded note from the table, watching her smooth the note over the table edge, then fold it once again and place one of its corners beneath a vase of wildflowers.

Beyond Thalang, as they crossed the causeway from the island to the mainland, Boone thought they were being followed.

"Don't turn around," he told Hatch, "but there's a blue Mercedes back there that's been keeping the same spacing since Phuket City. Orientals, four of them."

Hatch leaned his head to the side until he could see out the side rearview mirror. "Behind the bus?" he asked.

"Uh-huh. He's been keeping one vehicle back."

"Friends of yours? I don't think I have any here."

"Could be. Whoever, I can't drag them along to the airstrip. Buzz would have a cow."

"Whatever you need to do," Hatch said, bracing himself for the ride to come.

"Let them play along until we get into Phangnga. Unless they're better than they look, it'll be a snap to shake them off on one of the backwater mangrove trails there."

"Got any guesses?" Hatch asked.

"I don't think they're Thai, since they don't seem familiar with the area. Vietnamese? I can't tell. But one thing I do know, your presence seems to attract lowlifes like flies to shit."

"Thanks."

"You're welcome." Boone let out a laugh. "You are an entertainment, my friend. I'm sure gonna miss you this time."

Not like I'm going to miss you, old friend, Hatch thought.

As the road curved around the bay, hundreds of offshore islands, mountain tips puncturing the slate-gray surface, came into view, and Hatch watched a distant long-tailed boat disappear into a hole carved out of one of the limestone islands, only to reappear out the other side as Boone's white Mercedes rounded a curve that sloped down toward the natural rocky beach.

"Here we go!" from Boone interrupted Hatch's daydream of living like the skipper of that long-tailed boat might, going home to a wife, to kids, to a little night fishing, simple life as he imagined it, as he figured it had once existed for him, for one brief moment on Tuva. Suddenly the Mercedes swerved hard left across the oncoming traffic lane, bouncing over a slight depression at the ditch and onto a narrow trail composed of pea gravel and crushed white seashells. Rocking on its old shocks, the car yawed down the service road, kicking up a tornado of thick white dust, at sixty miles an hour.

Hatch gripped the hand strap and nodded to himself.

After a half-minute the road erupted into a wide, grassy field, beyond which stretched a rubber planation—rows upon rows of tall, wide trees with deep V's cut into them.

"Used to hunt monkeys here in the old days," Boone yelled over the roar of the wind coming through the open windows.

The Mercedes shot out of the dust cloud like a shell from a cannon, hitting the thick, wet, deep green grass going sideways. Boone worked the steering wheel back

and forth, just getting the car straightened as it raced
through the first row of rubber trees.

After opening his eyes, Hatch turned around just in
time to see the blue Mercedes wrap its side around one
of the first trees.

"*Adiós*," Hatch said to Boone.

Boone laughed and slowed down a little.

"Goddamn, just about makes you want to cream,
doesn't it?"

"Some driving, Boone."

"Thanks, buddy. Was some shit, wasn't it? Hatch, you
old pissant, you sure know how to put iron in a man's
britches."

Boone turned right and headed back out of the
plantation. At a safer speed, they were on the main road
in three minutes. Two uneventful hours later, half of
which Hatch napped, they reached the jungle airstrip
where Buzz Killion and his STOL airplane waited.

Hatch wondered who kept the airstrip cleared, and
why. The why, he figured, had to be drugs. What else?
But who? It would take a lot of effort, a lot of attention; it
was not a haphazard undertaking. Like walls, thick
jungle foliage lined both sides and each end of the
mowed field. It seemed hardly longer than a football
field, although Hatch knew it had to be. It would be
useless for any regular type of airplane; in fact, except for
helicopters, the only aircraft that could get off such a
small field was the Maule, especially built as a short-
takeoff-and-landing plane.

Buzz Killion did not inspire trust. Dressed in knee-
length shorts, one of the screamingest aloha shirts ever
made, shower thongs, and dark sunglasses with white
plastic frames, he was leaning against the Maule's engine
cowling, one hand resting on a prop blade and the other
holding a straw panama hat with which he lazily fanned
his face.

"Don't tell me that's the pilot," Hatch said as the
Mercedes squeaked through a narrow opening on the
road through the trees and onto the field.

"Buzz Killion," Boone said, nodding, smiling. "Don't worry, he always dresses fancy. That's not just for you."

"Some comfort."

"Good pilot, though."

The car stopped beside the small plane, and while Boone went over to greet Killion, Hatch began removing his gear from the trunk.

"Here, let me give you a hand with that," Killion said, taking the rucksack from Hatch and stowing it in a compartment behind the cockpit. He then took the shotgun from Hatch, pumping it twice to make sure it was unloaded. "Can't have this thing going off inside the plane, now, can we?"

Killion reached out and shook Hatch's hand as Boone introduced them. Killion's eyes went to the pistol in a holster at Hatch's side.

"If you don't mind, I'd just as soon put that *pistola* back there with the scattergun. Loaded weapons in the cockpit make me so nervous that I can't fly right." He smiled broadly and held out his hand, palm up, like a beggar.

"Yeah, sure," Hatch said, removing the clip before handing over the pistol. He put the clip in one of the rucksack's side pouches.

"Good man," Killion said, closing and locking the compartment door.

As Killion performed his final walk-around, Hatch walked Boone back around the car to the driver's side.

"No good-byes," Boone said, opening the door.

"Right," Hatch said. He reached out and shook Boone's hand. "But, thanks," he added.

"Don't forget to duck," Boone said, opening the car door and sliding behind the wheel.

"Boone," Hatch said, leaning on the window frame, "tell Jan that—"

"Sure, I'll tell her. She'll be all right."

"You be all right too, okay?" Hatch stepped back.

"Always." Boone started the engine and whipped the

car around. Once at the tree line, the car disappeared as if swallowed by the jungle.

When Hatch walked back to the plane, Killion started the engine. The right-side door was cracked open for Hatch.

"You ever been in a Maule?" Killion shouted over the engine noise.

Hatch shook his head.

"You're gonna love this, then."

He accelerated quickly and the small plane began bouncing forward. After the fourth or fifth bounce, the plane did not come down, climbing higher and higher until banking hard to the right and Hatch was looking out the side window onto a deep green carpet of the top jungle canopy.

"We're light," Killion said to Hatch's look.

The Maule Super Rocket had lifted off in four hundred feet.

Jan got back to Boone's house late that afternoon, when the sun was low over the Andaman Sea, turning the water purple and the jungle black.

She had taken a *samlor* into Phuket City to change some traveler's checks at the Bank of Bangkok office there. After that she wandered through the market district, almost able to feel like a tourist. She encountered groups of tourists at the shops, some Americans and some Australians, and for a while she walked the streets the way they did, went into the shops they did, and even had a drink in a bar filled with them. But their curious excitement and comradeship only served to intensify her feelings of boredom and loneliness. It was difficult to stay alone in the bar. Men came to her table and offered to buy drinks, to dance, to play. Finally their insistence forced her to leave.

She had not been able to decide what to do next. She did not know if she would ever see Hatch again, and if he did not come out of Laos, she would never find out what had happened to him.

There was no point in abusing herself with thoughts like that. She tried another bar, but again was not left alone to drink in private.

She bought five yards of brocaded Thai silk without having any idea what she would make from it.

At last, tired and bored, she went back to Patong Beach and to Boone's house.

She had to walk the last half-mile from the road. Boone's white Mercedes was parked out front instead of in the garage, and behind it was another car, a dark green Lincoln Mark V. The house was bright in the dusk light outside.

As Jan approached the veranda, she was stopped by the sound of a woman crying. Then the front door swung open and a tall man appeared in the doorway. Jan stopped, took two steps sideways, and hid herself behind a tree. Something was wrong in the house.

The tall man came out and looked around, then held the screen door wide open. Two other men came out then. The last one, dressed like an aging New England college boy, pulled off his sunglasses and dropped them into his shirt pocket. The first man hurried down the steps and opened the back door of the Lincoln for the third man, who ducked inside quickly. The other two men got into the front seat.

Jan moved around the tree, keeping out of sight, as the car turned around in the yard and headed back out the narrow road, its tires squeaking over the crushed coral and shells in the road like glass breaking underfoot.

Jan tried to catch her breath, leaning against the tree for support. She knew the third man. Once, in Wellington, he had come to visit her.

Linn was crying in the house. Jan ran inside.

Boone, looking like he had just witnessed a murder, sat on the wicker couch. Across his lap, Linn lay curled up in a ball, crying between gasping breaths. Boone stroked her back and said nothing.

Jan went to the couch and knelt on the floor in front of Boone and Linn. Boone said, "They know where he's going."

18

They had been flying northeasterly at wave-top level over the Gulf of Thailand for three hours when Buzz Killion first noticed the flash of the setting sun off glass or metal to his left and slightly ahead of their course. They were, Killion estimated, about ten minutes from landfall, then another fifteen minutes up the coast to the Pattaya airstrip. He scanned the area where the glint had been, but it did not come again. There was a lot of air traffic over the gulf and it had probably been an airliner climbing out from Don Muang over the Bight of Bangkok. The Maule was less than a hundred kilometers south of the capital.

Hatch had not been behind the controls of an airplane in twenty years or more, but the Maule had straightforward, basic instrumentation. Hatch remembered enough to know that Buzz Killion was good. After a while, Hatch had leaned his head against the side door and gone to sleep.

He was still asleep when a sudden roar seemed to force the small plane to lurch up and hard to the left.

"Holy shit!" Killion cried. "What the fuck—"

Hatch jolted awake and grabbed the side of his seat as Killion threw the plane over hard right and dove back down toward the water.

"Check our rear," Killion ordered Hatch.

Twisting his neck to look out the side window to the back, Hatch saw the black Hughes 500E helicopter rocking back and forth in their wake like a pendulum.

"Chopper," Hatch told Killion.

"Whose?" Killion wondered, climbing steeply. "That fucker's crazy!"

"I can't tell. It's black. Can't see any markings."

"He staying with us?" Killion yelled, the engine straining hard in the climb.

"Like on a towline," Hatch said, watching the chopper tail them about twenty yards back.

"What is it, can you tell?"

"Looks kind of like a Loach," Hatch answered, referring to the military version of the Hughes LOH used heavily in Vietnam.

"Must be a Hughes 500. He can cruise at about 250 knots, so we sure as hell ain't gonna outrun him. Some of your gun-toting pals?"

"Don't count on it."

"That's what I thought." Killion threw the airplane into a hard left bank and jerked the nose up. Talking to himself, he said, "Well, Buzz, old man, how many times have you told yourself to stay away from people with guns? Huh? If you weren't so bloody greedy . . ." After getting a stall-warning Klaxon when the airspeed dropped below forty-eight, he pushed the nose over and leveled out so low over the water that salt spray misted the windscreen.

The helicopter came up next to the plane on the pilot's side and they could see that the back door had been removed. A shooter with what looked like an M-16 sat in the opening with his feet braced on the skid.

"Jesus!" Killion cried, and threw the plane up and to the right.

Hatch unbuckled his seat belt and was trying to crawl back to the cargo compartment to reach his weapons.

"Look," Killion told Hatch, "don't you start shooting at them unless they shoot at us. Maybe they just want to make us land."

But before Hatch could get into the back, the shooter fired off a clip at the Maule, bullets riddling the cockpit and fuselage. Hatch, bent between the seats, felt pricks of glass nicking his back, and something warm, wet, sticky. The Maule's engine cried with the strain and the little plane lurched higher. Suddenly the stall warning sounded again, and adding full flaps, Hatch jerked back into his seat.

Buzz Killion had taken three hits and was slumped

against the side. Half of his face was torn away. The cockpit glass was shattered and wind roared through the openings. The remaining Plexiglas was covered in blood. Hatch grabbed the yoke and shoved it forward to get the nose down and recover some airspeed.

Anticipating a crash, the helicopter backed off.

Screaming into the wind, Hatch worked the rudder pedals to get the plane straightened out, and pushed the yoke forward to level off the nose. "Come on, baby," he begged the Maule, "come on, sweetheart. Fly, baby, fly!"

Through the shattered windscreen Hatch could see land approaching, a stretch of white beach and the thick multihued green jungle beyond. He had no idea where the airstrip at Pattaya was, although he could make out a clearing and a village to his ten-o'clock. He was too busy to think or to be afraid.

Then his vision was blocked by the Hughes dropping in front of him as if it had been lowered by a rope. The shooter was taking aim.

Hatch kicked down the right pedal and twisted the wheel. The Maule took the rounds in its belly, in a line stretching from the engine cowling to the elevators. The engine coughed six quick times, then smoothed out again, but smoke poured from the engine into the cockpit.

Blinded now, able to breathe only by putting his face against one of the bullet holes in the side window, Hatch fought to keep the plane in the air. The engine sputtered again, caught, sputtered, then died. The silence was short-lived, soon replaced by the chomping helicopter blades as the Hughes pulled up alongside the slowly descending aircraft.

Holding the yoke with one hand, Hatch managed to get his seat belt on with the other, cinching it tight. He reached over and checked Buzz's artery—flat. To keep Killion from falling onto the yoke when they touched down, Hatch, pulled him sideways and wedged him between the front seats.

The Maule was over the beach now. Hatch banked left

and kept descending, able to see ahead for only occasional moments. He was losing altitude fast and the stall warning sounded again. Then the yoke began shaking in his hand and the tail seemed to be sliding backward as the nose drifted up.

Then it hit. The plane came down on the surf line, the right wing over the beach and the left over the water. After the initial jolt as the landing gear folded up, the plane skidded in the wet sand for twenty yards before turning a hundred and eighty degrees and sliding tailfirst up the beach. Flames flicked from the engine cowling as soon as the plane stopped.

Hatch released his belt and kicked open the jammed door. By then flames had crawled into the cockpit. He had enough time to pull out his weapons and the rucksack from behind the seats before the fire, surging along the bulkhead padding, reached the cargo compartment.

Hatch darted into the tree line as the black helicopter made its first pass over the wreckage.

Boone had really had no choice. Jan knew it. Now they had picked up Linn's father and were holding him on narcotics-smuggling charges. They promised to have Linn arrested for prostitution and smuggling. Charges that would have condemned both Linn and her father to death in Thailand.

He could have lied, Boone explained to Jan, but they would have found out in a matter of hours, and that would only have made it worse for Linn.

"It doesn't matter about me," Boone had told Jan. "But I couldn't let them destroy Linn. Hatch knows how to take care of himself. He has a chance."

Jan hushed him. She understood. There was no point in discussing it further. The man who had made the threats might have called himself Perry Nelson, but he was, or had been, the chief of station in Sydney, or had claimed to be. He had been at her husband's funeral. His name was Tom Considine. That was the name Jan had known him by.

Why did the CIA want Hatch? This was not, she told herself over and over, the same organization to which Jason had given two decades of his life.

"They aren't playing games," Boone told Jan later that afternoon. They didn't go through all this just to have a talk with Hatch. They want to stop him from going into Laos, from finding Michael Laser."

"But the CIA wants Laser too. Every intelligence agency in the States has been after him since that aborted assassination attempt on the president. It doesn't make sense."

"They weren't surprised when I told them about Laser. As if they already knew. They only wanted to know Hatch's route and schedule. It's like they were more interested in Hatch than Laser."

"And if they already knew about Laser, then why didn't they just go get him? You can't tell me they couldn't have made some kind of deal with the Laotian government, a trade of some kind."

"The sixty-four-thousand-dollar question. But it doesn't matter. I've got to warn Hatch," Boone said, banging his fist on the table. "He's walking into a trap and it's of my making. I know his route, I can get there ahead of him."

"How?"

19

Hatch had watched the helicopter land on the beach, but he was gone by the time two men jogged over to the downed Maule to check it out. He pushed further into the jungle and waited until the helicopter, after circling the area for ten minutes with a spotlight on the trees, gained altitude and headed north into the evening sky.

They were probably Americans, Hatch figured, or at least Caucasians. The pilot had worn a dark baseball cap and mirrored sunglasses, which had once reflected the

sun into Hatch's eyes like a flashbulb going off. The
shooter wore a baseball cap turned bill backwards and
the same sunglasses. The second man in the cockpit had
on a coat and tie. And Hatch had caught glimpses of
another man in the cabin behind the shooter.

There was no choice but to keep going. Either they
would find him or not. Using a penlight, Hatch checked
the map against what he had seen of the coastline as the
Maule went in, and figured he had crashed almost fifty
kilometers south of Pattaya, along an outcropping of land
marking the mouth of the Bight of Bangkok. If he were
correct, then he had to be only a few kilometers north of
Sattahip, where, according to the map, there was a small
airport.

They would not be expecting him to get another
plane, Hatch hoped, and they would certainly be
checking the roads out of here. Road, singular, he told
himself. There was only one road and it ran along the
coast, either south until it ran into the Kampuchean
border, or north, skirting the eastern shore of the Bight
until it reached Bangkok. There seemed to be a number
of small rivers coming down from the interior mountains
onto the coastal plain. But they would only take him into
the densely forested mountains, beyond which lay
Kampuchea. An airplane was still his best, if not his only,
hope.

After checking and securing his gear, Hatch began the
trek inland, moving east from the beach to find the coast
road that led into Sattahip, which, if he understood
where he was, could only be a few kilometers away.

The airport, which Hatch stumbled across on the
southern edge of the town, consisted of a single short
asphalt runway and a fixed base operator with a few
sprayers. There were some planes Hatch could not
recognize, along with a couple of Cessna Ag Trucks and a
bi-winged Ag Cat. There were lights in the hangar, and
the faint sound of Bangkok radio rock-and-roll. The
stench of agricultural chemicals was strong. There were

a couple of dozen fifty-gallon barrels and a number of smaller drums stacked between the flight line and the corrugated tin Quonset hut which served as a hangar. A red windsock hung limply from a pole on the hangar roof. From inside the hangar, someone laughed.

Hatch made his way around to the side of the hangar, where an old rusting deuce-and-a-half truck sat wheel-less on concrete blocks. Near the hangar front were two aging Peugeots and one small Toyota truck. More laughter and an eruption of loud voices led Hatch to believe that some kind of game was in progress, probably cards. Pushing his rucksack in ahead of him to scatter the spiders and unknown critters, Hatch climbed into the back of the truck and made a place to sleep. Then he went out to reconnoiter the field and aircraft.

There were no guards; none of the planes were locked up or tied down. Fuel seemed to come from a large truck in braces about fifty yards from the hangar. The Ag Trucks were most similar to the Cessnas Hatch had flown in the past. They were also, although not quiet, signifi-cantly less noisy than the Ag Cat. Hatch knew he would have to fly out at treetop level and keep low through the moutain valleys to get across Thailand without being tracked on radar. One benefit of the Ag Truck, with the spraying pipes and mechanisms strung below its wing, it was obviously an agricultural plane and would not arouse too much attention flying over the treetops.

Hatch made himself comfortable in the back of the truck and while waiting for the men in the hangar to quiet down, rehearsed his route out of Thailand.

He finally got to sleep after eleven, when the party broke up and six men left in the Peugeots. Ten minutes later, the hangar lights went out.

Boarding the Thai Airways turboprop at Bangkok's Don Muang airport early that morning, Jan noticed how slowly Boone took the steps up to the plane, and how winded he was when they took their seats.

"Are you all right?" she asked him.

He only nodded and fiddled with his seat belt.

The thought had crossed Jan's mind that Boone could die and she would be alone in Laos illegally. What would she do with Boone's body? How would she explain to the Laotians what she was doing there and how she got there? Were the forged travel permits Boone gave her any good? Boone had said that most of the guards at the border were illiterate and accepted travel papers on whim anyway. She visualized herself spending the rest of her life in a Laotian prison, saw herself an old woman begging for food on the streets of what she imagined Vientiane to look like, she saw herself before a firing squad composed of little men in black pajamas; when the dream fell into a drama of rescue by Hatch, she pulled herself back into the moment and ordered a fruit drink from the attendant.

In a couple of hours they would land in Ubon Ratchathani. From there they would take a bus to the refugee camps at the border. They were carrying packs, the kind Jan was used to seeing on the backs of young American tourists. Boone had asked Jan to wear an oversize bra into which they had hidden folded paper money, both Thai *baht* and Lao *kip*; it was not painful, but just irritating enough so that Jan could never forget it was there.

Posing as medical personnel with Catholic Relief Services, with their visas and travel permits, Boone said they could take a Mekong riverboat south to Pakse in Laos. They should have beaten Hatch there by a full day, if not more. Moving on foot from the smugglers' airstrip in Thailand to the Mekong would take a long, hard day. If Hatch followed the plan they had outlined in Boone's backyard, he would take the river north from Pakse. There was no way he could get by them, Boone had told Jan. "I just hope you remember enough nursing to get us through a day with the villagers who live along the river outside Pakse," he had said, "because my notion of doctoring consists of 'Take two whiskeys, get laid, and hang loose, brother.'"

Jan looked out the window at the thick green jungle and the mountains. Fear knotted her stomach like a twisted rag and she wondered what had ever possessed her to think she could pull off such a thing.

She turned toward Boone, just to have his company, his distraction, but he was asleep. An involuntary shiver ran down her spine until she noticed that he was breathing.

The furious man had chased Hatch down the runway in his pickup truck, but the Ag Truck bounced into the air to the accompaniment of the man's shouts and the Toyota's honking horn.

Hatch noticed that he not only had a full tank of fuel, but a full chemical tank as well. Realizing that the fuel would stretch farther if he dumped the chemicals, he banked right on takeoff and sprayed the first field he saw, a tract of vegetables running perpendicular to the sea. Then, gaining only fifty feet in altitude, he cut northeasterly toward the distant mountains.

If his calculations were correct, after making his way through the mountain valleys, he would parallel the Thai-Kampuchean border to Laos, then land anywhere he could find a big-enough spot. Since he expected to fly undetected by radar all the way across, he might as well continue into Laos, rather than land on the Thai side and have to cut his way through the jungle for a day or more. If no airstrip presented itself, he could also skid it into the Mekong River where it widened just south of Pakse.

Until he got into the mountains, flying did not require much of his attention. He kept fifty feet over the jungle canopy, which in places seemed as solid as a carpet, and cruised at 170 mph. Soon he would need all the attention he could give the plane as it darted among the rocks and trees of the mountain valleys.

If he did not crash on the way, he would be in Laos in two hours.

Part Three

Ξ

Laos

20

Boone and Jan held the backseat of the rolling old green-and-yellow bus against the mobs filling the pus-colored vehicle from the front. When they boarded the bus at Phimun Mangsahan, the nearest town to the UN-controlled refugee camps, it was nearly empty; but after crossing the border—where the checkpoint guards simply waved—the bus seemed to be stopping every mile to add passengers for the short journey into Pakse.

As they passed through the Mekong's watershed, their view was of rice fields, although in the distance to the east they could see the dark purple rise of the mountains that would stretch up to nine thousand feet by the time they reached the border with Vietnam. Jan said it was startlingly beautiful. Boone told her that the scenery was deceptive, for they were in the country of Prince Phoun Som, and there was no beauty in that.

"This is all under direct control of Prince Phoun Som and his son, Kaysone Som," Boone told her. "It stretches south of the line made by the highway from the provincial city of Savannakhet east to the border town of Sepone, just south of the line that marked the old DMZ over in Vietnam, all the way down to the southern border with Kampuchea, or Cambodia if you don't like the new name. In landlocked Laos, the Soms control the only transportation route to a seaport, that is, the southern navigable section of the Mekong River. With no trains and few roads, the river's the conduit for heavy goods from the mountains to the sea, and in the business of the princes, heavy goods mean raw heroin shipped by the ton.

"Riding shotgun on river shipments through the pirate regions of Kampuchea, as well as protecting the poppy fields in the mountain villages under their control, requires a sizable army. The security force of the Soms, although nowhere near as large in number, rivals in its potential for fear and violence the army of the Lao People's Revolutionary Party. Laotian President Souphanouvong calls his country's drug lords 'tigers at the door,' but he's been too busy with counterinsurgents sponsored by an unlikely partnership between the Chinese and the Americans to send into the mountain camps an army large enough to put them down for good, although there've been rumors for weeks that the Vietnamese are fed up and have a plan to regain control of the pirate-held regions. For the locals here, it's just changing the name of a vicious master; it's all the same in the end."

The sight of a white man and woman, and the sound of English spoken, caused the normally shy Laotians to turn and stare at them. Jan smiled, then returned her attention to the passing scenery: water buffalo, field workers in their round, peaked hats, and the ubiquitous palms. The sound of Boone's voice helped soothe the tension she felt, which was why, she figured, he continued talking.

"Laos is no more or no less mixed up than any of these countries over here," Boone was saying. "It's certainly in better shape than Kampuchea, which is, even after the Vietnamese threw out Pol Pot, tantamount to living in hell. The Pol Pot regime was the epitome of everything that could go wrong with Communist theories. Half the population, *half*, was exterminated." Boone shook his head. "In 1975, when everything around here except Thailand fell like a house of cards, the Laotian monarchy was abolished and the Pathet Lao formed an alliance with Vietnam and, of course, with Russia.

"Here's the thing of it," Boone said, winking at a little girl, who quickly turned her face into her mother's black silk skirt. "In the center of the country, the area around the capital, you have control by the LPDR. But in the north, the area called the Golden Triangle, an unstable sort of control is in the hands of two not-so-friendly drug lords. Then, here, in the south, the Soms run everything. Scattered among them all are dissident Hmongs and a new, resurgent Pathet Lao aligned with the Chinese. What a bloody damn mess!"

Jan turned toward Boone. From somewhere forward, chickens squawked. A frightened baby cried. The bus lurched around a curve and people standing in the aisles swayed back and forth as if they were on a ship.

"You know the proverbial powder keg?" Boone asked.

Jan nodded, turning her head to follow the sudden attention toward the rear being given by some of the people in the aisle.

"Boone," she said, touching his shoulder.

Boone turned around to look.

Kicking up red dust from the road like an approaching storm, a chopped-top Toyota Land Cruiser painted in jungle camouflage and carrying four men and a pedestal-mounted fifty-caliber machine gun closed in on the smoking bus.

"Shit," Boone muttered.

Jan could feel the muscles tense in his arm where she touched him.

"What is it?"

"I don't know, but they're a little too rag-taggle for the army."

The Cruiser came up beside the bus and while the man behind the wheel honked the horn insistently, the men inside waved at the bus driver to pull over. The frightened and confused chattering of the Laotians in the bus sounded almost musical, like some fantastical Wagnerian opera made Oriental. Jan noticed that some of the people nearest them were hiding things below the seats, including, in one case, a child.

"What do they want?" Jan asked.

"I guess we're going to find out," Boone whispered, the effort to remain calm straining his voice. "Let me talk unless they ask you a direct question. Remember, look like you belong here. These people aren't good with words, they go on impressions. Remember to act indignant, but polite. Offer your travel permit right

away, as if they should have known we have the
permission of their superiors in Vientiane to be here."

The bus lurched to a raggedy stop in the middle of the
road, and the assault wagon swerved across the road to
block any further progress. Boone and Jan hid behind
the swarms of Laotians ahead of them, but they could
hear shouts from the front.

"Do you understand any of this?" Jan asked.

"Hardly any," Boone told her. "They're all too hyster-
ical. I think they want everyone out; the bus driver's
claiming party membership. This woman," Boone said,
nodding to indicate the woman who had hidden her
child beneath a seat, "is praying."

"She's afraid they'll hurt her child?" Jan wondered,
unable to believe any child could be in danger.

"She prays for us, the white couple," Boone said.

Jan could only look at him, her eyes wide, as the bus
emptied before them.

"Come on," Boone whispered, standing and taking
Jan's hand. "We should not appear to be hiding."

Jan nodded. She followed Boone and the last of the
Laotians from the bus.

At the doorway, two of the attackers grabbed Boone
and Jan, pulling them outside and shoving them to the
left, ahead of the bus, away from the huddled clump of
Laotians to the right, who were being held encircled and
guarded by the other two men.

All four of the armed men were yelling, their shrill
voices mixed with the cries of children and the passengers' pleas, so Boone could follow none of it. It was
happening too fast, too frantically, as if the attackers
were on a speed rush. One of the men kicked dirt in the
road, as if somehow that emphasized the point he
wanted to make, a point neither Boone nor Jan could
understand. All four men jerked their weapons around,
probing with them like pointing fingers.

Boone held out his travel permit unfolded around his
right index finger. Trying to make himself understood
over the shouting, he cried out in French, "Please, sirs,

we have official travel papers, official papers and visas from your consulate in Bangkok. Here, look at them."

Making no appearance of understanding, the man nearest them swung out with the barrel of his M-16, knocking the papers from Boone's hand and smashing Boone's finger at the same time. Boone doubled over and grabbed his finger, and the attacker yelled something, and in a movement like dancing, hopped closer to Boone.

"Oh, my God, please," Jan cried, trying to get Boone to cooperate. "Stand up, Boone, he wants you to stand up, please hurry and get up, Boone, please," she pleaded.

Boone straightened himself, but held the broken finger immobilized in his free hand, the pain stretched in a deep grimace across his face.

"United Nations," Jan cried. "United Nations Peace Authority," she repeated, saying anything that came into her head. "We are United Nations medical people, here to care for your sick and injured," she yelled in English.

"Please, sirs," Boone said in French again, "what do you want? What have we done? We are doctors, we are doctors with Catholic Relief Services. Catholic, you know? We have official travel . . ."

Without understanding the words, Boone could tell that the man had yelled at him to shut up. A pair of M-16's waved in their faces as two of the men herded Boone and Jan around to the front of the bus.

"I'm afraid I've really messed this one up good," Boone whispered to Jan.

She stumbled and fell to her knees. "Oh Jesus, Boone," she said, her voice cracking with fright, "are they going to shoot us? What did we do? Can't we give them something—uuhh," she cried sharply, interrupted by the shout of the man behind her and the barrel of his automatic rifle jamming into her back. Boone let go of his broken finger long enough to help her up.

"Hey!" Boone shouted then, spinning around.

But a punch to the stomach dropped him to his knees and he was jerked up and shoved forward.

It was suddenly apparent that they were being taken to the topless Land Cruiser. They were pushed ahead by the rifle barrels, forced up into the back of the Toyota. As Boone was helping Jan up, behind them two of the M-16's exploded like a string of firecrackers fired off, sounding as oddly innocent as the Fourth of July. Jan fell back into Boone and they turned at the same time.

The other bus passengers fell on top of one another like bowling pins, blood erupting from their bodies like fountains from a pool, red geysers spraying against the side of the bus. A man tried to run but was cut in half by a one-second burst that spit a half-dozen 5.56mm steel-jacketed shells into his body. A baby's arm, blown off its body by the fury of shells, rolled across the dirt like a kicked can. The screams faded all at once as if the volume of a radio had been turned down.

Boone and Jan were shoved into the Cruiser; then the two guards climbed into the back and sat across from them, rifles pointed at their prisoners.

The firing slowed as the men stopped to change banana clips, then, a few seconds later, stopped as the two shooters walked through the bodies looking for life. Boone and Jan did not look again. Three times they heard single shots, then a murmuring cry followed by another shot.

When all four men were in the Cruiser, the man in the front seat threw a hand grenade over his head back toward the bus; then with a shout the driver jerked the Cruiser forward and they sped away. Jan looked back at the explosion and saw the front of the bus lift up and disappear in a ball of dust, smoke, and fire. The sound wave blew her hair back, and she tried to keep from throwing up. Moments later, the Cruiser rounded a curve and all that remained of the bus was a column of black smoke rising in the thick, hot air.

They drove into the town of Pakse, which was not far, and on to the river southwest of the central city. Boone tried to tell Jan something once, but the shouts and threats from the guards cut him off at the first word. "No talk," one of them said in English.

By the open, even challenging manner with which their guards wheeled through Pakse, Boone had them figured as Prince Phoun Som's men, not members of the new People's Revolutionary Army. To Jan they seemed like Western desperados shooting up a cow town. Not a single person in the streets of Pakse looked directly at them when they passed, the Cruiser careening wildly through the narrow dirt streets, spooking dogs, scattering chickens, and raising clouds of red dust. But they might as well have been invisible for all the attention they received.

The Cruiser slid to a stop at the docks. There was an overpowering odor of fish and sewage, making Jan feel so nauseous that she feared falling down in a faint. The Laotian guards, again as frenetic as stoned monkeys, jumped from the Cruiser and ordered Jan and Boone to follow. They were prodded and shoved toward a large steel U.S. Navy Trumpy-class PTF patrol boat tied up between two native river sampans. The men on the boat—there were six visible—wore tiger-stripe fatigues and bush hats. They were heavily armed, including automatic pistols, M-16's—two with M-79 grenade launchers attached—and one man standing near the bow had an Ithica M-37 sawed-off pump shotgun.

As Jan and Boone were shoved toward the boat, its engines rumbled to life with such force that the ground beneath their feet vibrated with the might of 6,200 horsepower. In spite of the shouting and the engine roar, no one else on the docks or at the warehouses behind turned to look.

Jan and Boone went across the wobbling gangway and were immediately grabbed by their arms and taken aft. The men on the dock let go the lines and as the patrol boat eased out into the river, Jan and Boone were secured with ropes to cleats mounted on the gunwales.

"Lie down," one of the Laotian guards said in clear English.

Another man kicked Boone, knocking him flat to the deck.

Jan lay down quickly and then their feet were secured. The bonds were already cutting into their wrists. Diesel fumes mixed with the rich smells from the river and an undercurrent of stale urine.

"Be good," the English-speaking one said, laughed, then walked forward.

Boone looked up and back. A light blue flag with a gold circle in the center flew from the ensign staff. "Som," he said, recognizing the drug lord's emblem, a setting-sun symbol parodying the British slogan that the sun never sets on its empire.

The patrol boat increased power and its bow rose to plane, its wake slapping the opposing riverbanks like ocean waves.

Boone turned to look at Jan, who was staring at him in absolute fright, her face shaking with it.

"If they wanted to kill us," Boone said, "we'd already be dead."

"Oh God, I'm so scared," Jan said, closing her eyes tight.

21

Hatch had been watching the fuel gauge for ten minutes, as if somehow by staring at it, by wishing, he could jog the needle off the bottom peg.

He had seen Pakse just over the river and had turned north to follow the Done. With a time and speed calculation, he had estimated his position as approximately halfway between Pakse and Khong Sedone. Even low on the river, Hatch could see the Plateau des Bolovens rising to his right, and stretching out to the left the lowland watershed of the Mekong and its various tributaries, of which the Done was one of the larger.

There was very little traffic on the river, and what

there was of it seemed local and mercantile. He had not seen a gunboat, nor any vessel that appeared to be military. He doubted if any of the locals would bother to report a low-flying aircraft following the river.

Once men in a long fishing boat waved to him, and Hatch waggled his wings in return.

But now his attention was glued to the fuel gauge; even though he had been anticipating that sound for ten minutes, when the engine sputtered twice, coughed, and died, he tensed with surprise.

He hardly had enough altitude to glide any distance in hopes of finding a clearing. He had realized some miles back that he would have to put the plane into the river. He quickly checked the snugness of the shoulder harness holding him to the cockpit's single seat, then began easing the yoke back.

There was hardly time to plan an approach. The plane dropped fast, and a few seconds after the still prop began whistling in the wind, it was ten feet off the water.

"Keep your nose up, baby," Hatch, with the yoke held tightly to his heaving chest, coaxed the plane. "Come on, baby, come on, keep your pretty nose up."

The first impact sounded like a cosmic handclap, then the main landing gear dug in and pulled down the nose. The Ag Truck stopped as surely as if it had snagged an arresting cable, then flipped tail-over and landed on its back. Suspended by the large bubble of air inside and moving in the current, the plane began drifting tailfirst, upside down, with the flow.

Hatch struggled to stay conscious and to remember what he had to do next. The inertia of the sudden stop had thrown him hard against the harness, snapping his head forward into the top of the instrument panel. He was hanging upside down and looking through the cockpit at the underside of the silt-filled river, which had begun to leak into the cockpit like diarrhea.

Managing to twist sideways and brace against the side of the cockpit, Hatch shoved against the door with his feet, forcing it slowly open against the water pressure.

He took a deep breath and swam out, barely avoiding the tail rudder as it smashed by in the current.

Surfacing for a breath, Hatch watched the plane that carried his supplies and weapons glide smoothly down the brown river on its back.

Hatch dog-paddled his way to the near shore, suddenly aware of an extraordinary hammering inside his skull. He could not manage a deep breath without an accompanying stab of pain.

Tall trees laced together by the lattice of vines hovered over the river along each bank like parallel walls. Soon it would be night, and in the jungle it would be black like the inside of a cave. Lying on the bank in exhaustion and pain, Hatch realized he would not be able to move through the jungle as well, or as quickly, as he could by staying in the river and riding the current, even though it was pushing him in the opposite direction, back toward Pakse. He had to try recovering his weapons and the rucksack. Sooner or later the plane would bump into the bank or hit a snag. He really had no choice but to follow the plane, so he gritted his teeth and paddled back out into the strongest part of the current and let the river move him feetfirst downstream.

At sunset the patrol boat reached the splitting of the river at Khong Sedone, and there, secured to the shore with lines the crew members had tied around trees, it waited.

The crew sat around on deck smoking, chattering in their tonal language, occasionally making threatening gestures toward Boone and Jan, who were still tied in place on the flat aft deck. A steaming pot of fish soup sent pungent waves of steam and smoke over the prisoners.

Jan had tried twice to ask for a chance to relieve herself, and had twice been brutally kicked for speaking. The guards pointed at the stain on her pants and laughed, making crude, pantomimed jokes.

When darkness came, the boat's interior lights were turned on, and someone brought out a portable radio and tape deck with a cassette of *The Doors' Greatest Hits*. The laughter was still loud. Those men did not need to hide from anyone.

Disguised by the loud music and joking around, Boone was able to talk to Jan for a moment.

"How are you?" he asked.

"I guess all right. Why are we just sitting here like this?"

"I think this boat has too much draft to go any farther upriver. I suppose we're waiting, and don't ask me what for."

"Will they kill us, Boone?"

"I don't think so," Boone said, lying. He believed they were certainly going to be killed, sooner or later. "I'm sorry I got you into this."

"Nobody twisted my arm, Boone. I was determined to do this, and you couldn't have stopped me."

"I promised Hatch . . ."

"Promised what?"

"That I'd take care of you."

"Do you know where he is now?"

"He should have landed outside Det Udom—that's about thirty kilometers southwest of where we got the bus—he should have gotten there late this afternoon. By now he should have worked his way somewhere around Dam Noi Lake, where he'll probably spend the night."

"I mean, is he close to us?"

"No. Not close."

One of the guards dropped down from the cabin top and put the barrel of his rifle into Boone's face, yelling something in Lao. Jan squinted and turned her face away. The man kicked Boone hard before going back to the music, wine, and soup.

Hatch *was* close. If the Ag Truck had not run out of fuel when it did, he would have in less than ten minutes flown over the top of the patrol boat making its way northward. Even now, as he made repeated dives to recover his gear from the Ag Truck, which had jammed

itself between the bank and a large fallen tree rotting in
the river, he was less than twenty kilometers from where
the patrol boat waited at the split.

In the darkness, Hatch had to locate his gear by feel,
and working against the current used much of his wind,
allowing him only a few seconds each time he got inside
the flooded cockpit. Agonizingly he clawed through the
murky water, grabbing seat belts, twigs, and shredded
carpet, not finding the rucksack until the sixth dive. He
got the shotgun on the ninth dive. He gave up looking
for the pistol after the fifteenth. By then the pain was
debilitating.

He found his medical kit, which was sealed airtight,
and took a couple of the Percodan for the headache, then
moved into the jungle to find a place to sleep until
morning.

Suddenly the radio went off and the Laotian guards
moved to the river side of the boat. Then Boone and Jan
heard the engine.

They were pulled to their feet and pushed to a
boarding ladder at the stern. They were taken off the
patrol boat and put aboard a much smaller one. Boone
could tell almost nothing about the boat in the darkness,
although it looked like a U.S. Navy LCPL, a personnel-
carrying launch, with an added sun canopy of thatched
palm fronds. But Boone knew there was something
peculiar about the man at the wheel. His back was to
Boone, but the driver was either the tallest, darkest
Laotian Boone had ever seen, or he was a black man.

Boone and Jan were shoved into the stern cockpit and
secured to cleats. The patrol boat's crew exchanged what
seemed like friendly words with the launch's four-man
crew, then the launch shoved off.

The odor of marijuana was strong when one of the
guards bent over to recheck their ropes, and Boone
noticed the hand-rolled reefer hanging from the guard's
lips.

The launch moved slowly, steadily upriver in the

darkness. No running lights. Again, music from a tape machine played American rock from the cabin, and the smell of diesel curling over the stern sharpened the marijuana smoke. Now there was also the thick, sickly-sweet smell of jungle rot.

Boone strained his eyes in the darkness to get a look at the man steering. He was wearing khaki shorts and flip-flops, with a sleeveless army fatigue shirt. He wore a boonie hat with the sides rolled up cowboy style. A .45 automatic was in a holster hanging from a web belt around his waist. Boone figured he had to be an American or Cuban. But he had not heard of any Cubans in Laos. The man's hair hung long and curly, from beneath his hat. He never turned around to look at his passengers.

Clouds darted over a half-moon, sometimes laying a silver trail on the river. Boone and Jan could feel the turns in the river in their bodies, and sometimes the river narrowed to a point where the overstretching trees made a canopy over the water. The music and marijuana gave texture to the heavy, moist night air. The rain that had held back for hours now began as a heavy mist.

Boone could not help himself. Lulled by the engine rumbling through the deck against his back, completely exhausted from lack of sleep and constant tension, he fell asleep, his head rolling over onto Jan's shoulder.

Jan, eyes wide, stared at the back of the man at the helm as if he were going to be their salvation. She wished he would turn around so she could see what kind of face he had, to see if it was at all sympathetic.

Eventually Jan slept as well. It was hours later when the sound of the engines slowing woke both of them. Stiff, sore, aching from the bindings, Jan tried to scoot up as Boone lifted his head from her shoulder.

It was still night, although the rain clouds had cleared, and what there was of the moon gave the jungle a kind of shadowed reality as they idled to hold their place in the river's current.

Then, over the engine's low rumbling, Jan could hear
an ethereal tinkling sound, like small bells or dozens of
water glasses being tapped with spoons. The shadows
became more distinct, then bright enough for her to
make out individual trees along the bank. There were
tiny flickering lights somewhere ahead. There were new
smells, but none individualized enough for recognition.
Together they made her think of decay, rot, death.

The launch drifted sideways and the propeller went to
neutral, then reverse, as the boat stopped. The crew
tossed lines to shore and the boat banged against a
wooden dock. From her prone position on the aft deck,
Jan could see a peaked thatched roof. Hanging around
the edges of the roof in rows as neat and even as tassles
hanging from the rear window of a Bangkok taxi were at
least a hundred bleached white skulls. They must be
plastic, Jan thought, Halloween decorations; a few had
unlit cigarettes dangling from their teeth, and others
sported curly mustaches colored in with black wax
pencil. She looked again. Many of them had been
aerated by what looked like bullet holes. But when
Boone turned away and spit into the water, Jan realized
the skulls were real, and then she saw bits of rotting
tissue which still clung in a few places to the bone.

When Boone and Jan were pulled to their feet, she
shuddered at the gawking, dangling skulls. She slipped
backward, fell to the cockpit deck, and immediately one
of the guards began kicking her, yelling something she
could not understand.

Suddenly the guard disappeared like a fish jerked up
from the water, and Jan realized the helmsman had lifted
him up and tossed him over the side and into the river,
like an undersize trout. When the tall black man offered
his hand, Jan took it and shakily got to her feet.

"Sorry about that, ma'am," he said with a distinct
Georgia accent. "Let me help you off." He put his hand
firmly under her arm.

Behind the dock, the ground sloped immediately and
radically upward. The landscape blotted out the sky.

Throughout the jungle, torches illuminated small areas, although from the river the flickering lights looked like fireflies in a forest. With the engine now quiet, the eerie sound of bells was clear and distinct.

"Don't worry none about them bells, ma'am," the American told Jan, as if reading her thoughts. "Them's just some religious thing or another these folks get into. Spooky, ain't they?"

"You're an American," Jan said, stepping over the side, but stopping when the skulls blocked the way.

"No, ma'am. But I used to be." He reached up and parted the skulls like a bead curtain.

"What are you now?" Boone asked, his sarcasm barely masked, so that Jan held her breath.

"Just a war lover."

"Where are we?" Jan asked, clutching her arms to her sides and cringing as she rushed off the small dock.

"Hell," the man answered, and followed her.

When he let go of the skulls, they clanked together like bamboo wind chimes.

22

At night the jungle seemed alive. Breathing, moving, sensual, the enemy of reason. A leaf brushing an arm became a fingertip, the wind through the vines a voice, the crunch of dead twigs became breaking bones, a spiderweb across a face felt like the devil's embrace.

Their vision myopic with the darkness, Boone and Jan went forward, up the steep slope ahead, following the trail marked by the enigmatic American leading them. Two Lao men dressed only in loincloths, carrying M-16's, formed the rear, and they were flanked by hints of human movement in the high grass along their sides. Sometimes a man became visible for an instant, as if instead of simply passing through a thinning in the bush, he had formed from the air itself. And some of the Lao men they saw had painted their faces a deep, dark red, like dried blood.

Jan crossed her arms over her chest again and held her shoulders, stumbling forward and upward behind the American, who took the steep, dark trail with the surefooted familiarity of a mountain animal. Boone, Jan could hear, was having trouble breathing. Men became visible, then were gone. And there were the bells making a tinkling sound more like breaking crystal than anything metallic. Although sometimes, in an unsyncopated rhythm, there was another noise, like someone hitting a steel barrel with a metal rod. The only familiar human sound was Boone's shallow, raspy breathing in front of her, which barely tempered her frightening sense of aloneness and the weight of dread.

They climbed steadily, the salt of tears stung her cracked lips, and spirits of death danced through the jungle, which surrounded them like the walls of a cave.

The trail widened and moss-covered boulders erupted from the high grass and trees along the edges. There was light ahead and the trail broadened further, until it became apparent to Jan the area had been purposefully cleared. They had reached what seemed to be a highland meadow. Strings of multicolored electric lights had been laid in tree branches to mark the boundaries, almost like the approach to a carnival midway, or, Jan remembered, the strip of bars at Patong Beach.

The bells faded behind them, but remained the border within which all the other jungle noises were contained. The human apparitions no longer appeared in the light. There were only Boone and Jan, the war lover, and the two Laotian guards.

Because of the steep angle, Jan, who was behind Boone, did not see the place until they were very close. It rose directly from the boulders, the mountain itself its foundation. The top of it towered above the jungle like a peak ringed by clouds, so that all of the lower levels were hidden by dense forest. It was built of stone and wood, the lower walls solid, without doors or windows, perpendicular to the ground around it, and it was obviously very old, maybe an ancient monastery, Jan thought.

Now, although the lights strung through the trees were not very bright, they could make out smaller houses, huts, in the forest at the base of the monastery, from which poured light, and smoke, which clung to the treetops, lying there like a fog. Children, dirty and wide-eyed, watched in mute curiosity from some of the nearer windows. Twice Jan saw women's faces watching behind the children's. Somehow she felt more hopeful.

The procession continued another fifty yards along the rock foundation before the entrance became evident to them. A set of double doors, constructed from two six-inch mahogany slabs, enclosed an opening carved from the rock. The doors swung slowly open as the group approached, and four Laotians carrying machine guns stood aside to let them enter, Boone first, then Jan.

Boone and the war lover had to crouch passing through the low tunnel that led from the door into an inner compound. Boone's breathing reverberated off the damp rock walls, and Jan touched his shoulder with her right hand.

Inside the compound, there were more huts, and groups of Laotians squatted around campfires. There were groups of rifles stacked like tepee frames, and half a dozen filthy children played quiet chase games among them. The smell of food was strong, as well as a mild sewage stench and the sweet, spicy smell of marijuana.

Boone kept his head down, trying to breath and keep from stumbling with exhaustion. But Jan, as her eyes adjusted to the change in light inside the compound, realized that some of the men standing around the edges of the fires were not Laotians, but were probably Americans, like the war lover.

How could this be? Who were they? What were they doing in this place? Maybe it could be a good sign, she thought. If they were Americans, maybe they would help them somehow.

Boone stumbled, pitching forward to his hands and

knees. Jan hurried up and knelt next to him, but the
Laotian guards jerked her away. Then they pulled Boone
up, but he could not lock his knees and kept slipping
down. This infuriated the guards and one of them
punched him in the kidney.

"Help us!" Jan cried, looking toward the motley-
dressed Caucasians at the huts. "Please, dear God."

Two men laughed and said something to one another.
A third man picked his fingernails with a knife and
watched quietly. Another turned away and took a woman
into a hut.

The war lover put his hand on Jan's forearm and said,
"Just be cool." Then he said something in a harsher tone
to the guards. Cradling Boone between them, the
guards followed the war lover and Jan along the path into
the main compound.

"I'm all right," Boone said to no one.

They crossed the compound to a wall that towered
three stories above them. A door opened as they
approached and a man stepped out.

Unlike the rag-taggle varieties of military uniforms
worn by the other men in the compound, he had on blue
jeans, scuffed white sneakers, and a black T-shirt with
large, barely readable faded gold letters: IOWA HAWKEYES.
The hand he extended to Jan had left the butt of a large
pistol in a holster at his waist. Jan knew who he was
before he extended his hand to her and said, "How nice
of you to come by, Mrs. Moss. I'm Michael Laser.
Welcome to the kingdom of Prince Phoun Som."

With no other ceremony, and with Jan's mouth open,
Laser turned Boone and Jan over to the guards who
would take them to their rooms, saying only that it was
late, they must be tired, and that he would see them for
breakfast. Before leaving, he asked Boone if he wanted a
doctor to look at his finger. But Boone shook his head, he
had already wrapped the smashed finger and tied it to
the one beside it, which was still intact.

Boone and Jan were then taken through a series of
dark hallways to two connecting small rooms, each

furnished with the basic necessities: single bed, chair, washbasin, and table. There were no closets, only one door in or out, and only a small window that opened to a three-story straight fall to the rocks below.

Even in the darkness, Jan was able to tell that the fortress commanded a mountaintop view to the horizon in all directions. The spots of dim light in the trees below came from the huts they had seen while climbing up, she guessed, and she could see from the colored lights where the trail had opened up. She could no longer hear the bells. She took off her slacks and cleaned her legs. She could not stop moving in spite of her exhaustion; movement required some thought and helped her keep from focusing on the barely contained panic. She prowled the interior of the tiny stone room like a trapped bird.

At first light, Hatch moved back to the river. He could wait there for a passing boat, or he could begin moving north toward Khong Sedone. He ate a pack of dried peaches and a mix of dried tropical fruit. He finished the canteen of fresh water, then refilled it from the river, adding iodine tabs.

Hatch figured his position to be less than twenty kilometers south of the river split at Khong Sedone, but that was a full day's hike. Some of the land was open, marshy fields, but a good deal of it was jungle. On the other hand, he had no way to estimate how long he might wait for a boat to pass, and even then, no way to be sure he could either reach it or get its crew to come to the bank for him.

He wondered if the plane had been found. Would word of the Ag Truck's theft in Thailand have crossed the border? Hatch realized he should have removed the airworthiness certificate. At best they would assume the pilot had been killed and lost in the river. But there had been very little damage to the cockpit area. He might as well figure on search parties being out by now.

Hatch sat on the bank, hidden in the edge of a stand of

bamboo, and cleaned the shotgun with his shirt. He had been down that river once before, early in 1964, although his area of operation had been 150 kilometers to the northeast, in Toulan, at the border with Vietnam, near Khe Sanh. He knew that stretching ahead of him lay some of the most rugged tropical mountain terrain in the world. There were people living in interior villages who, because of the impassable landscape, never ventured two dozen kilometers from their homes; people who could not be sure that stories of a world outside their own were nothing more than rumors, fables, myths.

Hatch's thoughts were disrupted by the distinctive rotor beat of a pair of Huey Cobras, although they were still some distance away. He pulled back a few yards into the bamboo and blended in with the vegetation. A minute later the choppers came into view low over the river, following it like a highway, one after the other—a cow and calf. They were standard Army OD, looking a little worn in places, probably left behind when the Americans bugged out. Hatch could see the pilot and copilot in each one, as well as the door gunners manning M-60's in slings. As the choppers came close, he recognized Vietnamese Air Force markings on them.

The bamboo began whipping over his head as the Cobras went by; the rotor blast deafened him. They were too low and slow for a routine patrol; they had to be looking for something, someone. If they had been following the river for long, they would have spotted the Cessna.

When the choppers were gone, Hatch checked the shells to be sure they had dried, then inserted four in the magazine and one in the chamber. He attached the Kabar knife to his belt and put the Randall into his boot top. Then he buried the empty cans.

He no longer had the option of waiting for a boat. They would be watching for him on the river, where as a white man he would stand out like a tree in a plowed field. He pushed back through the bamboo and stayed at the edge of a field of elephant grass as he turned north toward the town of Khong Sedone, in tune with the jungle as if he had never left it.

23

The morning calls of jungle birds woke Jan at dawn. She rolled off the narrow bed and, wiping the sleepiness from her eyes, went to the small south-facing window. She had to lean far out and look left, toward the coral glow preceding the sun, before a sudden sense of the altitude jerked her back. The jungle top made a ragged black horizon line, as if it were cut from construction paper. Looking down the vertical drop to the jungle below, she had found no movement, heard no human sounds. The lights were off, the fires out. Wispy gray cooking smoke left over from the previous night hung low in the moisture-laden thick air at the tops of the trees. Jan shivered and pulled back farther into the room, as if to disguise herself from some unseen hand lurking in the smoke to pull her down.

Then she realized someone had entered the room while she slept. Her backpack had been leaning against the wall opposite the bed, but now it was lying down closer to the door. The thought that someone had been in the room while she slept, could have killed her, sent shivers through her body. In exhaustion, she had slept without dreaming. The intrusion was a horrible reminder that none of it had been a dream. She was trapped, they could do anything to her they wanted.

There was fresh water in the pitcher beside the ceramic bowl on the table. The used towel had been replaced, giving Jan hope. Would they do something like that if they were going to kill you? She washed her face, then went to her pack for a change of clothes.

She had lived through the night and no one had hurt her. They gave her a clean towel and her clothes. That feeble optimism kept her from tumbling screaming into a claustrophobic madness.

Just as she finished dressing, the door flew open and two Laotian men unceremoniously dragged her out.

Down the long, narrow, stone hallway, three doors removed from Jan's room, Boone lay absolutely still on his back in the bed, his eyes squinted shut, his teeth grinding together, as the wave of pain peaked and began to subside. He had not heard the commotion in the hall.

He had been told what to expect if he continued to refuse the chemical and radiation treatments, what would happen as the end approached. Although he might have hints of an appetite, he would not be able to swallow easily or keep down any food that made it to his stomach. He would be severely short of breath after only minor exertions. And the pain would come in waves, ebbing and flowing like the ocean's tides; sometimes it would be a fire in his veins, sometimes burning in his kidneys, and sometimes it would be a viselike constriction of his chest; there would always be headaches, ranging through the limits of his ability to tolerate them.

Boone knew, as he had always suspected he would when the time came, that he was dying. Maybe a day, maybe a week, but not a month. He would not see in six weeks the arrival of his fiftieth birthday. He had passed through the anger, the bitterness, eight months ago when the cancer was diagnosed. He had come to terms with the inevitability of his own death in ways he had never been able to do while a combat soldier. Boone had never believed he would die in combat, because he had never believed he would die at all. Now Boone craved immortality so desperately that he almost believed the very force of his desire could make it possible.

But, sweating through the sheet so thoroughly that he dampened the mattress, Boone lay still on the bed and felt the life seeping from his body as surely as the sweat from his pores.

The pain had almost subsided when he heard the key

twisting in the door lock. He urged himself to a sitting position and wiped the sweat from his face with a corner of the sheet.

The door opened and Michael Laser walked into the room, passing the two Lao guards, one of whom held a large key. Laser gestured to the guard, who then backed out and closed the door behind him.

"They will be just outside," Laser told Boone. "Looks like I didn't wake you."

Boone shook his head. He thought of standing, but rejected it for fear his body in its diminished condition was not yet ready to bear even his own weight.

Laser walked across the room, glanced out the window, then pulled up the chair and sat backwards in it, resting his arms over the chair back.

"Beautiful sunrise, didn't you think?" he said.

"Hardly," Boone answered. "No sunrise for a prisoner can be called beautiful; beauty is a province of the free."

"Nicely said. Although having a sunrise at all in your condition might be considered a blessing. And I am not referring to your status as our guest here."

"Guest?" Boone laughed.

"Keep your sense of humor, Boone. You'll need it."

Laser pulled a package of cigarettes from the pocket of his khaki shirt and lit one with a dented, scratched Zippo with silver jump wings engraved on the lid. He shook up another cigarette from the pack and held it out for Boone, who refused it. "Yes, I guess not," Laser said, replacing the pack and taking a long drag. "Another nail in my own coffin," he said on the exhale. "How's Hatch coming in?" Laser asked abruptly.

"Who?"

"Please, Boone, spare us both this charade."

Boone knew that Laser was right. He did not know how Laser got his information, but it was good and it was quick. He had obviously known ahead of time how Boone and Jan were coming into the country. And he probably knew about Hatch's flight out of Thailand. There was no point in pretending.

"You're afraid of Hatch, aren't you? That's what all this is about. You're afraid he can get to you, that he'll take you apart."

"If you believe that, your brain must be shrinking with the rest of you. Did you notice where you are? Did you notice that there is only one way to this mountaintop, and that's the river, which nothing passes, *nothing*, without our knowledge and consent? You'd have to lay a thousand-pounder directly on the roof of this fortress to make a hole big enough to get inside. We are inside a rock, man. No, you've got it all wrong. I'm looking forward to seeing Hatch again. He's a debt I have to settle personally, man to man. It won't be any other way."

"I hope I'm around to see that. Is there a place around here where I can make a substantial wager on the outcome?"

Laser laughed. "I like you, Buchannan. I like a man who's willing to grab his balls and give them a good shake as he's falling down the snake pit."

"Metaphorically speaking, I trust."

"Of course, metaphorically speaking." Laser's smile was quick, cold. "Now, shall we get back to the subject. Frank Hatcher. Let me tell you something, Boone. I know that you took Hatch to the old Air America helicopter field north of Phangnga, where he took off in a STOL plane piloted by Buzz Killion. The Maule was intercepted near the eastern shore of the gulf, just where it narrows into the Bight of Bangkok, and it was shot down, crashing on the beach near Sattahip. Killion's body was recovered from the wreck."

Laser stopped for a moment to watch the changes in Boone's expression.

"The next morning, yesterday as a matter of fact, Hatch stole one of those Cessna agricultural sprayers from a small field near Sattahip and intruded into Laos late that afternoon, crashing out of fuel into the Done River some fifteen kilometers south of Khong Sedone. No body, no blood in the cockpit."

Boone was smiling when Laser finished. So, Hatch was already in-country, already on the way to the Soms' mountaintop. No wonder Laser was so nervous. Boone was glad he had no further knowledge.

"So, my man, what's the story here?" Laser asked.

"I'd be inclined to cooperate with you, Laser, particularly since I don't think it'll do you a damn bit of good when Hatch does get here, but I've got a condition."

"You're in no position to ask for conditions, but I'll hear you out."

"Maybe my position depends on what I've got." Boone raised his eyebrows.

"Maybe. But no deals up front."

"Who says I'd trust you anyway?"

"Go."

"The woman, Jan—you release her, give her guaranteed transit off his mountain, down the river, and across the border safely into Thailand. She doesn't have anything that can help you, you don't need her, and I can be a lot more valuable if she's safe."

"What's the matter, Boone? You find yourself a little pussy-whipped so late in life? What's the difference to you with the woman?"

"Let's just say that I care about her, that I'd be prone to tell you what you need to know if I didn't have to worry about her."

Laser got up from the chair and walked to the window. He pushed open the glass and flipped his cigarette butt into the air. Then he leaned out and looked down.

"Come over here," Laser told Boone, gesturing to him with his hand while still looking out the window.

Boone urged himself up from the bed, slowly and painfully, and walked with as much dignity as he could toward the window. Laser moved aside when Boone got there and said, "Look down there, at the trail leading away from the mountain."

Boone leaned forward, bracing with his forearms on the window ledge, and peered down the sheer straight wall. There, on the trail just before it disappeared into the tall trees, two Laotian men dressed in olive-drab fatigues, one in a cowboy hat and the other bareheaded, pulled something behind them. Boone had to stare at the object a few seconds, because of the height, before he realized they were pulling Jan by her legs down the trail, her arms dragging behind her in such a way that Boone knew she was unconscious, or dead.

"What the hell have you done to her?" Boone turned, screaming into Laser's face. As Boone clenched his fists and stalked toward Laser, Laser pulled the pistol from its holster and held it in both hands, the barrel pointing into the center of Boone's face.

"Stand easy, hero," Laser told Boone. "Back up and sit down on the bed."

When Boone did as ordered, Laser said, "That's a good boy," and reholstered the pistol.

"She's not hurt. I gave her to the boy in the cowboy hat."

Boone jerked up from the bed, but sat back down when Laser's hand went to the pistol.

"Settle down, partner. Better than having her killed, which was the only other option. Wing's old lady—he's the cowboy—she died of some kind of flu a couple of months ago. Wing, he's a good little fighter, I owed him something. The woman's his reward. He's got no family. These people are into having a family. Now Wing can get himself some kids. You ever seen these Amerasian kids? They're something to look at.

"Look, Buchannan, it won't be so bad. Wing's all right for a Lao boy, he ain't no damn Meo. I've never known him to beat up his woman; you know, maybe a little slap when the need is obvious, when anyone would, but he's a good boy. My best scout. I want to keep him happy."

Boone was sitting with his face in his hands, shaking his head slowly back and forth.

"Don't fret, Boone. Hell, I mean, who can say? She might get to like it after a little adjustment period. I've seen Wing washing in the river. He's got a whacker on him like a mule. Some of these little guys got tools so big—"

Boone exploded off the bed in a single blurring motion, crashing headfirst into Laser's midsection, knocking him back against the wall, where both men fell in a tumble of fists, elbows, and knees. Boone cocked his head back, then smashed it forward into Laser's forehead, then, while Laser was stunned, got his hands around his throat. Jamming his thumbs deep into Laser's windpipe, Boone ignored Laser's fists pounding on his back.

Something struck Boone hard in the back of the head and he blacked out. He fell on top of Laser, who was coughing and trying to push his way out from under the body.

"Get this son of a bitch off me," Laser shouted, and the two Laotian guards, one of whom had just smashed the butt of his M-16 into Boone's head, jerked Boone off and threw him onto his back. One of the guards held out a hand to help Laser up.

"Secure that bastard to the bed," Laser said, ignoring the offered hand and getting up on his own.

Michael Laser went into the hall stroking his sore neck with one hand and headed down the stairs to find Considine—or was it Nelson this time? Laser hardly cared what name the man liked. All he needed to know was that he had the authority to make deals for the CIA.

24

Hatch crouched in the high grass between the river and the lowland rice paddies that stretched out toward the mountain slopes. Behind him, the river carried boat traffic into and away from Khong Sedone; on the other side, farmers and their buffalo walked the paddy dikes.

He had traveled steadily through the morning and afternoon, being passed by three separate patrols. He had not seen the last, only recognizing it as a patrol from the noises made along the river trail. Neither of the patrols he saw comprised government soldiers, Lao or

Vietnamese. They had the look of renegades, but Hatch
had no way of finding out if they were part of the new
anti-Vietnamese Pathet Lao or, more likely, some of
Phoun Som's bandits.

Hatch figured he was less than three klicks south of
town. He could go no further without increasing the
possibility of being seen. The thick vegetation along the
river was beginning to open up into grassland and rice
fields, which offered little cover.

Hatch needed a boat. From the river split at Khong
Sedone, it had to be at least fifty kilometers to Som's
base, which Hatch only knew was somewhere in the
mountains beyond Pak Song. He studied the terrain map
again, putting his finger on an unnamed peak just east of
Pak Song where the map showed a trail intersecting the
river. Here, he thought, right here. With an engine-
powered boat he could make it before midnight. Over-
land, on foot, it would take three, maybe four days.

He folded and put away the map, swallowed another
Percodan, then picked up his shotgun and started to inch
his way back to the river. A headache throbbed behind
his eyes, blurring his vision. He could not keep moving
against the painful pounding; he had to stop, sit down,
and hold his head in his hands until the Perc took hold.

In a few minutes he was moving again, the pain a
lurking memory.

As he moved northward in the high grass along the
river, the rice paddies became a large banana plantation,
and from somewhere on the opposite bank came the
distant occasional whine of a truck. In ten minutes, six
motor-driven long-tailed boats, humming with a noise
like a thousand bees, had passed him, as well as two flat-
bottomed pole barges moving slowly near the shore. In
the relative quiet between the long-tailed boats, he
could hear the singsong murmur of voices. After the
human silence of the jungle, so much activity seemed to
agitate the air, making Hatch feel apprehensive and
flushed with adrenaline. He had to move back into the
elephant grass; huts and small houses were beginning to

appear on the opposite bank. Since he had not yet come across any signs of outskirting villages on the eastern bank, he figured the town of Khong Sedone must be on the western side, which could explain the occasional road noises too.

The afternoon heat was oppressive, as heavy on his body as if anvils were strung from his shoulders. Although he had doused himself liberally with bug juice, a thousand darting black specks moved with him. The heat and headaches drained him, dulling his instincts, his concentration. Once he forgot to stoop low when a long-tailed boat passed, realizing too late that if the boat's two occupants had been looking at the eastern bank, they would have seen him. He cut back deeper into the grass and moved ahead.

Now there were settlements on the east side of the wide gray river. At first just the huts of rice farmers and plantation workers, but soon the beginnings of a trail, then a dirt road with thatched-roof houses on stilts. There were pigs and chickens and children. In midafternoon, Hatch figured, most of the adults would be in the fields. On the opposite side of the river, smoke rising, the sound of truck engines, and the sight of a couple of floating general stores along the bank formed the southern edge of the town of Khong Sedone. Hatch moved close to the river, which now was thick with coconut palms, and watched.

He had been there less than five minutes when he heard the distinctive rumble of a large diesel engine. As the engine sound increased, Hatch noticed that the children who had been playing by the river were disappearing like roaches in the light, scurrying in all directions to hide behind boats, stilts, or trees.

Finally the boat came around the southern bend and into Hatch's vision. He easily recognized it as an old U.S Navy LCPL personnel launch, despite the palm-frond roof that had been installed over the large open rear cockpit; the white paint on the low cabin had faded off to expose the primer. The 300-horsepower Gray marine

diesel made the shore tremble below Hatch's feet. Just
before ducking out of sight, he noticed a flag, a light blue
field with a gold circle in the center, flying from the bow
staff. He had seen that flag once before, more than
twenty years earlier, flying from a curved bamboo pole at
the river pier in Toulan. The day he walked out of the
war and the civilized world.

He could tell from the way the engine sound diminished that the boat had taken the right fork of the river,
which meant it was moving east toward the mountains.
Before the sound had completely faded, Hatch moved
into the edge of the village.

With the LCPL's passing, the children returned to
their play along the riverfront. A scrawny dog, probably
a pet, since it looked too skinny for eating, appeared in
front of Hatch, sniffed him for a few seconds, then
trotted off to hunt for food or play. Hatch flattened
himself in the grass behind a palm stump and watched a
half-dozen Laotian men standing on a barge, smoking
and talking. The barge had been secured to trees along
the shore with long ropes, and around its edges were
tied a few boats. There was a small thatched-roof
bamboo shack on one side of the barge, which seemed to
be a kind of store, selling a variety of things from bottles
of beer to cigarettes to dried fish. It looked to be a
semipermanent dock for the river ferry, which Hatch
could see tied up to a similar barge on the opposite bank.
He would have to move further into the settlement,
hoping to find a solitary boat somewhere else. This was
obviously one of the places where cross-river commerce
took place.

Just as he began scooting backward to turn away from
the settlement and into the cover of the trees, Hatch
sensed danger and turned, raising his gun at the same
time.

A boy, no older than ten, stood at the edge of the tree
line and stared, fixed with fear, at Hatch and the
shotgun.

"Jesus," Hatch said under his breath, feeling his heart
beating inside his throat.

The boy did not move. He stared wide-eyed at the barrel of the shotgun, arms held against his sides as if at attention, and shook so hard that Hatch could see the quivering in his skin.

"Please," Hatch said in Lao, and held a finger to his lips. He lowered the shotgun and got slowly up to one knee, keeping his head down and out of view from the barge. "I won't hurt you," Hatch whispered in the boy's language.

The boy, with eyes as dark and wide as a fawn's, took one slow, cautious step backward, as if from a coiled snake.

Hatch looked at him, not knowing what he should do. Clearly he could not kill the child, but neither could he allow him to alert the settlement. "Please," he said again.

The boy took another step, then started to turn, but Hatch held out his hand and the boy stopped dead in mid-step. "I need a boat," Hatch said then. "I am chasing some bad men," he went on, "and I need a boat to catch them. Will you help me?"

The boy put his foot down softly but did not respond. At least, Hatch thought, he no longer seemed ready to bolt screaming. Maybe it was hearing Lao spoken by a white man. It occurred to Hatch that the boy might never have seen a white man.

He decided to gamble that Phoun Som's men had terrorized Khong Sedone and the boy would understand the concept of bad men.

"The men on the big motorboat," Hatch said softly, holding one hand out, palm up, as if offering himself as a friend to the boy, "the one that just came by here. Do you know the boat I mean?"

The boy might have nodded. His head seemed to move.

"Yes, of course you do. It carries a flag the color of the morning sky with a big circle like the sun. They are bad men, yes?"

This time the boy did nod.

"Yes. You know. I am chasing them. I want to find them. Will you help me?"

Hatch noticed a movement and tensed, pulling up the shotgun. The boy flinched and closed his eyes. Then Hatch saw the skinny dog trot up to the boy's side and stop, its long tail wagging fast. Hatch put the shotgun down and took both hands off it.

"Yours?" he said, smiling at the dog. He reached out and patted its head.

The boy gave Hatch a look that indicated he did not understand the concept of ownership regarding a dog.

"What's your name?" Hatch asked, looking back at the boy.

"Bounkeut," the boy said so softly and tentatively that Hatch barely understood.

"I once knew a boy named Bounkeut," Hatch said. "But that was a long time ago. My Bounkeut would now be a man. He lived in Toulan. Do you know where Toulan is?"

The boy shook his head.

"Far to the north of here. It is a small river village, smaller than this one. Is this where you live?"

The boy nodded.

"Is this Khong Sedone?"

The boy pointed west across the river. The dog, bored and tired, sat down at the boy's feet.

"Khong Sedone is there?"

The boy nodded again.

"Will you help me?"

The boy said nothing.

"I need a boat to follow the bad men up the river. Do you know of a boat I can use? I cannot be seen by anyone. No one can know I am here. Do you understand?"

The boy nodded. "Will you kill them with that?" He pointed at Hatch's shotgun.

"Yes." Hatch nodded. "But I need the help of a brave young man, a young man like you, who loves his family and his town. Are you such a man?"

Bounkeut nodded, a smile just breaking the line of his lips and widening his eyes.

"A boat?"

"My uncle . . ." the boy said too loudly.

Hatch put a finger to his lips. "Ssh. We must be very quiet or the bad men might find me before I find them."

The boy understood that. He shooed away the dog with a kick of his foot and gestured for Hatch to follow. They moved away from the river into the trees, the dog trotting along behind, sniffing the edges of the narrow trail for diversion.

The boy suddenly stopped; Hatch stopped and went to his knee. The dog turned to see what was wrong before sitting on his haunches to watch. The boy put a finger to his lips and squatted below the grass line.

From somewhere not far ahead came voices and the squishing sound of sandals in mud. From his low perspective, Hatch saw only their round, peaked bamboo hats, bobbing like gulls on the water. The sound faded and the boy stood, waving Hatch forward. Walking behind the boy, Hatch smiled and nodded with admiration.

They were skirting the eastern edge of the settlement, an uncultivated jungle area between the village and a large field of banana trees. The sweet smell of rotting bananas was strong and Hatch figured there was a packing plant nearby, probably where many of the villagers found their employment.

They went completely around the village perimeter before cutting back to the river. They had lost the dog a hundred yards back when something with more interesting potential pulled him off toward the banana grove. Hatch could smell the river's proximity before it came into view as a gray movement through the green foliage. The boy stopped and squatted, Hatch knelt beside him, and together they looked through the grass and bushes. The boy pointed.

There, pulled up on the bank next to a footpath, was a small flat-bottomed boat. It reminded Hatch of the pole boats used inside the reef on Tuva, and of the bayou boats Louisiana Cajuns called "pirogues." There was no motor.

"It's a good boat," Hatch whispered, "but I need a motor."

Bounkeut signaled for Hatch to follow, then moved across the narrow trail to the riverbank next to the boat. He looked down the trail toward a small house on high bamboo stilts because of its nearness to the river's flood plain.

"Uncle keeps the motor in his house," Bounkeut said softly.

"Is there no one in the house now?"

"My uncle is at the boat landing with his friends of the Central Committee; his wife is in Khong Sedone with her sister, my mother. My cousin fights with the Pathet Lao, the shame of my uncle, his father."

Hatch nodded. "Go now, Bounkeut. I will leave your uncle's boat where it can be easily found."

"Sink it, I don't care," the boy said. "My uncle is friendly with the Vietnamese. They killed my father."

Hatch touched the boy's shoulder, then took his arm and pulled it forward to shake Bounkeut's hand.

"If Laos had enough young soldiers like you, Bounkeut, it would be a free country again."

Bounkeut smiled widely, showing his missing front teeth, then backed away at Hatch's insistence, turned, and disappeared as quickly and quietly as he had first appeared.

Hatch made his way along the edge of the trail toward the house of Bounkeut's uncle.

There were chickens pecking in the dirt in the shade below the house, six pigs prowled a bamboo enclosure at the rear, and tied to a rope wrapped around a palm was a milk cow. Bounkeut's uncle was rich.

Hatch quietly climbed the stair-ladder to the deck that stretched around the house, then stopped outside the door to listen. He took the Randall from its sheath and moved inside the house. Like most Laotian lowland village houses, it was mainly one large room with a cooking vent in the center of the high, peaked roof, and a sleeping area walled by a curtain or bamboo screen in the back. There was an unframed picture of Ho Chi Minh tacked to a wall, and below it, lying on its side, what Hatch was looking for—the small outboard engine. But before leaving, he raided the clothes closet, sorting through the meager offerings for something he might be able to get on.

Hatch found the gas can and hose in a box stored below the house, then made his way back to the boat.

After securing the engine and priming some gas from the tank, he slipped off his shirt and stowed it in his pack. Then he put on a black silk shirt, which he could not button, and added a round straw hat, tying it below his chin. He pushed the boat into the current and pulled the starter cord. When the engine caught, he turned the boat upriver, bent his head forward, and sat in the bottom so all that could be seen from the bank was the hat and black shirt.

A short distance away, Bounkeut, very pleased with himself, watched from the bank.

25

"I thought you told me these people controlled this entire area," said the man who used many names.

The name on his birth certificate was Peter Joseph Connors and he had been called P.J. by his fraternity friends at the University of Virginia, where he was first recruited by the Central Intelligence Agency.

"Didn't we have control of Boone Buchannan and his woman the moment they crossed the border, Nelson?" Laser said, pronouncing the name at the end with sarcasm.

"Then where's Hatcher?"

Laser had thought of this man as a thorn in his side ever since their first meeting over a year ago at the Lotus Bar in downtown Bangkok.

"We don't have to find him, he'll come to us," Laser answered.

"I don't like having a man like that on the loose; it's an element of unpredictability, and I don't like things I can't predict."

"Guess you don't go in much for horse races," Laser said.

Nelson ignored him. He turned and looked out the near window, which showed a view of the river twisting through the dense jungle, and the distant multihued green foothills to the west. Smoke lay low in patches just over the top of the tree line, marking villages.

They were in a large room inside the main section of the former monastery's living quarters, more lavish now than when the monks had been there; the living areas were away from the open compound where the Lao guards camped, and away from the noise of the training area. The room served as a meeting place for Prince Phoun Som, his son, Kaysone, and their top advisers, of which Michael Laser, as chief training officer of the Soms' armies, was one.

It was an opulently decorated room, designed to show off the spoils from piracy and poppy fields. A massive mahogany table, polished to the sheen of metal, dominated the center of the room. There were five ornately carved chairs down each side, with velvet-covered thrones on either end—the larger for the prince, and the opposite for his son. Stretched across one wall was a five-by-six-foot banner showing the golden sun on the blue field of heaven, the emblem of the Som family. The entrance door, six-inch-thick teak, was covered with hammered gold leaf, and when the sun from the opposite window hit it, the glare was blinding. The crystal chandelier hanging over the table had once hung in the foyer of the Paris Opera House. And the sun hitting it exploded into a thousand prisms across the velvet-covered walls.

Laser called it the pimp's room.

The door was pushed open by one of the Lao guards and two of the Soms' lieutenants entered. Nelson and Laser left the small table by the window, greeting the aides who were taking their places at the conference table. Laser showed Nelson which chair he should take.

The golden door opened again and the two Soms entered with their security chief, a Japanese man of indeterminate age named Nishioki, who, it was known, was a Ninja master in his homeland, and who, in payment of a debt of honor, had become Prince Phoun Som's bodyguard for eternity.

They were all seated. A pair of Lao with automatic rifles slung across their backs served wine from a six-thousand-dollar antique Waterford pitcher. Laser, who had an eye for the value of such things, had once asked the prince its value.

Prince Phoun Som, who was seventy-four years old and looked like a fat Ho Chi Minh, pulled at his chin whiskers and inspected the eyes of those seated around the table. Threat came first through the eyes. With a wave of his hand he banished the servants and nodded to his son, seated at the opposite end of the table.

Kaysone Som, his father's last child of four, and only son, was, at the age of forty, head of a band of pirates, thieves, and murderers the size and likes of which Asia had not seen since Genghis Khan; next to his ailing father, Kaysone was the most feared and powerful man in Laos, even to the Vietnamese Army.

Kaysone flicked a glance at Laser, who stood and addressed the elder Som.

"Mr. Nelson"—Laser gestured toward the man seated to his right, who smiled and nodded a greeting—"who speaks for the government of the United States, has come before us—"

Prince Phoun Som said something softly in Lao. Kaysone translated for his father. "Let him speak for himself," Kaysone said.

Laser nodded and sat down. Perry Nelson stood and bowed in *wai* to each of the Som men.

"I am honored to stand before the magnificence of
Prince Phoun Som," Nelson began, looking at the
prince. "And his courageous son," he continued, looking
down the table toward Kaysone, who nodded an accept-
ance of the compliment and translated it for his father.

"I am authorized to speak for the leaders of the United
States," Nelson went on, pausing long enough for
Kaysone Som to make a translation. "We are happy to
find in the great Som family, men whose distrust of the
Communists and vision for the future of their beautiful
and productive land is welcomed by the American
people with open arms and hearts."

Below the table, concealed from the others, Michael
Laser pushed his right index finger in and out of a hole
made by the thumb and index finger of his left hand.

"My government has agreed," Nelson was saying, "in
principle, to your counteroffer." Nelson's tone reminded
Laser of any of dozens of political films the Army had
made him watch in basic training. A smile appeared and
disappeared across Kaysone's face before he translated
for his father. "We will provide to you at the soonest
possible delivery date, all of the arms, ammunition, including the adequate missiles for ten hand-held launch-
chers, and ground transport you requested; as well as
making available to you data received from the ComSat
IV and our other Indochinese intelligence sources."

Prince Phoun Som nodded without any other sign of
his feelings as Kaysone finished the translation.

"Once the coup is finished and the puppet government of the Lao People's Revolutionary Party is over-
thrown, you will receive full and complete diplomatic
recognition by the U.S. government, along with a
foreign-aid package significantly more elaborate, and
profitable, I might add, than I'm certain you expected."

As Nelson seated himself, he added, "I will be happy
to answer any questions you may have."

Laser stopped screwing his finger into his fist and
placed both hands palm down on the table.

"Let's talk about how you intend to handle the threat from the Vietnamese Army," Laser said.

Jan had worked at the bindings long enough to realize she would not be able to break them or slip them off. For her efforts she had received only abrasions and cuts at her wrists.

Her arms were tied behind her back and secured to a thick roof-support pole inside Wingkhet Vongsai's hut. For a long time Wingkhet had squatted a few feet in front of her and stared, sometimes telling her things in Lao, sometimes quiet. He had not touched her since she was tied up. All Jan had managed to understand was, from context, that she should call him Wing. He had shown her a poorly taken black-and-white photograph of a Laotian woman holding a baby.

He had left three hours ago and she had been alone since.

The hut was squalid, stinking of urine, rotting fruit, and the rain-dampened straw matting which composed the walls. There was just one room, smaller than the average child's bedroom in a house at home. The roof was low, with a hole in the peaked center to expel cooking smoke, although it was evident the cooking wood had not been burned for some time. Crawling things and at least one rat shared the space with Jan, although none of them had come very close to her. The late-afternoon light in the hut was hazy and dim; sometimes she heard but could not see the things moving through the rubble on the dirt floor.

An hour or two ago she had heard shooting, individual pops that sounded to her like target shooting rather than fighting. Sometimes she could hear children laughing. There was comfort in that, as if perhaps, the presence of children would have to preclude any atmosphere of violence. But the children played far away, and most of the time she could not hear them at all.

* * *

Four men came in and two held guard while two released Boone from the bunk. They did not speak. When he was free, all four left, and Boone heard the lock click behind them.

He went to the window. It was, he figured, less than an hour to sunset. They had been in the Soms' fortress for almost twenty-four hours. Did they have Hatch? Where was he? What had happened to Jan? "Oh, Christ," Boone said softly, remembering the sight of her being dragged into the camp. He walked along the perimeter of the walls like an animal awakening inside a cage, his shoulder nearly touching the damp, cool stone.

It would not be long for him. Boone knew it. The lethargy was almost debilitating. There were hallucinations. When he could manage to swallow something, it came right back up. And the pain, even with the Dilaudid and Compazine, was excruciating. Death would come as a relief.

How would it happen? What would make his heart stop? Would it become more than he could stand, even with the Dilaudid, the opium? He had been told he would not die of the cancer, per se, that the cancer would make some part of his system break down. He would most likely die as a result of shock, maybe when the stomach exploded, or some vessel in his head burst.

Or, he thought, passing the window again as he prowled the barriers of his confinement, die from the fall from this window. He stopped and looked down. It was high enough. Probably fifty or sixty feet to the ground, a ground littered with boulders, stones, and sharp trees.

If it came to that, Boone thought, he could take himself out easily. He did not do it then, as a wave of agonizing nausea dropped him to his knees, because of Jan. He had to get her out, free. Then, okay. Then, with pleasure. God, whatever your form, whatever your name, I am at the mercy of your power, give me the strength to do this one last thing, Boone prayed. Then he was retching acid.

* * *

Wing came into the hut shortly after sunset. He crossed the small room and checked Jan's bindings, then took a match and lit a kerosene lamp hanging on a peg from the center main roof brace. The light was dim and yellow. Shadows danced on the woven walls.

Wing squatted across the room and did things Jan could not see. But after a few minutes he came back to her carrying a bowl with what smelled like smoked, dried fish, and an old army canteen of water.

"Eat, drink," Wing said in English.

"Let me go," Jan answered, shaking her head back and forth.

"Eat, drink," Wing repeated insistently.

Jan craved both food and drink, but she was afraid to appear cooperative. She shook her head, and again more violently when he picked up a piece of the fish and tried to put it into her mouth.

"Untie me," she said, twisting sideways as far as she could and looking back over her shoulder at the bindings.

"No run?" Wing said with the inflection of a question.

"I won't run," Jan said, shaking her head for confirmation. You really expect me to tell you the truth? she thought.

"Run, die," Wing said, bending behind her to release the hemp line around her wrists.

"Eat now," Wing said, moving back and squatting in front of her. "Fish," he said, holding out a piece to her. Jan ignored the piece in his hand and took one from the bowl, putting it into her mouth. It was pretty good, which surprised her.

"Drink," Wing said, sloshing the water in the canteen.

Jan took the canteen and drank a quarter of it in one long gulp. Only after she took the canteen away from her lips and noticed the earthy taste of the water did it occur to her that she would probably be incapacitated with dysentery by morning.

Wing left the bowl and the canteen within her reach,

and scooted back to squat on his haunches and watch her. It seemed to fascinate him that she ate and drank like other people. Jan ignored him as best she could and finished the fish and the rest of the water.

Putting the bowl and the canteen to one side, Jan looked at Wing and said, "Do you speak English?"

"Speak little English," he said, smiling because she was talking to him.

"Why am I here? I mean, what are you going to do with me?"

Wing shook his head. He did not speak that much English. His "little English" consisted of "yes," "no," some food terms, "water," and some military and weaponry terms.

"You don't understand?" Jan said, shaking her head and asking with her eyes.

Wing shook his head.

Jan pointed to herself and said slowly, "Me." She jabbed herself a few times in the chest. "Okay?"

"Me, okay," Wing repeated, smiling widely.

"Me go?" Jan said, making a walking motion with two of her fingers.

"Go?" Wing said, then shook his head and said, "No."

Wing scooted closer to her, got onto his knees in front of her. Jan pushed herself back against the wall.

"Beebee," Wing said, cradling and rocking his arms back and forth.

"Baby?" Jan said.

Wing nodded and kept rocking his cradled arms.

Shit, Jan thought, he wants to make a goddamn baby! The woman and the baby in the picture, they must have been his, they must have died or something. Jan shook her head quickly back and forth and said, "No, no baby with me," pointing at herself.

Suddenly Wing produced a Colt .45 automatic from the waistband at his back, the pistol looking gigantic in his small hand. He put the barrel of the pistol against the side of Jan's head, and as she tried to pull away, he held her with his other hand.

"Beebee, yes, you," Wing said.

Jan crossed her arms over her chest and held herself
tightly. She closed her eyes and tears dripped down her
cheek. She could feel the barrel touching her hair just
above her ear, and she could feel Wing's hand working its
way inside the barrier of her crossed arms.

26

The camp outside the walls of the Soms' fortress came
to life early. At dawn the jungle birds began their calls,
and minutes later the roosters, pigs, and dogs started up.
The banshee cry of a peacock announced the rise of the
sun over the jungle canopy.

The peacock's wail jerked Jan out of a deep sleep. She
sat suddenly upright and realized where she was, that
she had not dreamed it at all. She found herself naked
beneath the thin silk covering he must have put over her
during the night. But he, Wing, was not in the hut.
Sunlight coming through the open door stretched across
the dirt floor and up a wall; dust particles and tiny gnats
hovered in the light like black ice crystals caught in
moonlight.

Clutching the cloth to her body, Jan got up and
searched for her clothes, but they were not in the hut.
She had to run. Anywhere. She could go down the river
until she found a town. What about Boone? Could she
leave not knowing? She had to get away from Wing.

She began making a sarong of the silk cloth. It was
wide enough to wrap around her twice, and cover her
from just above her breasts down to her knees. She had
her back to the door, tucking a corner of the cloth into
her cleavage, when she heard him and turned.

Backlighted by the bright morning sun, he was a
shadow in the doorway; before him dust swirled in the
twin streams of light leaking around his body. She could
tell that he held a bundle in his arms.

Jan backed up until the wall stopped her. She shook her head back and forth, whispering the word "no."

Wing came into the hut and put the bundle on a low table near the middle of the room. He picked up a bamboo coolie hat and held it out to her.

"Work," he said.

He dropped the hat and held out a black silk shirt and pants.

"On," he said. "Woman work."

"Work" was not a new word for Wing, but he had just learned "woman." One of the Americans had taught him when he was getting clothes for her.

He dropped the shirt and pants, then picked up a pair of open-toed sandals with soles cut from car tires. He held them at arm's length toward Jan and jiggled them.

"Woman, on, work," he said, trying to explain that she was to put on the clothes and go to work.

Jan shook her head and repeated "no."

Wing threw the shoes down, reached out and grabbed the edge of the sarong, and ripped it away from her.

Jan turned her face away, trembling with fear, and tried to cover herself.

Wing threw the black shirt at her, repeating, "On. Woman. Work. Yes."

Jan nodded, picked up the blouse, and put it on. Wing held the pants out to her. Jan dressed quickly, put on the shoes and hat, then sat down on the low table for Wing to secure her ankles in leg chains.

With a rope tied loosely around her neck, Wing led Jan out of the hut. She shuffled her feet against the strain of the leg chains, leaving an odd track through the mud.

Once her eyes adjusted to the bright sunlight, she could see the scope of the encampment and the massive fortress rising out of the jungle rock above. Except for the thick, enclosing jungle, she was reminded of old prints of feudal villages: a walled castle surrounded by village huts and fields. Cooking smoke rose from some of the huts. There were a few children, but they were quiet, as if they had been taught to be respectful of the early hour. A dog trotted by. Chickens pecked in the mud around some of the huts. Steam seemed to rise from the dew-dampened vegetation. There was an overwhelming smell of life going to rot.

Wing pulled Jan along the trail for fifty yards until they reached a clearing. She remembered seeing it from the window the night before last and wondering what it was; a patch of green lighter in hue than the surrounding jungle, it had looked to be a crop.

Now Jan could see that it was a large vegetable garden. A dozen women with hoes and bamboo rakes worked on weeds. They were all dressed in the same black pajamas and coolie hats. Some of the women worked on their knees.

Wing called out something in Lao and one of the women got up and came quickly over to them. He said something else and the woman nodded, running to a nearby hut. Wing and Jan stood waiting until the woman returned carrying a large wooden bowl and a cup. There was fruit in the bowl, water in the cup. The woman held the bowl out to Jan and Wing gestured for her to eat.

There was mostly mango in the bowl, some guava maybe. Jan ate and drank, oblivious now of the dysentery she courted. She was too hungry and too dejected to care.

When she had finished, the woman took the bowl back to the hut, then returned. Wing spoke to her again, then handed over the neck rope. Then he walked a few yards away and squatted. The woman pulled Jan toward the field, made her kneel to her knees in the dirt, and began showing her how to pull weeds. No words passed between them.

Hatch knew it was Jan even before he got a closer look at her face. The woman in leg chains being led like a cow by a rope was a head taller than her guard, and much taller and sturdier than a Lao woman, not to mention the bits of blond hair hanging below the round, peaked hat.

Hatch had been working his way toward the camp for

three hours, after coming upriver to a point a few
hundred yards from the landing. He had sensed the
presence of the settlement for half an hour before
deciding to pull the boat to the shore and go inland. He
had not walked ten minutes when he began hearing the
gongs, bells, and drums. Then he left the riverbank trail
and cut up into the bush. He knew there would have to
be guards everywhere, but he had darkness and surprise
to his advantage. Once he was almost detected when
four men, drunk and ringing bells, wobbled along the
river trail singing a recognizable Laotian military chant.
They stopped ten feet from him and one of them pissed.

An hour back, he had come inside the perimeter.
There had been no mistaking the invisible barrier
guarding the camp. Staked on bamboo poles approximately twenty feet apart were decapitated heads in
various stages of deterioration; one seemed to be days
fresh, and another almost a skull with maggots hatching
in the eye sockets. Hatch felt fear crawling up his spine,
squeezing his lungs as he passed them.

From that point, he had crawled on hands and knees,
feeling for trip wires, watching overhead for booby traps.
It took him an hour to move two hundred yards.

He catnapped for two hours, jerked awake with the
same morning noises that roused Jan. He had been
working his way around the river-side edge of the camp
when he came across the women coming to work in the
garden. He could see the fortress rising from the jungle,
and was reconnoitering a safe passage to get closer when
Jan and the Lao man appeared. Hatch turned away for a
moment, then looked back. The catch in his throat
confirmed what his eyes would not accept.

But how could it be possible? How could Jan have
gotten here? She could never have gotten this far on her
own, which meant Boone must have brought her. Boone
was hardly *that* stupid. And he wouldn't have done it for
money. Hatch suddenly realized his mission of ven-
geance had become a mission of rescue. And that
changed everything, like having the rules change when
you thought you were one point from winning.

Hatch lay on the jungle floor and waited for something to happen, something he could work with, something to give him direction. Confusion distracted him, made his thoughts syrupy and muddled. There was very little he could do with a shotgun and a Ka-bar—at least not until he knew if or where Boone was being held.

There was a loud commotion, someone yelling from the trail leading back to the fortress, and everyone, including Hatch, turned toward it.

Hatch watched as a large black man dressed in tiger-stripe camos with the sleeves and pants legs cut off and a Detroit Tigers baseball cap came roaring down the trail, waving an automatic pistol in front of him. Who in the hell was this? An American?

Jan looked up, drawn by the shouts coming from behind her. When she turned around, she saw the man who had introduced himself as a war lover crashing down the trail, yelling and waving a pistol. He was not yelling in English, Jan noticed.

In Laotian, the war lover was yelling at Wing: "What the hell do you think you're doing with her, you little dog turd! You don't work an American woman in your fields. Get those chains off her right now or I'll have your shit-eating little face stuck on a spook pole in front of my hooch."

Wing jumped to his feet and yelled back: "Mr. Laser gave this woman to me; he said she's mine for whatever I wish; you don't like it, go talk to Mr. Laser."

"Gave? You say *gave*? Not on my piece of this block you don't be giving and taking people."

Jan could not believe what she saw then, a moment frozen before her eyes. The war lover walked right up to Wing, put the barrel of the huge pistol against the Lao man's forehead, said in English, "Fuck you," and blew off most of his head; Wing dropped straight down and folded up like a puppet whose strings were let go.

Jan was shocked into rigidity, although her hand flew up to cover her mouth to stop the scream trapped in her throat.

The war lover turned toward the women in the vegetable garden and put the pistol in a holster at his waist. The Lao women backed away from him, making themselves as small and unobtrusive as the cornstalks. Jan stared at him wide-eyed, hand over her mouth, and watched him approach.

"I'm sorry y'all had to see that, ma'am. I didn't know what Laser done . . . about last night, and all." He bent down and inspected her leg chains, then walked casually over to get the key off Wing's body. Jan looked away, but turned back to watch him unlock her chains, unable to take her hand away from her mouth. "I put up with a lot from these popcorn farts, and I let 'em go on in their way with their women, but this is something else again. I'm really sorry, ma'am." He pulled the rope off her neck, then stood back and offered his hand to help her up.

Jan uncovered her mouth and accepted his hand. "Thank you," she said, though not sure for what.

"My pleasure," the war lover said, and smiled. His teeth were bad. "Y'all like a smoke, or something?" He reached in his pocket to retrieve a cigarette pack.

"I don't smoke, but thank you," Jan said.

"I guess you'd like to get some decent clothes," he said.

Jan nodded. Then she noticed movement and looked beyond the war lover, who turned to follow her gaze.

Michael Laser, Perry Nelson, and two Lao guards were coming down the trail from the fortress.

"What have we here?" Laser asked when he saw Wing's body folded over in the mud. Laser's face expressed more curiosity than horror.

"I wancha ta know, Mike, I don't take to havin' a round-eyed woman treated thisaway. You know that about me."

"Did you have to blow his fucking head off, Harry?" Laser asked, bending over to inspect the wound as if Wing were a dog hit by a car.

The two Lao guards looked distinctly unhappy. One fingered his M-16 nervously.

"Y'all tell that boy to ease back some lest I shoot off his left nut." Harry, the war lover, put his hand on his forty-five.

"Everybody take it easy," Laser said, signaling to the nervous Lao guard. Then Laser noticed Jan staring incredulously at Perry Nelson.

"You two know each other?" Laser asked.

"Tom Considine," Jan said, although her voice was colored by a lack of faith in her eyes.

Nelson's mouth fell open a little as he stared hard, trying to recognize the woman dressed like a native worker. Then Jan tipped back the coolie hat.

"Well, I'll be damned," Nelson said. "I knew Boone came over the border with a woman, but I just assumed it was that Bangkok whore he lived with.

"Yes," Nelson turned and said to Laser, "Mrs. Moss and I have had the pleasure. I knew her husband."

"Well, I'm sure you and the lady have plenty to catch up on," Laser told Nelson. "Maybe you wouldn't mind escorting her back to the fortress while I try to get things calmed down out here?"

"Certainly," Nelson said, stepping forward and offering Jan his arm. "Not a very becoming ensemble," he told her.

"You touch me," Jan said, "and I'll . . ."

"Yes?" Nelson probed.

"Shoot off your left nut." Jan spit the words.

"Here, ma'am," the war lover said, holding out his pistol to her. "Be my guest."

"Put that thing away," Laser commanded.

"Don't push me, Mike!"

The war lover was on the thin edge, and Laser, wisely, changed the subject.

"Jan, I think you'd like a chance to clean up and change clothes." Laser turned his attention to her. "Please accept my apologies for your treatment. If I had known Wing intended to work you . . . well, enough of that. Please, you'll be better off back at the fortress."

"I don't intend to touch you, Mrs. Moss," Nelson said, gesturing for her to walk alongside him back up the trail.

Jan looked at the war lover and he said, "Y'all might as well, since you cain't exactly stay out here with these people."

"Thank you," she told him.

"My pleasure, ma'am. You're the first home woman I've seen for real in some years."

Jan nodded, then started up the trail, staying a pace ahead of Perry Nelson.

"I think we'd better have us a talk," Laser said to the war lover, putting his arm around his shoulder and guiding him in the opposite direction.

Hatch felt like a man who had just spent a year building a house, only to see it fall into a rubble of sticks and stones before his eyes. Nothing made sense. Who was the black man? A man with style, Hatch recognized, a way of shooting, the catlike walk of a leftover Green Beret. What was he doing with Laser? Hatch could not hear everything they were saying, but he recognized the other American with Laser as the same man who had visited him in the cell in Phuket City. If Nelson was in the CIA, what was *he* doing with Laser, a man every intelligence agency in the U.S. was hunting down with a kill order?

As the morning grew later, movement increased in the area. Four other Lao men carrying automatic rifles joined the two waiting by the vegetable garden. Hatch could hear human noises in the surrounding jungle. From inside the fortress he could hear faint but distinctive physical-training cadences. He was in a position close to exposure, so he pushed himself back deeper into the bush and then made for the river.

Everything had changed. Before, all he wanted to do was find the fortress and get to Laser and the Soms. Laser was for Jan, the Soms were for Hatch, a too-long-overdue debt that in paying might mend the deepest rip in his soul.

But that was before he saw Jan and realized Boone was probably also here. It was no longer three clean assassinations and gone. Now he had to start from square one.

27

Jan had a hundred questions for Tom Considine or Perry Nelson or whoever the hell he was, but she was unable to ask them, as if to speak to him would be in some way a recognition of his existence. He talked to her as they headed up the rocky slope to the monastery gate, but Jan kept her lips set and her eyes on the unsettled trail.

Nelson talked about his surprise over seeing her in Laos and, more generally, about life's ironies. He talked about the CIA as if Jan were still, through her husband, a part of the Agency. He talked about expediency as a value, the ultimate danger of world Communism, and the lack of backbone in the current crop of American politicians.

Finally Jan had to ask him. "Tell me that you've turned, that the Company doesn't know you're here doing business with these bandits. I need to hear that."

"To the contrary."

"Why? Why would our government have anything to do with these people? They're just drug smugglers, dope dealers—they're killers."

"Ah, yes, but they're *pro-west* smugglers and killers; they're anti-Communist. It's a vital distinction from our point of view."

"But, whatever your name is—"

"'Perry Nelson' is good enough."

"I don't care, really. But don't you see? They're only anti-Communist because they're pro-profit. If you're giving them money, they'll spew out whatever kind of tripe you want to hear."

"Of course, Jan. But they are also in a position to do

something for us that no one else can do as efficiently. We want this area back. We give them a few guns, a little money, and they give us a stronger foothold in Southeast Asia."

"For the first time in my life, you've made me ashamed of my nationality. God, we can't even vote you people out! You live in the baseboards of the government like rats."

Nelson laughed.

It occurred to Jan then, just as they reached the gate, that Nelson could speak with her directly—so unusual for the men in his profession—for only one possible reason.

She stopped and turned toward him, her eyes a mirror of recognition, of understanding, and said, "You're going to kill me."

Then, before Nelson could answer, she pushed her realization to the last logical step. "*You* killed Jason." She thought she would faint. It was like Hatch had told her: Jason was not killed by Michael Laser, but by agents from his own government, his Company. "Why?" she whispered, unsure of her voice.

"You really gave us a surprise when you blamed it on Laser," Nelson said. "It was supposed to have been a robbery. We made the mistake of using one of our lesser-known proprietaries. But of course you don't think it was me personally?"

Her hand seemed to come from nowhere, bashing into Nelson's face next to his left eye. Jan struck him with all her might. He saw her drawing back to hit him again, but he caught her arm at the wrist, twisting it backward until she collapsed to her knees, her arm bent back behind her neck.

"Nice right," he said.

"So do it," Jan muttered, grimacing with pain. "Just do it."

"That's not my style, Jan. Why do you think we employ people like Kaysone Som, Laser, their ilk?"

Nelson banged the door hard with the flat of his fist

and when it opened he pulled Jan to her feet and pushed her inside.

"Why?" Jan asked in a feeble voice as they crossed the compound under the watchful eyes of the Lao guards.

"Why what?"

"Why did you kill Jason?"

"Because he had found out that we knew where Michael Laser was and that we had some oversize secret arms shipments redirected. It was only a matter of time before he started adding one and one—that if Laser was in Laos and we were doing nothing about it . . . It wouldn't take a genius to see the implications. Your husband might have taken some time to see the big picture, but he had a very logical, deductive mind."

There was, Hatch learned, no way into the fortress except by invitation or suicide. It would take a bombing raid to damage it, and then only with direct hits. It held the high ground, with the jungle and the river serving effectively as a moat. The settlement of huts surrounded the perimeter so tightly that a team small enough to reach the fortress wall undetected would also be too small to breach the barrier. No wonder the drug lords had been able to operate with impunity.

It had taken him two hours to make those discoveries. Now he had a good idea of how the camp was laid out. There were altogether six large vegetable gardens, as well as some dairy cattle, goats, pigs, and chickens. There were bamboo fish traps in the river. The compound was probably self-sustaining. Hatch estimated that four or five hundred Lao men and women lived in the huts outside the fortress. There were some children, and even a handful of shamans with their gongs and drums and saffron robes.

There were signs of a training area—combat shooting range, physical-training obstacle course, and evidence of some kind of classroom instruction. Further upriver from the landing pier with the skull decorations, Hatch had seen a fully equipped dock facility, at which there were more than twenty LCPL's, half a dozen STAB-variety Boston Whalers, and four Trumpy- or maybe Osprey-class steel PTF's, as well as a fueling system, fuel tanks, and about fifty armed guards. The PTF's had too much draft to navigate that section of the river except during monsoon-season flooding, so Hatch figured those four were trapped there for at least another month. Finally, scattered among the appropriated military craft were uncountable small native boats similar to the one belonging to Bounkeut's uncle.

But Hatch knew nothing of the interior of the fortress. Three towers extended from a mass of buildings in the center, and the entire stone-and-mortar surface was covered by moss and a lattice of vines. Although Hatch had seen other ancient monasteries, he had never been inside one and could only guess at the layout.

There were guards along the walls with automatic rifles, a few with M-79 grenade launchers. And on the roof line were four sophisticated antennae, as well as a radar receiver. A guard on the wall above the main gate stood next to a hand-held SAM launcher, although Hatch thought it was some kind of bazooka.

As Hatch lay in the bush watching the entrance, the big double doors opened and a white man came out. He was, Hatch could tell immediately, another American. Who the hell are all these Americans? Laser, the black who shot the Lao, and now this one.

The one Hatch watched now came out the gate and started down the path toward the river. He was dressed in woodland-pattern camo fatigue pants with a brown T-shirt, a ranger bush hat, and flip-flops, with a .45 automatic in a shoulder holster, a Ka-bar in a Navy sheath taped upside down to one of the holster straps. He wore dark green aviator-style sunglasses and had a cigar stuck in his mouth.

Hatch, watching the man heading down the trail to the river pier, cut back through the thick undergrowth in the same direction, hoping the man would stay alone long enough for him to set up an ambush point.

The man kept to the rocks, avoiding the mud. He seemed to be daydreaming, as if he had no destination or purpose other than the walk itself. Hatch stayed ten yards ahead and off to one side of the trail, glancing back frequently to make sure the man was still coming.

Soon Hatch would be at the river. There were three Lao guards stationed at the pier there, and Hatch realized he would have to stop the man before he got that far. He eased over closer to the trail and disguised himself in the thick wet ferns growing wild throughout the stand of bamboo trees. He put the shotgun down carefully and withdrew his Randall. But after a second thought he put the knife back and reached out to the edge of the trail for a large stone; he would need the man's clothes without blood all over them.

The man must have heard Hatch an instant before the rock bashed into his skull, for he had started to duck and turn his head, causing the rock to strike him over his right ear. He dropped straight down, landing in a heap at Hatch's feet. Hatch pulled him quickly off the trail and into the bush, keeping his bloody head away from the shirt. When Hatch checked, the carotid artery in the man's neck was still.

"Shit," Hatch muttered.

He undressed the body and pulled it deeper into the underbrush; then, after hiding his own clothes, he put on the dead man's. He checked the clip in the automatic and the blade on the Ka-bar, then went out to the trail. It took a few seconds to find the cigar. He brushed off the tip, flinched, then stuck it into his mouth as he turned back toward the fortress.

When he heard the lock turn, Boone rose from the bed and stiffened himself to hide the pain. A pair of Lao guards came in and one of them said, "Come," in English, gesturing with the barrel of his M-16.

They took him out and down a long passageway enclosed by damp stones. Like going into a dungeon,

Boone thought. One guard led, the other followed at a distance just out of reach of an arm swing.

The hall ended at a tight circular stone stairway leading downward. They made Boone stop until the front guard started down, then they shoved Boone forward.

They went down three levels. Boone figured they must be at the bottom, at the open compound behind the wall where he and Jan had entered the night before last. Ahead, he could see sunlight streaming up the stairs. Around the next turn they came to the open doorway and took Boone into the compound.

The stairs had been hard for Boone, drawing deeply from what little remained of his energy reserves. He thought he would faint, that his legs would collapse beneath him, or that he might puke. If they were taking him out to shoot him, he was reconciled to it. Let's just get it over with, he thought.

Boone remembered a lot of the scene before him from when they brought him through earlier, even though it was dark then and midday now. The outer-perimeter walls of the monastery rose twenty feet high and were almost entirely covered by dark vegetation. Within the walls were scattered at least a dozen hooches, similar to the ones outside in the surrounding settlement, although nicer and with tin roofs. There were rifles in stack-arms cones. There was a large wooden frame building separate from everything else, and Boone took it for the ammunition-storage building; there were no fires within forty yards of it.

Most of the people Boone saw in the compound were Lao men; no women, no children. Some of the men wore only loincloths, while others were decked out in a variety of fatigues and BDU's. There were cowboy hats, baseball caps, boonie hats, and one five-foot-tall Lao wearing a white U.S. Navy enlisted man's cap with the sides rolled down.

Some of the men cleaned weapons, some napped, and some played card games. As his escort moved Boone around the edge of the compound, he began to notice that some of the men mixed in with the Laotians were bigger; and as they got closer, it became apparent they were Caucasians, maybe Americans. It was toward one of them that Boone was being taken.

The bearded man wore a tattered, faded green beret, a black sleeveless T-shirt, khaki shorts, and jungle combat boots. Definitely American, Boone thought; he was flipping a Ka-bar knife into the dirt next to his right foot, as if to see how close he could get without sticking it through the boot and his toes. He looked over at Boone as they approached, breaking into a smile and leaving the knife stuck in the dirt as he turned toward them.

"Boone fucking Buchannan!" he said, waving the guards away and planting himself before Boone, hands on his hips. "I heard it was you. . . . I'll fuck a mouse in the ear if I believe what I'm seeing."

The guards moved away and left. Boone stared unknowingly at the man greeting him.

"You old buffalo, how'd you get so skinny?" the man asked, then noticed that Boone had not recognized him. "Take away the beard, what do you see?" The man cupped his hand over his beard.

Boone still could not make a connection. "I give up," he said.

"Jerry Waters ring any of your chimes?" The man calling himself Jerry Waters threw his arms open wide.

"Sergeant Waters?" Boone could see it now, mainly in the eyes and the smile, the body shape, but seeing was hardly believing. "But you—"

"Dead? Right?" Waters gave out a loud, insane-sounding laugh, then grabbed Boone's arm and pulled him over to a wicker chair in front of the hooch. "Sit down, Boone. Shit. Man, of all the people I never expected to meet on this earth again, you're right up there."

"Same here," Boone said, still staring at Waters as if he was coming out of a dream, or maybe a twenty-year-old nightmare.

"I been lots of things, Captain, but dead ain't one of
'em. I been *missing*, ha! I been a POW—two years in a
work camp up-country near Lak Sao. It was the prince
got me out; me and Wesley, who's over there, and Harry,
he's not here right now."

Boone wondered if this was something coming out of
the pain, a crazy vision he was somehow able to animate.
Sergeant Jerry Waters, once a member of Boone Buchannan's recon team, had not returned from a patrol
that had been hit hard by a company-size group of Pathet
Lao. He had been listed MIA, presumed KIA, since
1965.

"All the Americans I've seen around here," Boone
wondered, "they're all . . . ?"

"MIA's? Nah, not all, Captain. But most, yeah. Most,
probably. A few of these guys"—Waters gestured inclu-
sively around the open compound—"are recent. Cowboys, you know? Guys who got bored sitting behind a
desk somewhere, who missed the shoot-'em-up, what-
not. A couple of bad asses came in with Laser two years
ago, when this screwy arms deal got going. The rest,
yeah, the rest of us just never left, if you get my drift."

"War lovers," Boone said, remembering the American
who introduced himself that way.

"Yeah, you could say that. Like old Harry, that's what
he calls himself. Harry was in the Fifth, Captain, but
long after our time. I think he first got in-country around
sixty-seven or sixty-eight. All the fun had gone out of it
by then, though, you know?"

"Why?" Boone asked, catching Waters' eyes.

"Why? Why what?"

"Why didn't you go home? Aren't you free to go?"

"Home? Shit, Captain. Where's home? This is my
home." Waters took off his beret and twirled it around
his finger before plopping it back onto his head. "This is
my father," he said, slapping the Colt .45 automatic in
the holster at his waist. "This is my country"—he
indicated his heart by slapping his chest. "The pay's good
too, although that ain't it by a long shot."

"Tell me something, Sergeant."

"Sure, Captain, if I can."

"Are there any MIA's being held in this country? In prison, or work camps, I mean."

Waters looked away, as if he would not be able to stand Boone's eyes, and spit hard into the dirt. After a few seconds he nodded, "Yeah. Yeah. Shit. I don't know how many, but a lot. Some over there too." He cocked his head to the east. "In the fucking Nam. We see 'em sometimes when we're moving product out." Waters shifted his gaze back to Boone.

"Don't give me that look, Captain. Where were you? Huh? Where you been? Me, I was there! I slept in a cage I couldn't stretch out in. I ate fucking maggots. I did things. They made me do things . . .

"Them that are left, well, most are pretty old and sick, and hell, to tell you the truth, I think almost all of them are crazy. Why do you think your old Uncle Sam abandoned us over here? Huh? How you think Uncle Sam's henchmen going to explain leaving all those guys over here, knowing they were here all the time, if now all they can get back are a rag-taggle bunch of fucking lunatics, half of whom can't even remember how to speak decent English? You answer that. I tell you, I don't think the U.S. government would take these guys back now even if the Laotians admitted they were here; they'd just deny it, say it was some Communist propaganda ploy."

Waters started laughing again, slapping his knee and rolling his head back to laugh at the sky, which was clouding over forebodingly.

Boone looked away. A searing pain cut through his stomach and chest. He bent forward and closed his eyes. When he raised up and looked, the sight was as unbelievable as the story Waters told. There, not twenty yards away, sauntering across the compound, wearing a ranger bush hat with a cigar stub in his mouth, was a man who looked just like Frank Hatcher.

28

Hatch moved across the compound as if he owned it. His insides boiled with fear, although evidenced only by the sweat stain spreading down the center of his back.

He had no plan. He had hoped that once he was successfully inside, something would come to him. Nothing had.

The guards were half-asleep in the rising heat. No one paid any attention to Hatch crossing the yard. He looked for an entrance into the fortress itself, and found three distinct possibilities.

He swept the compound with his eyes, taking in the placement of the guards, access to weapons, escape routes, probable holding cells, and then his eyes stopped on the building that must contain ammunition and explosives. He filed it in his memory and continued his scan of the compound.

When he turned his head to spit a wad of cigar juice into the dirt, something at the periphery of his vision demanded attention. He continued forward until he reached the wall, then turned and leaned back against the rocks, putting a match up to relight the cigar stub. Through the curling gray smoke he looked to the side again.

It was Boone, all right, sitting on a stool across from one of the American mercenaries. Hatch could not tell if Boone had seen him.

Hatch surveyed the compound before making his move. There were only eighteen to twenty men in sight, although evidence indicated a hundred could live there. Hatch figured the rest were on patrols, making a run, or in the training areas. There were a half-dozen children and three women. The women were cooking, the children occupied themselves with a soccer ball. It would be almost impossible, Hatch realized, to take out the compound guards without killing them. Prince Phoun Som was not stupid, Hatch thought, letting the women and children live among the guards.

Hatch worked his way along the wall to the rear of the hooch, where Boone sat with the American. He went down to his knees and crawled around the far side below the roof line, keeping out of view of the guard towers. If he could surprise the American, there would be no sound; it all depended on how Boone reacted when he saw Hatch come around the back wall.

Hatch took out the double-edged Randall and on his hands and knees moved closer to the front corner of the hooch. He could hear the American clearly then. He was in the middle of what sounded like a war story, punctuated at regular intervals by the phrase "I shit thee not."

Just as Hatch started to move into the open, something touched his left hand, the hand holding the Randall, and he froze. The tarantula went slowly up and over Hatch's hand, probed through the straw directly below Hatch's face, then crawled over the right hand before disappearing behind a water barrel. A large droplet of sweat fell off the tip of Hatch's nose and splashed on the straw.

He took a deep breath and exhaled slowly, quietly. Then another, which he held, and went into the opening.

Boone disguised his surprise quickly by looking down, and a second later Hatch's right hand closed over Waters' mouth, jerking his head back to expose his throat to the Randall's razor-sharp blade. When the throat opened, blood fountained out over Boone's head. Together Hatch and Boone pulled Waters into the hooch.

"Ssh." Hatch put a finger to his lips, then put Waters' body against the back wall, covering it with a sleeping curtain.

Boone bent over the water bucket and cleaned the blood off his face. "What took you so long?" he whispered when Hatch came near.

"What the hell are you doing here? How could you let her talk you into this?" Hatch whispered back.

"They knew you were coming," Boone said, but a wave of nausea stopped him. He turned away and went to his knees, doubled over with dry heaves. The pain was indescribable, and he had just thrown up the Dilaudid. He fell to his side and pulled his knees against his chest, as if he could contain the pain in a smaller space.

Hatch dropped to his knees next to Boone and held his shoulders. "What is it, man?" he whispered. "Tell me what to do, what can I do?"

Boone just shook his head, squeezing his eyes closed.

"There's got to be something I can do for you, man, just tell me what it is."

"Nothing," Boone said in an expulsion of breath.

"I've got some Percs in my pack, hidden out by the main trail," Hatch said.

Boone shook his head. "I've got Dilaudid in here"—he patted his shirt pocket. "Can't keep 'em down."

"How bad is it?" Hatch asked.

Boone just gave him a look.

"Yeah, never mind," Hatch said. He knew Boone was dying, maybe enough life left to count in hours, or at best, days. "Where are they keeping Jan?"

"I don't know exactly. Somewhere inside, probably high, on the second or third level. That's where they had me. You can forget trying to waltz in there. She'll be dead before you see her, and so will you. The hallways are a maze and it's guarded better than Alcatraz."

Hatch nodded.

"He used to be sergeant with my team," Boone whispered, looking at the body covered by the curtain. "Jerry Waters. I thought he was KIA."

"Later." Hatch cut him off and began looking around the hooch. "Here," he said, tossing Boone a camo shirt, then a bush hat and a blue bandanna.

Boone began changing clothes.

"What else can you tell me?" Hatch asked while Boone dressed.

"You must know more about the outside—it was dark when they brought us in. You've seen as much of the compound as I have."

"Inside?"

"Just the room they kept me in, a couple of narrow hallways, and a long spiral stairway. But it's full of Lao with submachine guns, grenades, M-16's, and no sense of humor."

"Okay," Hatch said, helping Boone to his feet. "Can you make it?"

"Yeah, but listen, Hatch, if I can't, drop me, leave me back, shoot me if you have to. I won't be opening any Christmas presents this year anyhow."

Hatch nodded, unable to look into Boone's eyes when he did. "We walk straight out, straight across the middle to the main gate, then down the trail. Just stay with me, and when I cut right, you cut right."

"Like glue, my friend."

Hatch picked up a pair of aviator sunglasses from the table near the door and slipped them on as he went outside. Boone picked up the M-16 leaning against the wall and cradled it in his arm. They nodded to each other and began strolling into the open.

Hatch kept the pace slow, almost a saunter, partly so Boone would have it easier. A woman looked up for an instant, but went back to her work. Hatch kept his head turned so no one could get a full-face-on look at him. They were ten yards from the gate when the soccer ball hit Boone's right hip.

Boone turned and positioned the M-16 at the same time. He was a blink from squeezing off a short burst when he saw that his target was a half-naked little boy whose eyes were staring back as big as a pair of peach pits. Hatch kicked the soccer ball back to the boy and put his hand on Boone's shoulder, able to feel the nerves jumping beneath the skin.

"Jesus," Boone exhaled, lowering the weapon.

Hatch tapped him on the shoulder and they continued toward the gate.

The gate guards were smoking and talking, their backs to the two Americans heading out. They did not turn around. Once outside, Hatch and Boone turned down the trail and picked up their pace. They marched straight through the settlement toward the river until, a hundred yards from the fortress wall, where the trail curved out of sight from the watch towers, Hatch suddenly cut right into the bush and Boone followed.

Jan had seen everything, from the incident with the soccer ball to where the two men disappeared from the trail.

From the window in the tower room where they had put her, she could, by looking tight to one side, see half the compound, and straight out, her view overlooked the trail to the river and the foothills to the west. She had only by chance seen the boy accidentally hit Boone with the soccer ball, although from that height and distance she could not be certain the two men were Boone and Hatch. The one man walked slowly, bent, as if sore, and was very thin. The other man walked exactly like Hatch, determined, but gracefully athletic. If it was him . . . Jan held her breath with hope. She had not seen his face, except in profile, and he wore sunglasses and a hat, but if Boone was the other man—and she felt sure it was—who else could be walking him out, letting him have a gun? No, it had to be Hatch. He had found them.

Jan turned away from the window after the two men were out of her sight, and smiling to herself, sat on the edge of the bed. She had to help them. Somehow she had to get to them or let them know where she was. If only she could find a way out of the tower room and down to the more accessible areas below.

In another room in another tower, where three men were holding a meeting, no one was looking out the window.

Kaysone Som, Perry Nelson, and Michael Laser sat

around a small table on which was a bottle of Perrier, a bucket of ice, three glasses, and a liter of Jack Daniel's. A quarter of the Black Jack was gone.

Nelson took a piece of paper from one of the pockets on his khaki safari jacket and unfolded it on the table in front of him. Reading from the list, he said, "One hundred cases, new in the grease, AR-15's, with ten thousand rounds of 5.56mm ammunition; fifty cases, also crated, Heckler & Koch HK-91's with retractable butt stocks, and ten thousand rounds of 7.62 NATO's; fifty Remington model-870 twelve-gauge riot guns, with one hundred boxes Federal 00-nine pellet buck; a hundred standard Smith & Wesson 9mm semiautomatic pistols and appropriate ammo; twenty belt-fed fifty-caliber machine guns, appropriate ammo; four cases of M-79 grenade launchers, with ten cases of 40mm HE rounds, ten cases canister rounds, and one case illumination rounds.

"Okay, let's see, coming down to the end of the light stuff, we have fifty M-60 machine guns with ten thousand ball cartridge rounds, five thousand armor-piercing, five thousand armor incendiary, all 7.62 NATO."

Nelson made a fold halfway down the list, poured two fingers of whiskey into his glass, added some ice and Perrier, then continued.

"Let's move to the middleweights now. Two dozen LAAW M-72 antitank weapons with the following ordnance—ten cases M-18 warheads, ten cases of 66mm rockets . . ."

Michael Laser stood, took his drink over by the window, and gazed at the horizon while Nelson went on listing 60mm and 81mm mortars, a variety of explosives including 80/20 Amatol, Pentolite, Tetryl, and various plastique compositions including B and B-2, C-3, and C-4, with the necessary Primacord, fuses, caps, and wires. Then he moved on down the rest of the Soms' shopping list, a list Laser had written, to finish off with the hand-held SAM's and SSM's.

Laser had never been scratched in battle; neither

bullet, nor knife, nor shell fragment, nor piece of
shrapnel had touched him. He had suffered leeches,
ants, mosquitoes, rats, snakes, dysentery, trench foot,
and severe hangovers, but never a wound by man.
Avoiding wounds during a twenty-five-year career as a
professional soldier was not the luck of the draw, Laser
believed. Mike Laser was a man who first cultivated and
nurtured his survival instincts, then put complete faith
in them. That, in combination with the fact that he never
hesitated to act, to kill rather than wound, to depart
when faced with superior force, had kept him safe from
harm.

Only once in his life had he been wrong. And now
Laser looked out the window at the jungle carpet
stretching to the horizon and *knew* without a doubt that
someone was out there waiting for him. He could feel
Hatch's eyes on him, found himself edging away from the
window and turning back to Kaysone Som and Perry
Nelson. Maybe Frank Hatcher was the only man alive
who might come close to having Laser's instincts and
skills, but as long as he held Hatch's friend and the
woman, Laser had the upper hand.

Kaysone Som was talking to him.

"I'm sorry, what was that?" Laser said, coming back to
the table and refilling his glass with only Perrier.

"I said, Nelson claims you told him we would drop the
aircraft."

"That's right, I did."

"I want the helicopters and the airplanes, as
promised. That was our deal."

"We can't get them in without calling attention to
ourselves. How are we supposed to get them here? Fly
them? Crate them and haul them upriver? We've got
enough trouble getting the weapons upriver without
alerting Souphanouvong's people. This coup can succeed
only if we surprise the Lao and Vietnamese armies.
Nelson and I agree that once we have taken the
government buildings and killed the Council of Minis-
ters, we'll have access to all the airfields and the planes
we want.

"It's the Vietnamese regulars I'm worried about," Laser said, turning to Nelson.

"If that's the only thing you're bothered with, you might as well go have yourself a nap or something. Seven days from tomorrow, the Chinese are going to mass along the northern border, and the following day, Khmer mercenaries are going to begin systematic attacks against posts along the southern Cambodian border. In short, my friends, the Vietnamese are going to be so bloody busy holding on to their own piece of the pie that you'll have this country locked up tight before they can shit, shave, and shower."

"That's it, more or less," Laser said.

"I suggest we toast the new president of the independent, democratic nation of Laos." Nelson picked up his whiskey glass and held it out, waiting for Laser to join him. When he did, Nelson added, "To Prince Kaysone Som, friend of the American people, beloved leader, and the new president. To you, sir."

As they touched their glasses to their lips, one of the guards knocked loudly and persistently at the door.

"Enter," Kaysone called out in Lao.

A breathless guard rushed in and went directly to Kaysone's side, speaking quickly in Lao.

Mike Laser jumped to his feet.

"What the fuck is it?" Nelson asked, standing with Laser.

"They found one of our men with his throat cut, and Boone Buchannan is missing."

"So what?" Nelson said, following Laser out the door. "How far can a dying man get in the jungle?"

Laser had no reply. He knew who had killed Jerry Waters, and it had not been Boone Buchannan.

29

Jan's fingers trembled as she worked at the buttons of the black shirt. She left only the bottom closed so that the shirt would open far enough to expose most of her breasts. Then she positioned herself on the bed, hiding the ceramic water jar behind the pillow.

She moaned as if in pain, but nothing happened. She tried crying out. Finally the door opened and the two Lao guards came in, leading with their automatic rifles.

Oh no, Jan thought, one at a time, one at a time. She held her stomach and rolled her head, moaning as authentically as she could. The shirt gaped open as Jan shifted her weight, exposing her right breast to the nipple. She closed her eyes as if in pain and said, "My stomach hurts."

One of the guards came forward, and the other held back with his rifle at the ready. The approaching guard said something in Lao that Jan did not understand, but she understood the meaning of his eyes riveted to her chest.

The guard put his M-16 on the table, then bent over Jan. She reached out and took his hand, placing it on her stomach and moaning again. "Hurts," she said.

The guard pressed slightly and Jan began moving his hand off her stomach and upward. When the guard looked up at her, she closed her eyes and let her mouth stay open slightly.

As his hand bumped into the underside of her exposed breast, Jan opened her eyes and looked at the guard standing back at the door, then picked up the other guard's hand and pushed it away from her body, keeping her eyes on the guard by the door.

The guard by the bed looked over his shoulder, then, with a smirk, told the other guard to leave them alone. With an anticipatory smile, the other guard backed out the door with the knowledge he would be next, closing the door behind him.

When the door closed, Jan moaned a little and closed her eyes. She felt the guard's weight on the edge of the bed as he sat down beside her. Then she felt his hand on her stomach again, pressing gently, and he was saying something to her. His breath smelled heavily of pungent fish sauce. The guard's hand slid up her stomach to her breasts and she could tell he had pulled the shirt completely open. He took a breast in each hand and leaned over her. Making a grunting noise, he put his body against hers and she felt his mouth closing over a nipple as he kneaded the breast toward his face.

Jan raised her arms above her head and slipped her right hand inside the mouth of the water jug. She made a fist to keep the jug from falling off. Slowly she eased the jug from beneath the pillow and held it up to the full extension of her arm.

Then, taking aim on the back of his skull, she brought the jug down with all her strength just as he opened his mouth and started to raise his head.

The jug and the skull cracked together, making a sound like a handclap. The guard went unconscious immediately.

Jan slipped herself out from under him and hurriedly pulled him onto the bed. She laid him on his stomach with the pillow beneath him. Then she took his rifle and went to the door.

"No, no, stop it, please, no, no," she said loud enough to be heard through the door. Then she kicked over the chair.

Ten seconds passed and Jan wondered what else she could do to get the other guard to come through the door. She looked around the room for something to make a noise. But before she could move, she saw the door handle lift.

Grasping the M-16 by its barrel, she lifted it over her shoulder like a baseball bat.

The guard opened the door and started inside. Jan saw

the smile on his face, his eyes on the bed, just before she swung the rifle around and bashed the butt stock into his face. The guard dropped to his knees, but before he could fall over, Jan swung the rifle again and hit him in the back of the neck. Then she quickly buttoned her shirt and picked up the hat Wing had made her wear.

Her heart pounded as she stepped over the fallen guard and checked the hallway. She started out, but suddenly felt dizzy and had to lean against the wall and steady her breathing. Her head felt like it was going to float away.

She squatted in the hallway, angry with herself for her fear. Why now? she asked herself. How can you let this happen now, after what you just did in there? Get up! Move! If you sit here, you will die!

She looked both ways down the hall. They had brought her in each time from down there, she remembered, looking to the right. She put on the round hat, slid the rifle back into the room and closed the door, then turned left and went down the hall.

Boone had told Hatch everything he knew, everything he had seen inside the fortress, which had only served to confirm what Hatch already knew: to breach the fortress's defenses would be a suicide mission. There were too many guards and too few entrances.

They were thinking the same thing, so when Hatch said, "Let's take as many with us as we can," Boone knew what he meant.

Boone nodded. "Will you let me have Laser?" he asked.

"Sure, buddy."

Hatch's score was older and deeper than anything Michael Laser had done to him, a debt going back over twenty years to another village in the Laotian jungle, to a time when Hatch was still young and hopeful, still able to love and dream and plan; back to the man who had destroyed the woman Hatch loved, planting a rat inside her womb to gnaw on the fetus of their son, and with the same act ripping out Hatch's soul. Prince Phoun Som. Hatch made pacts with God and then with the devil to be given just five minutes with the prince.

Hatch put his hand on Boone's shoulder. "Let's do it, brother."

Boone nodded, smiled, then picked up his weapons and followed Hatch up the slope toward the massive rock monastery.

Now Jan was lost. She had tried to keep moving down, but the sound of voices ahead had twice turned her back and through side doors. She had found herself once in a storage room and now in a circular hallway with only doors opening to the interior, none to the outside. She had no choice but to go back the way she had come. At each door she could hear human sounds—voices, water running, metallic clanking. She turned back and started up the spiral staircase.

She came to her room again. The door was still closed. She hurried ahead and took the stairs they had brought her up before. She knew that this way led directly to the central courtyard, but now she had no choice but to cross it in the open, her hope of finding another exit crushed by the maze of halls and doors.

Jan reached the compound door and stopped. The afternoon sunlight was blocked by the high fortress walls, as would soon be the jungle outside when the sun dipped below the top canopy of trees. There were cooking fires burning in the compound, and in a few of the huts there were lantern lights, but most of the compound was in shadows. Jan figured she could use the darkness near the walls to reach the door. Then she would either get by the guards at the door, or not. Period.

She pushed the hat further down and tilted her chin to her chest, then folded her arms in front of her and went out.

She walked without looking forward, keeping her eyes cast down to the ground, and tried to maintain a steady, not-too-fast pace.

She was ignored completely. Most of the men seemed to be gone. The other women in the camp were too busy to wonder. She was going to make the gate, which was now only a short distance away. She kept inside the shadow line and picked up her pace, hoping she could walk straight through without being stopped.

Then a hand fell heavily on her shoulder and spun her around. Jan gasped and tightened her body for whatever would come next. The hand went beneath her chin and lifted her face.

"You'd never have made it," said Harry, the war lover. Nobody comes into or leaves the compound after dark, except the Americans, unless they have a pass from Laser."

"Please help me," Jan said, her eyes wet and wide.

Harry nodded, and kept nodding for what seemed like a long time, as if he were convincing himself of something. "Yeah," he said finally, "I always was a sucker for a woman in distress."

He reached out and pushed the hat farther down on Jan's head, then told her, "Don't make a sound and don't, for Chrissakes, look up, no matter what I do to you or what I might say. You dig?"

"You can go out?"

"I can do any damn thing I like. Now turn around and do what I told you."

Harry turned her, pushed her head down, then shoved her in the back and said, "Move your ass," in Lao.

Jan stumbled forward with Harry right behind her. He kept pushing against her back, shoving her pretty hard sometimes, saying things she did not understand.

"Open the door, you dog suckers," Harry called out in Lao to the entrance guards, then gave Jan another hard shove and said, "Shut up and keep walking, you female vampire bat."

One of the guards pushed open the door and the other two stood aside. Harry pushed Jan through the door, giving the guard there a wink when he passed.

When they had cleared the door and he heard it close behind them, Harry whispered to Jan in English, "Keep doing what you're doing until I tell you otherwise." He came up next to her. "I'm sorry, ma'am, but I'm gonna have to get a little personal to make it look good, us going into the woods."

Harry put his arm around Jan, resting his hand on her ass, and pulled her against his side.

In that fashion, they walked down the trail and through the first row of hooches.

Hatch heard noise on the trail and signaled Boone; both men squatted in the high bush to wait for the source of the noise to pass them.

At first Hatch could only see that it was one of the Americans and a native woman. But then, when they were nearly parallel, the woman raised her head slightly and Hatch recognized her. He turned back to Boone and pointed. Boone nodded, his eyes showing surprise.

Hatch held his hand out, palm down, toward Boone and withdrew his knife with the other. Boone pulled out his own knife to cover Hatch.

The war lover heard the rustling of the grass first, then sensed the movement to his rear. He was starting to turn and crouch as Hatch jumped. Jan, just starting to turn, saw the knife blade before she saw Hatch. Harry saw it too, and his arm came up protectively as his other hand reached for his pistol. Jan cried, "No," and pushed Harry aside. The knife caught Harry's upper forearm, making an inch-deep, four-inch-long slice before Hatch saw Jan falling in front of him and pulled back.

"No," Jan said again, putting herself between Hatch and the war lover.

By then Boone had recognized Harry and came out of hiding.

"I know him," Boone said.

Jan put her hand over Harry's to keep him from drawing the pistol. "He helped me." It was then she realized the assailant was Hatch and saw Boone coming

out to join him. Jan fell into Hatch's arms and buried her
face into his shoulder.

"Ain't this the shits?" Harry said, watching the blood
flow out of his arm.

30

Using Hatch's knife, Jan cut strips of cloth from her
pants and wrapped Harry's forearm to stem the flow of
blood.

"You won't get by the first door," Harry told Hatch and
Boone. "But even if you did, somehow, you'd never get
inside the fortress—ouch, shit."

"Sorry," Jan said, easing up a little on the knot she was
tying in his makeshift bandage.

"Forget it. Do what you have to do," Harry told her.

"Then we walk away," Hatch said. "There's always
another time."

"Not anymore, no way," Harry went on. "By now they
know he's gone"—nodding his head toward Boone—"and
maybe the lady too. You can forget going through the
jungle, 'cause it can't be done, not being chased. That
leaves the river. You won't outrun Som's boats, and
there's no place to hide. We . . . these people *own* this
country down here. You'll stick out like a naked nigger
trying to hide from the Klan in the middle of a Methodist
Ladies' Guild picnic."

"To coin a phrase," Hatch said.

"Right," Harry said. "And you're running out of time
too. Look, man, you think the Vietnamese are going to
turn this country over to the Soms? They been infiltrat-
ing this place for weeks, and no way we've tapped all of
'em. Let me put it this way; a hard rain's gonna fall, it's
time to be a-going."

"I won't run," Boone said, meaning he could not.

Hatch knew that. And he understood what Harry was
telling him. He looked at Jan, but she was occupied with
Harry's arm.

"Tell y'all what, though," Harry said, looking over the arm Jan had bandaged, declaring it fine with a look. "There is another way, a kind of secret entrance. Me and Laser went out that way once, about two years ago. I don't think any of these gooks know about it, 'cept of course the Som clan and their personals."

"Into the compound?" Hatch asked.

"Into the fortress, direct."

"No shit?"

Harry nodded. "We have to pass through a portion of the castle, but after that the cave leads back to the river. It's a way."

"Sorry about your arm," Hatch apologized.

"Hey, you just helped me remember how old I'm getting. Five years ago I'd of got you at the first sound."

"Five years ago I wouldn't have made that sound," Hatch said, smiling.

"Okay, so what? She got out. Let her go. What chance do they have of getting two miles from here?"

Laser stopped at the door to the room Jan had been held in and turned back to Nelson, who had stopped by the window and looked out at the thick jungle as if to emphasize his point.

"Who said they'll try to get away?"

Nelson followed Laser into the hall and said, "Of course they'll run. They wouldn't be stupid enough to come back here. So what if they did? A walking dead man who can count his remaining breaths on one hand, some derelict Green Beenie, and a woman, for Chrissakes. Those three against this!" Nelson held his arms straight out from his sides.

"You are such a fucking bureaucrat, Nelson. All you government assholes are alike. You're so myopic you're dangerous. Make yourself useful and go find Wells and Marlar, tell them to get a couple of patrols together; cover the boat docks and the river landing. I'll get things beefed up inside."

All Laser could see was an image of falling dominoes, one by one, until the whole line was down.

It was difficult moving through the jungle in the dark, and it took them fifteen minutes to make a hundred meters. They avoided the trails. Harry was familiar with the terrain, and by taking the point he was able to move them around the fortresses's perimeter without being seen or heard by any of the patrols.

In what seemed to be the dark middle of nowhere, Harry stopped and signaled the others to get down. He crawled back to Hatch, who had taken up the rear. "We should be close, maybe ten, fifteen yards," he whispered. "Let's bunch up so we make one quick pass through the cover."

"Any lights in the cave?" Hatch asked.

"Further back, far enough so you can't see any light from the entrance. The guards will be at the light. There are usually only two."

Hatch nodded, then said, "You didn't have to help us."

"That's right."

"Why?"

"If the Vietnamese get into here, well, I'm not going back to no fucking bamboo prison camp. Can you dig it? Besides, I don't like that fucker Mike brought in here, that pasty-assed spook. And I guess you can also say that this is a down payment on a long list of debts I gotta pay before the big General up there lets me take a break."

"I can dig it," Hatch whispered, grasping Harry's hand in the old Special Forces style.

Harry went forward and stopped next to Boone. "Let's kill 'em all, eh? Let God sort it out." Boone smiled, but it was hard. He could feel life leaving him like a bird taking flight.

Hatch crawled up to Jan. "The cave's close," he whispered. She nodded, the fear and excitement twisting her face into a grimace. "I want you to stay right here until we come out." He put a finger to her lips to hush her. "Listen to me. If it goes bad, at least out here you'll

be alive. You can try to escape when you get a chance."
Hatch lied badly. Jan knew as well as he did that one way
or another they were all going to die, inside the castle or
later, running.

She pushed his finger away from her lips and shook
her head. "No chance, Hatch. You're not leaving me
here. If you try, I'll just go in alone following you. If you
aren't coming back, well, I'm not going to be a prisoner
again, I'm not going through that again. I'm going with
you, or I'm going behind you." There was no doubt, no
hesitation in her expression. But there was inside her,
where Jan wished with all her might she had never let
Hatch leave Tuva. She felt like she had murdered him,
and Boone, and now this man too, Harry, the war lover.

"Can you use that?" Hatch looked down at the
Swedish K submachine gun Harry had given her.

"What's to know? Point and pull the trigger."

"Pull the trigger, then immediately let up; you can
empty a clip in a second or two. Remember, short bursts
or you'll be out of ammunition in less than a minute."

Jan nodded. Hatch gave her a bag of 9mm clips and
showed her how to insert and eject them.

A signal from Boone, passed back from Harry, said it
was time to move out. Hatch indicated that Jan should
go ahead of him, that he would keep to the rear. Jan
started to tell him something, the words just forming at
her soft lips, but Hatch stopped her with a hand signal
and backed away.

The fortress's security force had been fully alerted and
had taken their defensive positions. Outside, in the
compound, the Lao mercenaries had formed into squads
and were searching both inside the compound and
around the fortress perimeter.

Prince Phoun Som, with his bodyguard, Nishioki, was
hardly to be worried about such a motley little threat,
and went back to his nap, Nishioki sitting cross-legged
on the floor by the sleeping mat.

An hour before, Kaysone Som had gone into his lavish

quarters with a couple of his favorite boys, leaving strict orders to be disturbed only for the most dire emergency. Kaysone's guards did not believe that the slim possibility of an assault on the fortress by a woman, a dying man, and some ghost warranted interrupting their leader's evening of pleasure. Nor was the odd flurry of coded radio activity over the Vietnamese air channel worth incurring the prince's wrath.

Perry Nelson went to the kitchen and made a sandwich for a bedtime snack; he expected to be asleep within the hour. Early the next morning, he was supposed to be taken to the airfield outside Khong Sedone to meet a chopper for the ride into Thailand, where at the airport in Ubon Ratchathani he would hop one of the Company's Transamerica planes back to Bangkok. He had a lot of work to do before the coup that would overthrow the Lao People's Democratic Republic, which would also make him a hero at Langley, maybe even in the White House.

The bells, gongs, sticks, and drums erupted suddenly from the surrounding jungle like a radio turned on, only louder, much louder, as if amplified, only the sound was live, not recorded. It came from everywhere, above and around them, growing louder by the second.

"Laser's just trying to spook us," Harry said to the others as they bunched up behind him in the darkness.

"It's working," Jan said so softly that only Hatch could hear her.

"It won't be so bad inside the cave," Harry said, turning around and moving out again.

But something stopped him, something in back of all the noise, something he had heard before, something that did spook him. "Wait," he said, turning back to the others. He put out his hand to keep them quiet. "Hear that?"

Hatch strained to hear whatever it was that had stopped Harry, but there was only the noise, the godawful gongs and the drums that his heartbeat struggled to match.

But then it was there, faint but clear, something rhythmic behind the unsyncopated drumming, something mechanical . . .

"Holy shit," Harry muttered. "Choppers, a whole bunch of choppers. Man, this is the big time!"

They could all hear the rotors then, although there was nothing to see in the night.

"What kind?" Hatch asked.

"Might be more appropriate to ask whose," Harry said.

"Russian," Boone said as if to himself.

"Give that man a Kewpie doll," Harry said. "Hinds, D's or E's, my guess."

"Russians?" Jan said, unable to believe they were now, on top of everything else, going to be invaded by Russians.

"Vietnamese," Harry told her, as well as informing Hatch, who had turned to look quizzically at the pitch-black sky. "Russians gave some to the Vietnamese Air Force.

"Ha!" Harry exclaimed, looking up at the fortress above their heads. "Fuck you, Laser, fuck you all to hell!"

The Mi24's, six of them in straight-line formation, were so loud that they seemed right on top of the fortress, although no one on the ground had seen them yet. Then, suddenly, the eastern sky lit up like a thousand sequential strobes.

"Incoming!" Harry screamed at the top of his lungs, and began burying himself in the wet jungle floor. Hatch threw himself on top of Jan as the fleet of Swatter missiles screeched over the top of their heads and impacted against the walls of the fortress, showering them with thousands of shrapnel-size pieces of ancient rock.

In the near-quiet between the missiles and the following UB-32 rockets, the jungle's cacophony stopped.

"Rockets!" Harry cried as they streaked overhead, leaving a contrail of fire and smoke. "The cave," he yelled, scrambling to his feet and lurching through the bush toward the entrance.

Hatch pulled Jan up with one arm and grabbed Boone's hand with the other, all three stumbling forward through a hail of rocks and sticks into the hole Harry had made bursting through the cave's camouflage.

There was smoke in the cave, some dust falling from overhead, but it felt safe from the storm outside. At the sound of an M-16 burst, Hatch shoved Jan and Boone against the side.

"Clear," Harry called back. "Come on."

Hatch, Boone, and Jan ran down the dark cave toward the lights glowing fifty feet ahead; just before reaching the lights they passed the bodies of the two guards. Harry waited by a large wooden door.

"We can ride out the storm in here," he said, his eyes wild, crazy with apprehension. "This doorway's a bottleneck, and ain't nobody coming through here if we don't want 'em to."

"And we can't get out, either," Hatch said. "Some grave."

"Some could," Harry said, "if some stay."

"I'm going in after Prince Som," Hatch said. "I'll block this exit for you."

"Look," Harry said then. "You got two ways to go on the other side of this door. Left goes up and into the castle; right goes down one level and exits back into the cave, where it widens again; a hundred yards more, give or take, and you come outside again, not far from the river, but a long way from the boat docks; still, it should be clear."

Hatch nodded. "Take Jan and get her the hell out of here."

"Somehow I figured you'd say that." Harry smiled.

"No." Jan protested.

"Shut up," Hatch told her. "Please, do this, Jan. I'll meet you back at the river. We're all going to get out of this."

There were six loud booms, almost of top of one another, and the cave walls shook like rattled tin.

"More Swatters," Harry said. "You'll find the prince on the top level, end of the wide hall, the double doors; that is, if there still is an upper level," he told Hatch.

"Thanks, troop." Hatch reached out and jerked the submachine gun out of Jan's hand and ripped the bag of clips from her shoulder. "Go!" he yelled, and shoved her hard into the war lover's grasp.

"No, Hatch, God damn you!" Jan cried out, but by then Harry had swung open the door and jerked her to the other side.

"Okay," Hatch said, breathing hard as he turned to Boone, who was leaning against the wall; it seemed to be as far as he could go. "Go with them, my friend. Haul your ass."

More Swatters hit above and dirt fell heavily over their heads and shoulders.

"You always had a taste for the melodramatic, old man." Boone smiled, pulling open the door and going through. When Hatch rushed through behind him, he saw that Boone had gone left and up the stairs into the crumbling former monastery.

At the first landing, Hatch came up beside Boone and they ran through the opening, firing in sweeping arcs, spilling a half-dozen Lao guards in the hallway. Rockets exploded in the compound and parts of the ceiling had caved in at the back of the hall.

Hatch passed Boone and started up the next set of stairs. Fires from burning huts outside the perimeter made dancing shadows on the walls as Hatch ran past windows; the smell of burning rot and cordite was strong.

As they crossed the second landing and started up the last stairwell, they heard voices yelling orders, others screaming in pain coming from the far, dark end of the second level. Boone stopped and touched Hatch's shoulder. "Laser," he said, recognizing one of the voices.

Hatch nodded and gave Boone a thumbs-up sign. Boone backed up and headed down the hall; Hatch took the stairs two at a time.

Boone followed the sounds, the screams and the confused orders, through the rubble in the hall. It took the last of his strength to kick open the door at the end.

Inside a room with the look of a treasury, Michael Laser, with Perry Nelson hanging on to his arm like a coat, was stuffing gold and cash into a large bag. Nelson's left leg was crushed. When the door burst open, Laser shoved Nelson away and jerked the Browning from his belt.

As Boone stumbled into the room, tripping over the body of a Lao guard, he sent a short burst from his M-16 across the floor and up the wall, three of the shells passing through Nelson on their way across. As Boone got up on one knee and tried to level the M-16, Laser squeezed off three rounds that impacted inside a four-inch circle in the center of Boone's chest. The force of the bullets lifted Boone off his knees and threw him back against the wall. He was already dead, his eyes and mouth wide with surprise, when Laser put a fourth bullet into his forehead.

There was no third level. When Hatch got halfway up the stairs, he met a pile of rocks and debris, beyond which he could see the dark open sky. The missiles had blown the entire top off the old monastery. Coming now from outside there was the clear and distinct sound of small-arms fire, mostly AK-47's.

Hatch turned back for Boone; there was still a chance they could get back to the cave and to the river. He hit the bottom of the stairs on a jump and turned into the hall. . . .

. . . just as Mike Laser, arms full of loot bags, came through the far door and saw Hatch turn the corner.

Through the open door, Hatch could see that the entire wall behind Laser was gone; through it he could see the tops of the tallest palm trees.

It was that one second of hesitation, whether to drop the bags and pull his gun, or protect the gold, that gave Hatch the edge he needed. But as he aimed the M-16 at Laser's chest, the space behind Laser suddenly filled with the nose of a Hind D chopper. As Hatch squeezed the trigger, the Hind's weapon operator—a helmet glowing in dim red light behind the flat nose screen—let go a pair of rockets, one of which passed straight through Laser's back without detonating, and continued on to deflect off the wall halfway down; the second, passing through the explosion of the first, whistled out the window directly behind Hatch, who went with it, blasted into an infinite blackness.

Glancing back as the war lover pulled her through the stinging, wet jungle, Jan watched the fortress collapsing on itself, fires raging out of control in the area of the boat docks and from the huts around the castle. The six Russian helicopters danced at the edges of the flames and smoke like bees teasing a flower.

They had been hearing shooting for ten minutes, since they left the cave and forged into the thick black jungle that sloped downward to the river bend. Harry told her that most of the firing came from AK-47's, "very little of our stuff."

Jan begged him to stop and wait for Hatch and Boone, but Harry would not. He moved fast, pulling her, dragging her when necessary, making for the river.

"If they were still inside," he told her, "they're gone."

"But maybe they were in the cave before it collapsed."

"And maybe the hand of God's gonna pluck us the fuck up outta here and set us down in the Ping Pong Bar, Bangkok."

They made the river. Harry's and Jan's arms and legs were shredded by the vines and brambles they had plowed through at the end. The shooting became more sporadic, and then the choppers banked right and headed for Vietnam. The single, distinguishable shots sounded more ominous than the firefight, which had sounded to Jan like a Fourth of July show in Coronado.

"You can run away if you want to." Jan turned to Harry with her hands on her hips. "But I'm staying here until Hatch and Boone show up."

"They ain't gonna show up. How many times I gotta tell you that?" He grabbed her arm and jerked her toward the river.

"Leave me alone. I'll scream." And to prove it, Jan opened her mouth and let go a yell.

"Aw, lady," Harry said, just before he threw a right cross and knocked her unconscious.

31

He came to facing a night sky. It frightened him, as if it were a continuation of the nightmare he was having, a dream of falling, falling, falling into a dark, deep abyss. He was on his back, that much he could tell, but it did not feel like the earth he lay against. The messages his brain was receiving were confusing and misleading. Dark clouds against a dark sky, cracked in one place, where a sliver of moon blinked in and out. He strained his eyes to see it again, but the clouds closed and raced down the mountainside.

It was quiet, yet not. He heard nothing human. There was the sound of wood creaking, like branches rubbing slowly against one another, and a rustling noise, like mice in straw. In the distance, so faint as to be barely audible, monkeys chattered. A bird. Another. Water somewhere, dripping, moving.

There was the smell of jungle, green, wet, rotting, and pungently alive. But something else, something acrid, stinging, sharp, foul. Like . . . what?

Flesh. Burnt flesh.

And cordite.

Bare metal. Or . . . blood.

Parts of him came back individually, sequentially, beginning at his head, which ached, throbbed, and burned like the first day in hell; he found his eyes, although the images passing through them were blurred and weaving; his ears tingled with a low humming noise, backdrop to the jungle sounds; a tongue swollen inside his mouth only tasted blood; his back felt punctuated like a braille card with sharp pricks, as if from needles the size of pencils; his arms were heavy, sheeted in iron sleeves; there was nothing, nothing below the waist.

Slowly the world turned upside down before his eyes, and he closed them, sinking deeper and deeper into the dark, empty tunnels inside his mind.

When his eyes opened again it was dusk, the evening after his second day there. Where? There was no sensation of time, neither of moments nor of days passing. He did not think to ask how long, only where. Then, who.

He could move a little, and tried to turn himself; but suddenly the world began dropping out from under him and he grasped wildly for a hold. His berth, whatever it was, held him only precariously.

Why could he see only the sky, the close, cloudy, threatening sky? Where was the earth?

He turned his head slowly to the side and looked across the ragged green carpet of treetops, like the puffy upper side of a cloud bank seen from an airplane.

Trees? His vision remained undependable. His swollen, painful head was filled with everything but relevant facts. How could he see trees from the top, looking across, like seeing the sea from a raft?

Unless . . . How did he get into the top of a tree? And how would he get down through the thick lattice of vines and branches?

From the color of the sky he could not tell if it was dusk or dawn, if he faced a night or a sun-searing day. He tried to move again, but even the smallest turns brought pain throughout his body. The pain rattled his brain and knocked him back into unconsciousness.

The next time he opened his eyes it was day and the sun was high. He did not know if he had been out for ten hours or ten minutes.

It was then that his instinct for survival began pouring adrenaline and endorphins into his system. He still could not see clearly. The humming in his ears sounded like a bee hive, and the pain in his limbs burned like acid; he could not breathe through his nose. But he moved, turned, and faced the ground four stories below.

It was slow. He moved by inches at first, working his way across the mattress of vines toward the larger, thicker interior branches. Then it was down, down one branch at a time, one branch every few minutes, for two hours. A quarter of the way down, he stopped and lay on a branch the thickness of his own body, falling asleep there for an hour. It was nearing dusk of the third day since he landed on the jungle's top canopy when he reached a point near enough to the earth to risk a fall. His impact with the sodden ground knocked the breath from him and sent electrical surges of pain through his body.

Destruction surrounded him: bodies everywhere, some blackened, all bloated so fat that shirts had ripped at the seams, pants exploded; the residue of burned-out huts, fences, and trees; and a mass of smoldering wood and stone heaped so high it looked like a collapsed city.

How could he remember nothing?

Some instinct drove him toward the water. And although he could only crawl, the trail, except for some bodies and shell casings, was open. It ended at a rickety platform over the riverbank. What had once been its roof was now collapsed onto the dock. As he crawled over it, his hand touched a bare skull, too old, too clean to have been part of the carnage behind him.

He could see the river flowing beyond the edge of the dock, but he could not raise himself. The gunwales of a dinghy floated at the top of the water, a line running up from the sunken bow to one of the dock poles. Another small boat, like a narrow wooden canoe, was wedged against the dock, its stern being tugged by the current.

He tried to stand again, but it was no use. The effort

sent his head spinning and, trying to crawl forward, he fell over the end of the dock, landing hard on his back in the canoe. His inertia pushing the canoe into the current.

The canoe and its unconscious occupant turned two circles getting to mid-river, then spun backward and drifted south.

Bounkeut first saw just the front of the little boat wedged among the exposed root structure of a big tree where he sometimes went to pretend he was a soldier like his father had been. Maybe it was a good boat. Bounkeut thought of stealing it and going down the river into Thailand, where his uncle could not find him, so he could no longer beat him like a dog. If it was a good boat, maybe his mother and his sister and his two cousins would come, and he, Bounkeut, would take them to safety over the border.

The boy approached the boat cautiously. Things not in their right places often meant death in Bounkeut's world. One of his friends had been killed when he picked up a fine metal box and it exploded. Bounkeut's mother had warned him in the most serious tone to never touch something unfamiliar. But a boat is certainly familiar, he thought.

He moved closer, and the rest of the boat came into view. But now it no longer seemed empty; there was what looked like a bundle of clothes inside. Bounkeut approached, leaning forward as if the riverbank were the edge of a cliff.

When a moan came from the bundle of clothing, Bounkeut jerked backward and cried out, turning to run with all his speed to escape from the spirit of the boat.

But he was a curious boy, and after five minutes, when the spirit did not give chase, Bounkeut went back to the boat. Maybe it had been the river sighing, a sound he had heard before at night. He leaned out over the bank, holding the vines on the tree, and looked in.

"Help me," the man said weakly, his eyes open, staring straight into Bounkeut's soft dark eyes.

Bounkeut remembered him. It had not been so long ago. The man to whom he gave his uncle's boat. The man who said he would kill the bad men. And everyone knew that the bad men *had* all been killed, that the village was now safe from the pirates, if not those Vietnamese dogs.

Bounkeut moved closer to the boat. "I will get my mother," he whispered, as if to speak louder might injure the hero. "You wait here," he said. "I will go get my mother and come back quickly."

The man, wondering how he thought in one language but understood the boy speaking another, smiled.

Bounkeut ran.

Tuva

It had been raining steadily for two days. The sea and the sky shared the same gray lack of color, one blending into the other, offering no sense of horizon. The seaplane had flown over from Tahiti on instruments, but now, as it dropped below the cloud layer, Tuva could be seen half a mile ahead, its highest mountain, Kilohana, lost in a misty haze. The atoll seemed only to be a disorganized swatch of color wedged between two layers of gray, particularly through the rain-streaked round window that the plane's only passenger peered through. The plane banked hard and she looked down on the surface of the ocean. Then, just before the plane leveled off for landing in the lagoon, she saw the reef, a ring of pearl-white froth marking the line between gray and foam green.

There were few people waiting on the pier as the plane taxied close and turned: two small boys, two old men fishing, and the two men who reached for the mooring lines tossed from the cockpit hatch. It was raining hard by then.

The woman climbed through the hatch and accepted the hand offered to pull her to the pier. She smiled, then turned back to get one small suitcase and a plastic-covered cardboard box.

The copilot said, "Tomorrow, noon," before dropping back out of sight and closing the hatch.

The two native men pushed on the plane's wing tip to turn it out, then stepped away as the propeller's increased RPM's mixed salt spray with the warm rain. The boys stared at the white woman, who had walked over to the two old fishermen.

"Makavaana," she said to one, who turned to look at her. "Do you remember me?"

"You only woman come Tuva from sky; two time now," the old man said, holding his hat with one hand and his fishing pole with the other.

The plane moved out into the bay and made its takeoff run, climbing out with water pouring from its floats to the awestruck amazement of the two boys.

"I have brought something for Mr. Jolly." Her eyes went to the plastic-covered box. "Could I find him at the Government House?"

"Same-same," Makavaana said, nodding as well.

"Thank you," she said, then turned and thanked the men who had held the plane and given her a hand.

When she left them and started walking up the pier toward Papa Jack's bar, the two old fishermen chattered to one another in their native tongue and the boys trailed the woman at a brave but discreet distance.

From the window of his office in the Government House, Mr. Jolly Malcolm watched the woman walking off the pier. He had thought of going to greet her, but his chair-bearers were home and he decided not to send for them. After all, it was raining, and even a warm rain caused problems for a man with no legs.

When she turned left at Papa Jack's he knew she was coming to see him. He rolled behind his desk and waited.

Her knock was light and he told her to come in. She set the suitcase and box down just inside the door and strode directly to his desk with her hand out, which he accepted and shook for a long time.

"Well, well, Jan," he said. "The last time a plane came to our island, you were the reason. Here we are again. And may I say that you look—"

"Wet," she inserted. "How good to see you again, Mr. Jolly."

"Please, take that chair." Mr. Jolly indicated a wicker chair by the desk and Jan sat down with some expression of tiredness. "I was about to say that you look stunning, even wet."

"Mr. Jolly, you are a lying jewel."

Their eyes averted suddenly and there was a silence. Then Jan got up and retrieved the box.

"I have something for you, as promised."

"Books." Mr. Jolly's eyes brightened and he sat up straighter in his chair with clear anticipation.

Jan ripped open the plastic rain covering and cut through the masking tape with her fingernail.

"Oh Lord, what have we here?" Mr. Jolly craned his neck to see inside the box.

Jan began pulling them out one at a time, laying them on the desk in front of Mr. Jolly, who immediately picked up each and fondled it. Jan read the titles as she removed them: *"The Philosopher's Pupil, The Sea, The Sea,* and *Nuns and Soldiers,* all by Iris Murdoch." Mr. Jolly nearly squealed with the joy held in his hands, stroking the covers like one would a baby's cheek. *"Brighton Rock* and *A Burnt-Out Case,* by Graham Greene."* She handed those over. "Oh, I hope you'll like these two: *The Magus* and *Daniel Martin,* by John Fowles. He's one of my favorites."

It was like Christmas, with Jan as Santa and Mr. Jolly the good, expectant child.

"Here's a strange little book, but I liked it quite a lot," she said, handing over Robin Moore's *The Doctor's Wife.* "He's British, you know? Reading it gave me quite a flush."

Jan kept pulling out books and handing them over until, piled high on the desk, blocking Mr. Jolly from the eyes down, were sixteen books, hard- and paper-bound.

"I hope these are all right," Jan said finally.

"All right, my dear? I have died and gone to heaven."

"Not for a long time, let's hope."

Jan sat back down and Mr. Jolly pushed an aisle between the books so he could see her.

"Could I have something brought for you? Coffee, perhaps? Something stronger, if you like?"

"Please, don't go to the trouble. I won't take much more of your time. If Mr. Lee still has a room over his

Emporium, I would like to stay on Tuva overnight. The
plane will come back for me tomorrow."

Jan could have made the delivery of books while the
plane waited, and taken it directly back to Tahiti. But she
wanted a night on Tuva, a night to walk through the
village and remember Hatch. She already felt closer to
him, being here.

"And maybe," Jan continued, "it might be possible for
me to see Hatch's little girl? Do you know if that would
be all right?"

"Why ask me? Ask Hatch."

His last two words shocked her like an electrical jolt,
but she must have misheard, for even Mr. Jolly would
not see humor in such a joke.

"I don't understand what you mean." Jan sputtered
the words out.

"What's to understand? Didn't you come here to see
Hatch?"

"Hatch is alive? Here? Alive?"

"Of course he is, and getting better all the time, I
must say. You mean, dear one, you didn't know he was
here?"

"But, I didn't know he was *alive!*"

"Oh, goodness, do forgive me, Jan. But I thought—"

"I paid three different men to go back into Laos to find
him, or his body, and I bugged the State Department
until they contacted the highest officials in the Lao
government, who cabled confirmation that Hatch had
been killed during an attack against a pirate stronghold
in a joint operation by Lao and Vietnamese troops. They
said he was buried in a mass grave there. I gave up.
That's why I came here now, to see his daughter, to tell
her . . . Jesus Christ, Mr. Jolly! He's alive?"

"Would you like to see for yourself?" Mr. Jolly said.

The rain had stopped, although dark, heavily laden
clouds still rolled in from the sea, as everything came to
the island. Shafts of sunlight streaked through thin

places in the clouds and seemed to explode in sparks off the bright sea.

When Jan was a little girl, she believed those shafts of sunlight were the rays of God's eyes, and if you were ever caught standing in one, you would be the focus of God's sight, which to Jan was an alternately glorious and terrifying thought.

On the path ahead, as she neared Hatch's beachhouse, a large bright circle of the sun weaved smoking through the trees and ferns, washing over the path like a spotlight. In a moment she would be caught in the light. As she came into it, the light was so bright she had to shield her eyes. Jan looked up, squinting through the overhanging trees. "God," she whispered, "can you see me? Please let this be true, please let Hatch be all right."

She lowered her head, nodded to herself, and moved on through the light until its warmth left her shoulders.

Then she pushed aside the last of the bushes and came into the clearing.

There he was. And there she was. Hatch was sitting on the steps to his porch, his legs stretched out in front of him, leaning back on his elbows, eyes riveted on the little girl tossing a ball to a heavyset woman Jan recognized as Hatch's sister-in-law.

Emma, the child, saw Jan first, missing the ball when Jenny Makani tossed it. Both Jenny and Hatch turned to follow Emma's gaze.

Hatch stood and Jan noticed how slowly he moved, how one leg seemed not to bend when he rose. She smiled broadly, with what she hoped was a contained and controlled look, but the beating of her heart urged her faster and faster, until she was running when she and Hatch came together at the corner of the beach. She was crying in spite of herself.

Emma was saying something, but neither Jan nor Hatch seemed to be hearing her. Jenny took Emma's hand and, under protest, escorted her toward the trail back to the village.

"Come, honey, and don't be like that," Jenny said. "Let Daddy have some time to visit with his friend."

Hatch, looking over Jan's shoulder, saw Jenny and Emma leaving, but before he could say anything, Jenny waved, Emma waved, and Jenny called out that they would be at her house.

Hatch nodded his thanks and put his hand on the back of Jan's head, letting her cry hard into his shoulder.

"I couldn't remember anything at all for the first week," Hatch told Jan as they sat on the porch with their drinks, watching the sun sink in a splendid purple splash below the layer of black and blue clouds. "Then it began returning, in dreams at first, but I knew the dreams had been real. Even then, I lost everything that happened that last night, when the Vietnamese attacked the fortress, all the way up to when I came to in a cave, tended by the boy and his mother."

Jan sipped her drink and kept touching him, as if testing his reality, putting her hand over his, or leaning her head on his shoulder for a moment, just sitting close enough for their arms to touch, or their legs.

"They kept me hidden in the cave for four months, feeding and caring for me, until this thing"—Hatch slapped his stiff right leg—"was stuck together well enough to walk on, or rather, limp on. Then we made it over the border. That kid saved my life at least three times."

"They're all right?"

"Yes. They've been adopted by a church in Iowa. I have a letter from Bounkeut I'll have to show you later."

They were quiet for a while, watching the sun dip below the water. It was so quiet there that they held their breaths, as if they might hear the sun sizzle when it touched the water.

"What happened to Harry?" Hatch asked, coming back onto the porch with a kerosene lantern.

"He didn't think too much of America, it seems. The press hounded him a lot over the MIA thing, and the government rattled its saber about prosecution for desertion. I saw him three or four times before he took off again. He's somewhere in the Philippines. He told me there was a good little war brewing over there."

Hatch smiled. "Good for him."

They left the porch and walked along the far edge of the beach to a tiny trail leading upland behind the house and into the jungle. Hatch held out the lantern and Jan held tight to his free hand.

In a few minutes they came to a clearing that for Hatch, working just with hand tools, must have been hard-won. There, as the lantern light revealed, was a spirit house, like the one Boone had shown Jan on his land at Patong Beach.

Hatch set the lantern down on a rock ledge, then stood before the spirit house and bowed in *wai*.

"For Boone," he said, turning to Jan, the moisture in his eyes shining in the yellow light.

"For Boone," she repeated.

And they held each other for a long time.

BANTAM
SHOP·AT·HOME
C·A·T·A·L·O·G

Special Offer
Buy a Bantam Book
for only 50¢.

Now you can have Bantam's catalog filled with hundreds of titles plus take advantage of our unique and exciting bonus book offer. A special offer which gives you the opportunity to purchase a Bantam book for only 50¢. Here's how!

By ordering any five books at the regular price per order, you can also choose any other single book listed (up to a $4.95 value) for just 50¢. Some restrictions do apply, but for further details why not send for Bantam's catalog of titles today!

Just send us your name and address and we will send you a catalog!

LION'S RUN
by Craig Thomas
☐ (25824 • $4.50)

"When it comes to keeping the story moving and stoking up the excitement, Mr. Thomas knows his business."
—*New York Times*

"He knows how to make a chase scene drive the reader from page to page ... A damn good read."
—*Washington Post Book World*

"Not to be missed."   —*London Daily Mirror*

Sir Kenneth, Director-General of British Intelligence, is the victim of an elaborate and brilliant KGB plot. At its heart is the murder of a British agent. Having discovered his role in it, the Soviets have found the one weapon against which Sir Kenneth cannot defend himself. The truth will convict him.

Time is running out as the KGB moves to bring Aubrey to Russia where he will quietly disappear. There are only two slender hopes for Aubrey's survival, one a persistent friend who refuses to believe the worst, the other Aubrey's bodyguard, who is only one desperate step ahead of the KGB assassins who are attempting to track him down before he can find proof of Aubrey's innocence.

In LION'S RUN Craig Thomas has created a masterpiece of suspense, a thrilling novel of intrigue, friendship and betrayal that has all the ingredients of a major Craig Thomas bestseller.

THRILLERS

Gripping suspense . . . explosive action . . . dynamic characters . . . international settings . . . these are the elements that make for great thrillers. Books guaranteed to keep you riveted to your seat.

Robert Ludlum:

☐	26256	THE AQUITAINE PROGRESSION	$4.95
☐	26011	THE BOURNE IDENTITY	$4.95
☐	26094	THE CHANCELLOR MANUSCRIPT	$4.95
☐	26019	THE HOLCROFT COVENANT	$4.95
☐	25899	THE MATERESE CIRCLE	$4.95
☐	26430	THE OSTERMAN WEEKEND	$4.95
☐	25270	THE PARSIFAL MOSAIC	$4.95
☐	26081	THE ROAD TO GANDOLFO	$4.50
☐	25856	THE SCARLATTI INHERITANCE	$4.50

Frederick Forsyth:

☐	25113	THE FOURTH PROTOCOL	$4.95
☐	26781	NO COMEBACKS	$4.50
☐	26630	DAY OF THE JACKAL	$4.95
☐	26490	THE DEVIL'S ALTERNATIVE	$4.95
☐	26846	DOGS OF WAR	$4.95
☐	25525	THE ODESSA FILE	$4.50

Robert Littell:

☐	25831	THE SISTERS	$3.95
☐	25416	THE DEFECTION OF A. J. LEWINTER	$3.95
☐	25457	MOTHER RUSSIA	$3.95
☐	25432	THE OCTOBER CIRCLE	$3.95
☐	25547	SWEET REASON	$3.50

Prices and availability subject to change without notice.

Buy them at your local bookstore or use this handy coupon for ordering: